Run, Alice, Run

Lynn Michell

Linen Press

First published by Inspired Quill: 2015
Second edition published by Linen Press, London: 2018
8 Maltings Lodge
Corney Reach Way
London
W4 2TT
www.linen-press.com

A CIP catalogue record for this book is available from the British Library.

Cover design: Louise Santa Ana

ISBN 9780993599774

Dedication

To My OBF. Again.

Praise for Run, Alice, Run

'Run Alice Run traces the breaking points of a young girl's heart and the ways in which each fracture moulds her into the woman she's become at the novel's start and end.'

– Isabelle Coy-Dibley, The Contemporary Small Press

'In this eloquent novel, Lynn Michell ultimately weaves a poignant tale of hard-won freedom.'

– Jenny Garrod, Dundee University Review of the Arts

'A very rare thing – a literary novel about female ageing and sexuality that pulls no punches, and it should be applauded for that.'

– Chapter and Verse

'With a voice as unique as its heroine, Lynn Michell tells the story of one woman's attempt to understand and acknowledge her past in order to secure and save her future. Her characters are strong and believable. Her settings in Birmingham and Edinburgh are recognisable and fresh, yet coloured by the emotional baggage that Alice brings to them.'

– Brook Cottage Books

'Melodrama interlocks with irony and subtly paints a portrait of the ageing beautiful woman in Western society. Alice feels she becomes invisible. Her husband is married to his computer. And instead of breaking that computer over his head, she starts stealing and stealing becomes a habit….The strength of the book is its humour and that humour remains, despite the drama and the serious issues posed in the narrative about women in today's society.'

– Laura Martignon. Amazon reader.

'Engrossing and believable. It even made me understand better my own time of acting oddly. I wanted to keep reading until the end.'

– Odaline. Amazon reader.

Run, Alice, Run

Prelude

Alice

Chapter 1

2007

I Shot The Sheriff

NOT TODAY! PLEASE not today. Give me one more hour and I can get out of this. I'll never do it again. Never. Never.

SHE WILL RERUN this inch of tape loop for the rest of her life.

She indicates left and drives slowly round the corner into the street where she has lived, quietly and anonymously, for the past seventeen years.

Two police cars are parked outside her house.

Down comes the jam jar trapping Alice Green.

FOR THE PAST week, Alice has not bothered to cover her tracks. She's left evidence strewn all over her bedroom for anyone to see. Two days ago she pulled off her most outrageous binge – she might as well hold out her hands and tell the police to click on the handcuffs.

Quick. A plan. An escape.

Some lies.

IT'S LIKE DROWNING. Like that book Pincher Martin she read at school, where the whole of a man's life flashes in front of his water-logged eyes. She watches her personal documentary and in re-watching the beginning, knows the predictable, inevitable ending.

The cars are not exactly discrete, with their brazen PO-LICE sign and the orange and yellow squares all over the bodywork. You can hardly mistake them for a taxi or a Molly Maid car or a green-painted florist's delivery van.

One is parked right outside the big house opposite hers; owned by a portly property developer who on Sunday evenings pressure-washes his three silver cars. One for him, one for the wife, and one for emergencies. Boy, this man loves his nozzle of shooting water. Having hosed the cars to within an inch of their lives, he turns his hose on the dead leaves and debris outside his house, whooshing his power-squirt of soapy water all along the pavement to the gutters. Sometimes, when Alice draws her bedroom curtains at eleven at night, he is still at it. He doesn't speak to Alice Green, perhaps because she owns an old Citroen Diane and never washes it.

The second police car is parked in the spot reserved, in invisible writing, for the very proper and upright couple who inhabit the flat below hers. Theirs is the more prestigious ground floor conversion with its own barricaded front garden and main door. In the driveway sits a red, phallic convertible with personalised number plates. He is a sheriff – something to do with the Scottish courts – and suddenly Eric Clapton is singing along in accompaniment. Appropriate, but inaccurate. She hasn't shot the Sheriff. Nor his deputy. Nor his wife. She hasn't shot anyone but she has been very bad.

ALICE GREEN IS on her way back from an after-work swim at the local baths; council, not private, because it is only a dream that she might one day plunge into the infinity pool at One-Spa where the monthly membership fee is more than her salary. Instead, her passion for swimming is precariously balanced against the discomfort of public baths with eye-reddening chlorine, screaming children and water that is far too hot for exertion. There she contends with testosterone-charged men who stir up the entire pool and sluice water over her head and capsize her gliding breaststroke. Recently, a friend with a strong interest in these matters, informed her that men at the baths eye up the young mothers. The acronym is MILF – Mothers I'd Like to Fuck. Alice knows that she falls about a hundred lanes outside this category. Not even the very old, skinny-legged pensioner in baggy swimming shorts notices her.

While she travels up and down her lane, she dreams of an empty, embracing sea with a shimmering horizon. Alone, she glides through cool cobalt water that caresses her skin with each wide-open stretch of her arms. She is a sharp silver blade, cutting into the silky fabric of the water and leaving in her wake only a murmur of disturbance.

Alice passes briefly under the public shower which is positioned at the end of the pool. Children must wear swimming costumes to shower. Grown-ups, too, if they want to avoid arrest. On she pads towards the exit and into the confined space of the changing room where she bumps hips and elbows with other damp women. She towels briefly, and pushes her sticky-wet limbs into grey track suit bottoms and an old T-shirt. Her hair drips chemical-water and will later paint dark spots on the seat of her car. Her face is pink and shiny from the exercise and naked of make-up. All this she will amend but only after she has walked her dog, who has been left alone in the house and waiting for his exercise.

Alice Green does not shoot sheriffs or shower naked in public baths or neglect her beloved dog.

HEART POUNDING, IN the three remaining seconds before she comes to a halt, Alice considers her options. She could do a runner; drive straight on past her house, head for Morningside then speed along the city bypass to the ring road. And head for....um...where? Obviously she doesn't have her passport with her so she can't catch a plane and start a new life in Mexico. Nor can she fly to a tiny island in the sun, where, in the thrillers she reads, bank robbers and tax evaders flee and live happily ever. Or she could drive round and round Edinburgh until the police get bored and go away. Surely they won't hang around all evening. After shuffling the cards she has, she settles on the obvious option. Pull up, park nicely and express shock and bewilderment at the police presence. She is just minding her own business and will ask in alarm if there has been an accident. This is nothing to do with her. They have no proof, and it's innocent until proven guilty, right? Don't they need a search warrant to look inside a house? Having never tangled with the police, nor committed any crime worse than parking on a double yellow line, she is ignorant of her rights. Perhaps she can persuade them that they need a search warrant, so she can bin the evidence and slip back into her normal self; an ordinary, middle-aged, law-abiding citizen.

That's a lie. In fact, two lies. First, she did have an encounter with the police, but it was thirty years ago and she dismisses it as irrelevant. Nothing after that. The second lie runs deeper. Who are you kidding, Alice Green, when you describe yourself as ordinary? Ordinary middle-aged women don't steal clothes from high street shops. They don't come home to two police cars parked outside their door.

Absorbed in this emotional stocktaking, she doesn't notice the much younger woman, an erstwhile Alice standing on the pavement beside her. Alice stares at the model of herself made more than thirty years ago. *Now I'm hallucinating. It's the shock of four very visible policemen outside my house. I'm cracking up.* She looks at the waif with the waterfall of fair hair and khol-rimmed eyes in a long gypsy skirt and jangling bangles. Her feet are bare.

"You'll catch your death without shoes." Maternal instinct is stronger than fear. Stronger than guilt.

"You never wore shoes when you were my age. We all went barefoot. In the summer, anyway. The summer of love!"

"It's not summer. And we're in Edinburgh with an East wind. You need warm shoes."

"I'll go back and get my red boots later. I've come to help."

"I'm beyond help."

"No, you're not. What's happened?"

"I honestly don't know. I'm about to be arrested."

"Goodness…what did you do?"

"I've been on a bit of a rampage."

Alice is comforted by the presence of this sympathetic young woman, even if she is an apparition. She's about to talk to four angry policemen so why not entertain a ghost, too? At least the ghost is friendly. The day became surreal some time ago.

"You won't know this yet, but even when you're middle-aged on the outside – wrinkles and greying hair – you still feel twenty on the inside, only with more luggage. Though not all women go shoplifting when they hit fifty, I suppose."

"Why did you do it?"

"I felt diminished."

The young girl shrugs and Alice somehow knows what she's going to suggest before she speaks. "OK. Let's go back. Let's tell the story and see when we went off the rails… it all sounds a bit tragic."

Alice agrees. Close to weeping, she lets her gaze wander over the girl's youthful beauty and wonders how anyone so lovely morphed into the tired person she is now.

"You know, you're more of a shock than the uniforms," she says finally. "There's so much joy and hope in your eyes. It breaks my heart to know it will fade."

"I'm pretty dismayed too. Sounds like you lost the plot."

"It's true."

"Then tell me what happened."

"I haven't time. The police are waiting for me."

"OK, the bottom line. Who hurt you first?"

"Julian," Alice says, not missing a heartbeat.

Act 1

Julian

Chapter 2

1967

When I Saw You Standing There

LEFT ALONE ON the pavement, unable to focus on the face of the boy who broke her heart, her mind pulls up several images, as if shuffling postcards. The first is weak and water-coloured: the not-quite-awake walk across fields from her house to the local train halt made of a single platform and the twenty minute ride with doors opening and closing and school kids climbing on board until they finally shunt into High Wycombe station. The second image shows Alice elbowed out of the train and carried on the youthful human tide through the town to the cross-roads where green and black uniforms part company. Last is the muscle-memory of the long, reluctant, steep climb that hurt her thighs no matter how many times she did it and, on cold mornings, squeezed her breath into painful asthmatic wheezes.

TWO HILLS ROSE above the town, each topped with a grammar school. On one sat the old, prestigious enclave where boys studied science and played rugby. At the end of their school careers, the clever lads, including Julian, were packed off to Oxford and Cambridge to cope with culture shock and meet the privileged boys who had slid down a ready-built slide greased by class and wealth and influence. Those who had got there through hard graft and clever genes remained, for three years, baffled and alienated by a species who strolled the green lawns as if they owned them (some of their fathers probably did) and turned their well-bred noses up at intellectual pursuits. The grammar school boys and the future leaders of the country had nothing to say to each other.

On the other hill, the girls were split into Latin or Domestic Science, played Hockey in winter and Lacrosse in summer, though today Gillian and Alice were lying hidden among tall stalks of tickling grass where the extensive school grounds sloped away down the hill and into the valley.

Only a small bi-plane could cross the divide between the sexes.

THE AFTERNOON WAS too hot and cloudless for running up and down a rectangle of dried mud with heavy butterfly nets. From under half-shut eyelids, Alice cast furtive, astonished glances at her friend's F cup, fortified bra and the great globes of wobbly flesh contained therein, and understood why, on meeting her, boys' eyes dipped immediately to this stunning sight. Gillian was tiny in height but bounteous in bosom. Beside them were their cast-off clothes and satchels, stuffed with homework because both worked hard, baffling the staff by being both clever and rebellious. Other girls who were about to finish O levels were either steadfastly on course for university or, to the equal relief of the school and the girls concerned, ready to leave to become hairdressers at the first opportunity. This pair could not be pigeonholed.

"I'm too hot," Alice said, sitting up to examine her legs and shoulders. They were tanned golden but starting to tingle.

"Yeah. Me too. We'll go soon." Gillian propped herself on her elbow and stared at her friend. "You meeting Julian?"

Alice's heart tripped. She held her breath and didn't reply because no-one, not even Gillian, could imagine what it was like to be absorbed, to the point of obsession, by a boy she had met only a few weeks previously. For another ten minutes, the two girls lazed in the slanting rays of the afternoon sun before it dipped below the wooded horizon. Perhaps Gillian drifted into sleep, but Alice was wide awake, tracing in her imagination a sharp-boned, wide-mouthed, symmetrical face and tasting long, summer kisses. If it had been suggested to her that other girls of fifteen or sixteen were similarly smitten, she would have shaken her head. This was different. She knew she had found her soul-mate; it had taken less than two minutes.

ON THAT PARTICULAR afternoon – which Alice would later describe as earth-shattering – the boys had gathered as usual near the bus stop outside Woolworth's and were making a combined effort on their homework to save doing it later. Four brilliant minds were better than one and thanks to Peter, they had the algebra tied up in minutes. The Latin translation and the English précis took a bit longer, completed in shaky writing because the lined exercise books were propped up against a wall or held in midair and bumped by passersby.

The boys who blocked the pavement did not think of themselves as a gang. They were a group of misfits who had found one another while using public transport or singing in the choir or playing in the orchestra. They were the oddballs who deliberately ruined rugby games by staring into space instead of hurling their bodies on top of the ball. They were the ones who argued on political grounds against Cadet Training and did care in the community instead. They were defined by negatives; not the shiny academic ones on the treadmill to medical or legal degrees; definitely not the loud, sporty ones; not the thugs who'd landed in the wrong school with the wrong academic curriculum.

ALICE HAD SPOTTED the familiar group from way back and had noted the new person. Not that she could have missed him, since he towered nine inches above the others and had a shock of raven hair. Later, when she asked him why he went around with that particular group of lunatics, he told her that despite being a giraffe, or rather because of it, he was equally low in the male pecking order and was taunted with the name Tripod or Bones. He said the thugs at school had quickly singled him out for taunting, and there'd been fights, but one day he'd lost his temper and broken a guy's leg. After that the tough boys left him alone.

Now, as she made her way along the crowded pavement, the tall boy looked up and, as if he had been expecting her, shot her a look so blue, so direct, so penetrating, that she stopped walking. People cursed as they bumped into and squeezed past her until someone nudged her on. She resumed

13

walking, unable to look away, crashing into women with shopping bags and tripping over the feet of preoccupied children. When she finally reached her friends, her breath tight and jagged with anticipation, the tall youth was still staring at her and in that look, she saw determination and incredible strength.

ALICE HAD MET her match.

"HELLO," ALICE SAID, blushing heavily. What a stupid thing to blurt out. How childish.

"Hi!" he replied. He didn't try any charm offensive or flirt with her or play the fool as others usually did to win her over. He was quiet, confident and matter-of-fact. As if the mission was already accomplished.

"Are you new?'" she asked, and then wished the pavement would swallow her. Of course he wasn't new. The other boys were falling about and digging each other in the ribs, looking at Alice because their revered and wondrous goddess had turned really dumb. Yet amid the teasing, the others knew exactly what was going on. Their quick-fire, mocking repartee wound down, stalled by the static that sparked off this pair and their intuition that their queen bee was about to be caught and netted. Julian would succeed where they had failed.

"New!" said Peter, creasing up. "He's only been here since the first day of first year, whereas you, Alice, fell from the heavens into our midst at the end of last term. Alice, this is Julian. Julian, meet Alice."

"No, I'm not new," Julian said. Was he patronising her with his lopsided smile? "But you are. This lot told me all about you."

"That's right," Alice replied. "I've been to loads of schools because my Dad's in the army and we keep getting posted, but…"

"Whereas I've been to two schools. First primary school, then up that hill for the past five years."

"Oh," Alice said, not even batting her eyelashes or flicking back her blonde hair. "I've never seen you here before. I mean, I always bump into Andrew and Peter and…"

"They bussed us to Cornwall last month to label the flora. I'm just back." And with that, and a light but firm grasp of her arm, he steered her away from the others, casting a don't-dare-follow look behind him. Alice willingly let herself be led. She loved the sureness of his hand and the way he towered over her.

"WHERE TO, MADAM?" He was deadpan and wry which, as she would learn, was his norm. "Your wish is my command."

"The station," she replied, amused. "I get off at Gerrard's Cross. Five stops-"

"Same as me."

"Then why haven't I seen you before?" Alice repeated.

"I've seen you. Several times. Before I went wandering around Helston staring at wild orchids."

"You must be doing Botany."

"Botany, Biology, Maths, Chemistry and Physics. You?"

Oh goodness, five subjects, so he was brilliant as well as gorgeous looking. "English. That's what I love. Reading

15

novels and poetry. I'm doing Art, though they say that won't get me anywhere and it's a waste of time, but I enjoy it. And Latin because you need it to get into Oxford."

"We're on a collision course then."

"Are you sitting Oxbridge?"

"Yup. Which college?"

"Um...I'm not sure." In fact, she hadn't a clue. The exams were challenge enough for now. No member of staff had bothered to ask her about colleges.

"I want to go to Trinity."

Such sureness. Such composure and certainty. "Do you work very hard?" she asked, then regretted such a stupid question. It was considered weak and pathetic, even amongst her own clever friends, to admit to trying. While Alice put in four hours every evening declining Latin verbs and pondering the merits of Silas Marner, the boys were out kicking a ball around or drinking cider in a pub garden, having lied about their age. No bartender believed them, of course, but what harm did it do to let a group of lads get a bit noisy and opinionated in rural England? Everyone knew everyone, so if things got out of hand, the pub staff knew whose parents to call.

"Hardly at all," he replied, with the same self-mockery. "At the weekends, I walk for miles in the woods. Thinking. In the evenings I listen to music and read."

"What do you do read?"

"Nietzsche and Freud at the moment."

Alice had heard of neither. "For pleasure or homework?"

"I don't make a distinction. Do you?"

"Some of us have to read Scott and Dickens. Thousands

16

of pages."

"I'll rephrase the question then. Which writers do you like?"

"Jane Austen and the Brontës and the Romantic poets."

Alice waited. Was her answer acceptable?

"Would you like to come for a walk after school on Friday?"

It was.

AS THE TRAIN pulled slowly into the station, the tall boy took Alice's hand and kept hold of it as they walked the length of the platform in search of an empty compartment. He held it as they rode the five stops in a sweet silence, and kept it when they climbed out and walked through the small town until their paths diverged. When Alice turned round, he was standing still, staring after her.

Chapter 3

2007

Every Breath You Take

THE SCENE OUTSIDE her house in the here and now rolls again, and Alice sees that the police are about to play their very conventional parts in it.

TWO POLICE CARS.

Alice opens her car door.

Their doors and hers are perfectly synchronised. Four car doors opening.

One policeman is crossing the road and walking towards her.

Three other uniformed police wait by the vehicles.

Alice swings her legs out of the driver's seat and twists round to grab her handbag and the gym bag that leaks chlorine from her wet swimsuit and towel.

The officer on the other side of the road walks his policeman walk.

ALICE MOVES. NOT fast, because fast is guilty. Not slowly, because her dog is waiting for his walk. She clicks open the latch on the gate. Fastens it behind her. Walks up the driveway which she shares with the occupants of the top flat. Her own front door is at the side of the detached Victorian house, the entrance to the top flat is round the back. The main door is at the front, shielded by very high hedges. Maybe the Sheriff and his wife are hoping to sleep for a hundred years. If they are, four policemen are about to wake them.

Please God, don't let the already disapproving neighbours be there, sipping tea at their garden table on the other side of the greenery.

Alice will walk down her drive and greet Hunter who will be on his hind legs, clawing at the glass panes in equal parts of welcome and anxiety. His whimpering will escalate into excited little howls of joy as she turns her key in the lock. She will dump her gym bag in the hall at the bottom of the stairs, grab Hunter's lead from the hook on the wall and set off again, dog in tow. No, the dog will set off with Alice in tow. Hunter has been shut in the flat for more than half the day and needs a pee. Needs a crap. Needs a walk. Alice inserts the key and turns it.

This is usually a deliriously happy moment for dog and owner, when Alice buries her head in her collie's long black fur and breaths in his comforting mud-and-dust-and-dog smell. She fetches the dog lead and clips the end to his red collar and sets off, head bowed, eyes down, and walks slap bang into the uniformed officer. Fuck! She arranges her features in an expression suitable for a resident of the Grange. We don't do police cars in this leafy up-market area. We do not do petty crime. We have a Neighbourhood Watch scheme. We house the city's lawyers, property developers, bankers, architects – all with petrol-guzzling four-wheel drives and convertible Mercedes. Not forgetting the sheriff with the shiny red BMW and personalised number plates.

ALICE IS A mistake who slipped into the area on a stroke of luck when an out of town lawyer missed a deadline, and so her canny solicitor was able to put in a quick and cheeky offer which, to her astonishment, was accepted. Here, at the side of the house, she has her own front door and front steps where she crams as many plant pots as possible. Where, on a fine weekend morning, she sits with a mug of heavily leaded black coffee, face held up to the east light, visible to those who pass her gate and stare up her drive and signal that this is not the correct code of conduct.

"MRS GREEN." IT is a statement. Not even so much as a good afternoon.

"Yes," she replies, looking aghast. She is aghast. "Is something wrong?"

"Just wait here please." He lifts his walkie-talkie. "I have Mrs Green here… yes… if you would."

"What's the matter?" she asks, the question itself a lie.

"We'll just wait for my colleagues to arrive. We've been waiting all afternoon."

"I was at work. Then I went for a swim. My hair is wet." She pushes back her dripping locks, knowing her appearance is of total irrelevance. "I'm just on my way to take my dog for a walk. He's been shut in all day and needs…"

"You won't be walking your dog now, Mrs Green. We need to have a word with you." His face is blank. His eyes are blank. No, his eyes are dead. He's seen too much.

"I'll be quick then. I'll just go over the road – over there – he's desperate for a pee."

Hunter is straining impatiently at the lead, pulling too at Alice's conscience because she can't satisfy her dog's simple needs.

"You aren't going anywhere." The policeman places a hand on her arm.

Chapter 4

1967

I Got You Babe

A LICE AND JULIAN started hanging out together, although that wasn't the word they used back then. They started going out together. Almost straight after the electric storm of a meeting on the streets of High Wycombe, they became inseparable.

JULIAN LIVED AT the end of the most distant lane of a pretentious and exorbitantly expensive commuter town which he despised. His home was a child's drawing of a house, planted in a clearing in the woods with the railway line behind it. The land had cost a few arms and legs, and his parents weren't well off so there wasn't much left over for the building. The windows had steel frames which rattled. There was no heating. Julian shared bunk-beds with one of his brothers – the one who was already at university and so not there much. The land around the house, too tree-root-infested to culture, remained a wilderness of beech trees and secluded places for two people who wanted to be alone. Julian's mother seemed blithely oblivious of mess, and content to expend maternal energy cooking enormous roast dinners and fruit pies and custard for her three sons. Mostly, she kept out of their hair. Julian's father was a mad professor who built contraptions in the garage and sometimes didn't recognise his own children.

Alice pretty much moved in. Compared with her lower middle class bungalow with its square of grass and border of hideously overblown roses, this place was Wuthering Heights and Alice wished she had dark, tumbling curls like Cathy to better play the part.

SUCH A TRITE phrase, love at first sight, and yet that's what happened. Their eyes, which were exactly the same shade of blue, had met, though not across a crowded room but an ordinary pavement in High Wycombe. Alice adored Julian's towering height, his wide pillar-box mouth and his thick black hair that managed to stay sleek and shiny without a brush or comb. It's why God gave us fingers, Julian said, the same way he would give other explanations, with absolute certainty and a wry smile. He was a facts sponge that swelled with information. But he also loved to negotiate the twisted thought corridors of philosophy and theology and politics. He told Alice he had argued heatedly with his mother since he could talk, and they both got a kick out of it. Alice, on the other hand, had never argued with anyone because in her family it was considered rude and upsetting. Having never debated anything, she felt her way through life using emotional antennae which were finely tuned to people and places. Her ideas and assumptions were instinctive, intuitive and usually very accurate.

The love between them was all-consuming. It ripened under the sun's freckling touch as they crossed acres of flower-sprinkled meadows and walked barefoot across trickling, tumbling streams to reach forbidden territory. Julian had a sense of direction as sure as a mariner guiding a boat by the stars, unerringly prompted by an inner compass which Alice did not possess. He led and she followed. On hot days, they lay in the sweet-scented dips in haystacks where the brittle stalks scratched their skin, squinting up at the sky through daggers of light that pierced the dome of leaves and painted dancing polka dots on their retinas. Until the puffs of yellow dust made Julian sneeze and swelled his sensitive eyes to bloodshot red. Despite the difference in their height, or perhaps because of it, the contours of their bodies slotted together, two pieces made by the same sculptor. They folded into each other and kissed until their lips were swollen.

ONLY WHEN THEY talked seriously did Alice feel a shiver of insecurity as she tuned into a faint, faraway voice which whispered that she wasn't a match for him. In her family, no-one discussed anything more contentious than the weather. No-one read books or played music or looked at art. Julian already had strong opinions which he articulated with total confidence while Alice fell silent, and felt stupid. When they were with the others, Julian argued vehemently about the rights of the labour party and trade unions. About the stinking rich and those who lived in poverty, without power. He laid open the flaws in the arguments for Christianity and defended the rationality of atheism. He talked about his passion for Bach; about Shakespeare, and though that was her subject, he still had more to say than she did. On her birthday, Julian gave her a blue bound volume of the plays and sonnets which, thirty years on, Alice still has. She gave Julian an LP of Mahler's Fifth which he hated. Nothing after Mozart, he told her. That's when classical music died. Alice was chastened and ashamed.

"LET'S GO TO Stratford," Julian suggested one day, out of the blue, while they lay together in long grass.

Alice propped herself up on one elbow to better see if he was kidding. Distracted, she touched his beautifully boned face. Every girl she knew fancied him. He could have taken his pick.

"Why not?" He read her hesitation and continued chewing on a blade of grass. "We both did Richard II for O level. Peter Hall is directing. A chance to see the real thing, Alice, not remember the play as something we read in class with boys using falsetto voices for the female parts. I thought you'd jump at it."

Alice, still amazed at this boy's sudden decisions, leaned over and kissed him. "I've never been away from home. Not for a single night."

"Well now you have the perfect excuse."

"They'll never let me. Not with you. My mother is a walking wreck of anxiety, wringing her hands about her daughter getting pregnant. She's terrified because she knows how much I love you."

Julian let her words hang in the air for a moment too long. It was a subject they avoided. The fear of pregnancy, especially for a nice girl like Alice and a boy as principled as

Julian, was a very effective form of contraception. Unlike other boys she had gone out with, not once in their insistent exploration of each other's bodies had Julian given the slightest suggestion that they should become lovers. It worried Alice that he was so definite. If he had asked, she would have said yes. Without hesitation.

"You don't want to talk about it, do you?" she asked.

"No. There's no point."

"Perhaps we should…"

Julian's mouth hardened into a tight line. "Look, Alice, we both know it's impossible."

"It's not impossible. Not if we're very careful."

"I'm not risking it." He stood up and stretched. Without looking at her, he wandered off through the trees, stopping to snap off a branch which he swished hard, left and right, at whatever got in his way. Subdued, Alice followed.

WRONG MOVE, ALICE. He wanted to talk about Shakespeare.

INTERVAL

A LICE IS SO lost in her story that she stares right past the older woman standing on the pavement beside her.

"I can hear you telling the story in the background like a distant radio station and it's terribly distracting. It brings back such strong, sad memories. And I have a question."

"What?"

"Why did Julian put up the barriers?"

"Didn't I explain? We were sixteen-"

Young Alice is shedding tears that make dark spots on the pavement where just now a heartless policeman walked. "It was too intense. I should have keep it light. It was my fault."

"I don't think it's about fault."

"I pushed too hard. I behaved badly."

"We don't learn, do we?"

"But this is different. *This* isn't your fault."

"The judge is out. In fact, he hasn't even entered the court room."

"Hadn't you better pay attention to what's happening now?"

"Oh heavens! I'd much rather not; I know what's going

to happen."

"Now or in the past?"

"Both."

Chapter 5
2007

Would I Lie To You

A LICE DECIDES TO skirt the policeman, but he takes her arm, keeping her still. Three other policemen are opening the gate and walking down her drive, slow and steady, slightly rocky as if they've just stepped off a boat. Oh, she's mistaken. One is a woman, but with her hat pulled down low, it's hard to tell. They must be hot in all that padded clothing and attachments. Hats, jackets, bulletproof vests, boots, walkie-talkies, tear gas, hand cuffs, truncheons, guns, hand grenades. OK, maybe not hand grenades. Guns, maybe. They are armed, these days, aren't they?

Oh my God. In her heart Alice knows it is all over but she's not giving up without a fight. Policemen are not that bright, are they, whereas she, long ago, obtained a degree in English Literature and now works as a librarian with floor-to-ceiling books. They haven't actually accused her of anything. They have no proof. Oh who is she kidding? The proof, and plenty of it, is on the back of the bedroom door, in the wardrobe, and even laid on the bed as if she were staging a rehearsal for this very crime. Keep up the charade, she says to herself, but she knows it's over.

STUPID, STUPID. YOU were always going to get caught.

"PLEASE, CAN I just take my dog over the road?" she tries again, aware that her voice is jittery. Hunter is quietly whining because he expects and deserves and needs to trot off to the nearby woods to relieve himself, to sniff his familiar territory for fellow canines and foxes, and to roll in the mud and dust and fallen leaves. The same routine at the end of his owner's every working day.

"You won't be walking your dog now, Mrs Green. We're going inside." The policeman has no heart. The tin man. *Somewhere Over the Rainbow* pipes up right on cue.

"In the garden then. I'll just take him in the back garden."

"The dog is not going anywhere. Nor are you, Mrs Green." A don't-grapple-with-me voice.

"He doesn't deserve… he doesn't understand…"

She is close to tears. The man's implacable expression makes her tug Hunter in a U-turn, and while the dog gazes at her in sorrow and puzzlement, she unlocks the door and pushes him back inside. Damn you, she says to the policemen, but not out loud. She could hardly do a runner with an old dog and wet hair while four uniforms stand in the driveway watching.

ALICE'S HEART SKIPS a beat and then sprints to catch up as they all file over the step and up the stairs to the mezzanine level. Perhaps she will have a heart attack before they reach the landing at the top. She is a fit woman who walks over hill and dale with her dog but at her age you can never tell, especially with the stress of four policemen following you.

She can feel her mask of respectability hanging by its elastic from one ear. I am Alice Green, she reminds herself. I am Alice Green who recycles everything into separate boxes, and picks up her dog's crap with a little shovel before dropping it into a black plastic bag to take home. I pay my parking tickets the same day I find them taped to the windscreen, and I have never been caught speeding. I even pick up other people's empty bottles and sweet wrappers in the hospital grounds where I walk my dog.

TIME TO FACE the music, Alice. You might consider yourself invisible to most of humanity but someone has spotted you. Someone has seen you up to your tricks.

Chapter 6

1967

Hitchin' A Ride

"COME BACK…" ALICE begged as Julian crashed away from her, swiping at bushes and plants that had done him no harm. "Please come back and talk to me. I do want to see a Shakespeare play on a stage. Come back. Let's plan it."

It was the right move. Get his attention back on something factual and interesting. She ran after him and caught him round the waist. He turned, threw down his stick and put his hands on her shoulders, bent to place his mouth on hers. His kisses, long and gentle but insistent, sent shivers down her spine. *A Taste Of Honey*. She shut her eyes.

"I love you." It was a simple statement meant to explain everything else. "I love you and want you but I can't see beyond today and tomorrow. Let's just enjoy what we have now."

Whether his words were meant to comfort or warn her, Alice did not know. She accepted them regardless.

THEY WALKED ON, Alice carrying her sandals, until they came to the stile that led to the open fields below Julian's house. The light dazzled after the pulsing strobes of sunshine in the woods. Alice let go of Julian's hand and ran. While he watched, an amused smile on his lips, she danced in the long grass, whirling and swaying and flinging her arms in the air. A will o' the wisp. A wood spirit. A skinny, starry-eyed girl on the cusp of womanhood. Julian raced after her and caught her in a gentle rugby tackle, pulling her down with him. Her skirt went up like an umbrella in the wind and her hair spread out, a perfect match for the ripe wheat-grass. Julian leaned back to look into her face, sighed, then found her mouth again with urgent kisses. Alice unbuttoned his white shirt and stroked his hard, smooth chest, all collar bones and sticky-out ribs. She pressed her fingers into his shoulders and the tops of his arms where the muscles were starting to bulk. Working her way down, with difficulty, because they lay so tightly-coiled together, she opened the zip of his jeans and pushed her hand inside, closing it around his erection. As she stroked, gently at first circling with finger and thumb, then harder with a tight fist, Julian threw back his head and moaned. It took two minutes for him to come. Afterwards, he lay panting and spent while she wiped the semen off her hand and bare legs with tufts of grass and gazed at him in amazement. This is what they did. This was the red line they never crossed.

LIKE A PRICKED balloon, he lay on his back while Alice curled into him. Freeze this moment, she thought. Keep it like this for ever. Let me live in this love story.

LATER, JULIAN PICKED spears of grass to torment Alice, first tickling her ear, then making a shrill whistle by blowing on the blades between his thumbs.

"OK, so we'll go to Stratford," he said, picking up where they had left off an hour previously. "We'll hitch there and back and buy standing room tickets before each performance."

"And stay where?"

"A cheap B & B."

"What do I tell my parents?"

"That your teachers say you have to see the plays."

"They don't care about my A levels. Do you know what my mother told me the other day? She sat me down for a talk…"

"She told you not to get pregnant or the world would end."

"Shut up! Just listen for once! She said when I leave school, I should train to be an air hostess or a secretary, then I can either marry the pilot or my boss."

"Honestly? Funny…I thought you were going to university to study English and read a thousand more books."

"Honestly. Yes, I am. Mum's still in the 1950s. Dad is basically absent on active service except there's no action in Bucks and he's a very frustrated man. Do you know what he called me when I told him my O level results? A parrot! He said, 'You're not clever, Alice, you've just got a good memory like me. You're a bloody parrot.'"

"Wow! What praise."

"It's not funny! I cried."

"But seriously, you're a clever girl!"

"Unproven. Anyway, it's the duty of even clever girls to get married." Alice tugged down her skirt and lay in a straight line beside him. "OK, I'll try to pull the wool. I'll tell Mum the school says I have to go. She'd never dare phone them to check."

"I'll just tell my mother we're going."

Alice pulled a face. "She's so relaxed."

"Yeah. Wish yours was."

"Mine has daughters. She can't be relaxed until we're safely off her hands."

"Nothing we can do about that then. When shall we run away?"

Pulling down the shutters on the future, Alice wished that really was the plan.

"Soon." Alice replied, snuggling against him.

They clung to each other until only a red half-circle was hanging above the horizon.

A WEEK LATER, around lunch time, two young people who caught the eye of passing drivers were standing at the side of the A1, Alice holding up a big card that read STRATFORD-UPON-AVON. On the pavement, a carrier bag contained clean knickers, a nightie and her sponge bag. A girl must always wash her face and clean her teeth before bed. Julian's otherwise empty rucksack contained two sleeping bags. When a car came into sight, they pulled apart from hurried kisses, and Julian shoved Alice forward to the kerb side where she grinned and wagged her thumb and hitched her skirt a little higher to attract the driver. Julian hung back. If he'd hidden in the bushes, the first car would have skidded to a halt.

A HUGE LORRY stopped within minutes, the driver's attention caught no doubt by the slim girl with blonde hair that blew into a halo with every car that whizzed by. The long articulated vehicle rumbled to a halt twenty yards further down the road while Alice and Julian picked up their bags and ran. Oh wow! Alice elbowed Julian. Hey, we're getting a ride in a juggernaut!

"Hello, Sweetheart!" the driver shouted over the idling engine. "Want a ride?"

She didn't miss his eyes assessing her body, maybe giving it a mark out of ten, nor his glee when a car raced past and whipped her skirt high above her thighs in a Marilyn moment. She rewarded him with a sweet smile, still eager to please. The driver leant over to push open the passenger door, and after Julian had shoved Alice up the step, leaned over and grabbed her hand to pull her on to the bench next to him, leaving Julian to haul himself up. Ignoring him, right from the start. The driver was a heavily built bloke with a heart-shaped tattoo pierced with 'Mother' on one forearm and a shapely, naked woman on the other.

"Running away together, are you?" he asked into the awed silence that settled over the two of them, even Julian, as they registered the drop to the tarmac that raced past under the noisy roll of the double wheels. The bloke grinned. This pair seemed to amuse him. The man drove one-handed with experienced ease and didn't hide his appreciation of Alice. It was his payment for giving them a ride.

"No, we're going to see Shakespeare's plays." Alice replied, seriously.

"Shakespeare, eh? Sure you don't want to go to Gretna

Green? I'm heading north." He laughed at his own joke. "How old are you anyway?"

"Sixteen." Alice replied.

"Under age too. Better be good. Don't do anything I would do. Name's Stan, by the way."

The banter continued, Alice responding politely to the man's repartee and smiling a lot, while Julian withdrew into himself. Alice read his mood. This is simply the means to an end, she told herself. When other male eyes devoured Alice, one glance from Julian's steel blue eyes usually withered them into passivity. But in his driver's cab, the older man was in control. Right now, he was offering Alice a Jaffa Cake from an open packet that had scattered crumbs, including some under Alice's thin skirt. The princess and the pea, she thought, trying to brush them out from under her bum.

"Can I help you, Miss?" Stan asked, leering and grinning.

AFTER THE CHAT and the biscuits and more jokes, Stan turned up the volume on his radio and he and Alice sang along to Radio 1. When the DJ played *We Gotta Get Out Of This Place*, Stan managed to steer the juggernaut one-handed while linking arms with Alice and belting out the lyrics at the top of his hoarse, off-key voice. It earned them a filthy look from Julian but Alice was having a ball.

AN HOUR AND a half passed between Gerrard's Cross and Stratford. Stan announced their arrival as they rolled slowly through a suburb of expensive mock-Tudor houses and ironed lawns. Traffic clogged the road; they weren't bowling along now but shunting forward, yard by yard. Big bumper to small bumper.

"Bloody tourists," Stan said as he changed down to second gear.

"Like us," Julian replied.

Stan heard the criticism but didn't respond to the taunt. "Yeah, but you're young things and getting away to have a bit of fun, whereas this lot pay through the nose to eat expensive scones with expensive jam and pretend they've gone back a few hundred years. It's a commercial theme park, this place, put on for the Americans 'cause they've got no history, have they? The locals do a good trade in summer…don't begrudge them that. Anyway, I'll stop over there and you can walk the last half mile down to the river. You'll see the theatre. Can't miss it. If that's really where you're going…" He squeezed Alice's thigh.

AFTER PROFUSE THANKS from Alice and a curt nod from Julian, the massive vehicle growled into motion and rolled on its way. Stan leaned out of the open window.

"Shakespeare!" he shouted. "I've heard better excuses!"

They walked on in silence, Alice bewitched by the magic atmosphere, the crowds who walked with careful poise in the lush gardens as if they too were on stage. Not far away stood the red-brick theatre and the swans who rode up and down the river, claiming majestic ownership.

"What's the matter?" Alice asked eventually, emerging from her dreamy trance to notice Julian's mouth set in a grim line. After a year, she knew his moods and this one was flashing blue lights. Police cars and ambulances. He was coiled and ready to spring. Oh for heaven's sake, she thought. Now what? We're here. It's romantic and exciting. We're alone together for the first time. Surely you're not going to spoil it.

"You were flirting," he said. He might as well have spat in her face.

"I wasn't flirting."

"You treated me like a piece of luggage. Sorry I took up space."

"You're jealous! I don't believe it."

"Of him! Spare me, Alice."

"He gave us a lift and I was polite, which was more than you managed."

"Polite! For God's sake, Alice! Which century are you living in? It's polite to let an old geezer grope you? You're the one who spouts women's lib."

"I do believe in women's lib…"

"So I'm suggesting you put the philosophy into practice. You're pathetic, Alice!"

ALICE DIDN'T CRUMPLE, not immediately. She managed to stay upright on her high horse for two minutes longer. Then she sat down hard on the grass and buried her head on her knees. Hot tears accompanied the self-recrimination.

"I'm sorry," she sobbed. "I didn't know…"

"Didn't know?" he lashed. "Of course you did."

"It was nothing…"

"It isn't nothing." Ice coated each word. "When I met you, you'd been flirting with every boy in the whole bloody school. *Arte* they called you. Did you know that? Goddess of unexpected happenings. Oh, they were all in love with you, Alice, but only because you're prettier than the others. But prettiness will not always be a passport. If we're going to carry on together, you have to grow up a bit."

"Why are you saying all this now?" she asked, lifting her head to see what she could do to make it better. "Why have you waited? Today was supposed to be special."

He knelt down beside her, breathing heavily – did he take pity on her, or was his anger simply spent? – and put an arm around her shoulders. "I want to respect you. I want others to respect you."

"Don't you respect me?"

"I'm not putting this very well." he continued more quietly, stroking her arm. "You don't have to let yourself down…"

"No, Julian." Alice flung down her arms and leant back to look up at him. "What you're saying, in that clever way you have, the way you argue about everything, is that I've let you down."

"You sometimes behave as though you're quite dim, Alice," he replied, ignoring the criticism. "Before I met you, I went out with a string of pretty girls who had turnips for brains and used their looks to get what they wanted. I expect more of you."

"Aren't you over-reacting?"

"No. What happened in the lorry is one specific example of how you sometimes behave…in ways that diminish you. You played along and gave him everything he wanted."

"He gave us a lift," she said, agitated.

"He offered us a lift. We thanked him. There was no

40

legal agreement that his payment was a bit of skirt and a hard on."

IMPASSE. THE SILENCE stretched away as far as the river, as far as the fields beyond its banks, as far as the horizon. He's just told me he's ashamed of me, Alice thought. I'm not good enough for him.

JULIAN STARED AHEAD. Unrepentant, Alice thought. Unforgiving.

INTERVAL

A QUIET VOICE filled the gap when Alice stopped talking and sighed.

"I don't remember this much crying," the older woman said softly. "I remember a head-over-heels, walking-on-air happiness."

Alice wiped her eyes with her finger tips so as not to smudge the mascara. "It was happy. Impossibly happy."

"But you're remembering the sad parts."

"No, I remember being happy too. You remember...we were so saturated with each other that we needed nothing else. No-one else."

"Was it too perfect to sustain?"

"Perhaps. That's why I'm looking for the fault lines."

The pair stood together, watching the same images and hearing the same soundtrack, trying to rerun the past with more exactness.

"You didn't remind me what happened after that row."

"Sorry," Alice gave a rueful grin. "I didn't finish. We made up. We saw the theatre exhibitions and walked along the river and ate scones with expensive jam. We saw two performances each day, standing right at the back of the auditorium where we could hardly see or hear the actors. Then we slept in the theatre gardens, on a wide patch of grass in our sleeping bags. Julian named the stars. Everything was perfect."

"But still no sex."

"Come on. You know the answer to that," Alice teased. "It wasn't on the agenda. We made a plan though."

"I remember the plan." And with that Alice was gone.

Chapter 7

2007

You Aint Seen Nothing Yet

F ROM ALICE'S BAY window, with its fine view of poplars and the north-facing sweep of Blackford Hill, two policemen are clearly visible to the houses opposite up and down the street. How many people are discretely observing? How many are openly staring? Not many dramas unfold in the leafy Grange in Edinburgh.

We might as well all whistle, Alice thinks, to fill the silence intended to intimidate. It's their standard game plan – waiting for me to crack. She runs her hands through her chlorine-rinsed hair as if to excuse her appearance.

WHICH ALICE GREEN do the uniforms see?

Mrs Green, faithful wife and dutiful mother, librarian, dog walker and responsible citizen?

Or Mrs Green, suspect, criminal, shoplifter and *English*?

Really, it couldn't get much worse.

"I'VE JUST BEEN swimming," she announces for good measure.

The chief uniform ignores her comment, or doesn't hear her.

"Now that my colleagues are here, Mrs Green, we can get down to business," he says in Scottish plainsong. "Do you mind if we sit down?"

Do, Alice thinks, and I'll just pop into the kitchen and make you all a nice cup of tea and arrange some shortbread on a plate. We can talk about what life is like in the police force and I can get some material for another unpublished novel.

FOUR UNIFORMS REMOVE their checkerboard-rimmed hats and place them neatly on chair arms or pine floor boards: one heavy, I'm-in-charge guy whose eyes fire only blanks, one tall, clean shaven one (policemen, like doctors, grow younger every year and this one is about twelve), one older crumpled one with no-one to iron his shirts, and a pretty female whose lovely brown hair is pulled back in a Schemie Facelift.

Creases sits on the very edge of an armchair near Alice. His glance is not unkind. Cynic lowers his stocky self onto the sofa opposite, legs splayed to accommodate the bulk between. From a black wallet, he produces a notebook, a cheap ring-bound thing with lined pages, and a plastic biro. Alice wonders why they don't supply him with a decent A4 notepad and a good pen. Pads and pens are her genies and jujus, her magic wands and good charms. She finds plenty of excuses to go to the posh stationers in Morningside and to slip one into…

Don't go there.

"Mrs Green, I won't beat about the bush. We have reason to believe that you've been shoplifting items from a number of shops in Edinburgh." He looks straight at her, and Alice can't help mentally comparing his eyes to currants, buried in suet folds of pockmarked dough.

Bull's eye. What other reason could there be for this gathering? Alice shivers, her mouth is dry, and a hot flush courses down her body. Sweat mingles with the remains of pool water between her breasts and on the backs of her legs. No, she is not blushing. She wants to tell them it's the menopause, not guilt, that makes her cheeks look like lollipops.

Alice says nothing while her mind revs, throwing up denials. She feels an utter fool. Not a criminal, but a total idiot. To have been caught; that is her crime.

"Mrs Green, I need to tell you that you don't have to say anything at this point in time. However, the more you cooperate with us, the more leniently you will be dealt with if, and when, you are charged. Do you understand? We've spent a lot of time on this case, Mrs Green, a lot of time." He flashes a plastic card. "We'll be carrying out a full search of your home in due course."

Alice, knowing what awaits him in her bedroom, feels that she might faint.

"I'm not a thief," she says, half believing her own words.

Silence.

"Have you, Mrs Green, at any time stolen anything from any of the clothes shops in Morningside?"

"No. Never."

Silence.

Acres of silence.

Alice stares at the floor. Strokes Hunter's head who remains at her side, shuffling to remind her that he is still waiting to go out. Alice glances at her watch and sees that half an hour has passed in slow motion.

Cynic sighs and flips his notepad open and shut. Open and shut. Flip flap. Flip-flap. "Look, Mrs Green, as I have just informed you, I advise you to cooperate with us. If you cooperate, we can include that in our report, and in the event of an arrest, it will be taken into consideration. Do I make myself clear?"

"Yes."

"Do you sometimes visit a clothes shop at the bottom of Morningside High Street called Temptation?"

"Um…only if there's a sale. Their clothes are too expensive otherwise."

He isn't listening. "Did you go into Temptation last Thursday afternoon?"

"I've no idea. No, not last Thursday because I was still at work. I'm a librarian."

"Temptation is open late on a Thursday. Last Thursday, at six fifteen, immediately after a woman answering to your description had been in the shop, the owner noticed that a garment was missing. She saw the empty clothes hanger straight away. It was an expensive item, a designer label, and Temptation is the only shop in Edinburgh that stocks that particular brand. We replayed the CCTV footage…" here Cynic looks up and stares long and hard at Alice, "…and I would say that it was you in the shop at six fifteen, Mrs Green."

"I didn't steal anything from Temptation." Caught and dangling, Alice continues to wriggle on the line but she knows that any minute now they will cosh her and put a swift end to her futile squirming. They'll tread on her to crush her lies. They have big feet. Their boots are hard.

She's furious at herself. She has stolen an expensive designer top without even knowing it. She is a crass amateur of a thief who doesn't know her Top Shop from her Stella McCartney. They are all looking at her. Creases flashes a look of sympathy because he knows that she is trapped. She peers at him from under the jam jar. Begs him to be kind.

"When we watched the CCTV footage," Cynic continues, "the owner said she recognised you from the local library. Said you'd recommended something for her the last time she went in. And so we found you. It was going to happen one day, wasn't it, Mrs Green?"

They all stare at her.

"So we'll start in the bedroom, shall we?"

ALICE IS CRYING. It took so little. As she leans over to bury her scalding face, tears plop one by one into Hunter's black fur. He turns his gaze upwards to meet hers and to ask his silent questions: Why are we still sitting here? Why are we not running through the leaves? What have I done wrong?

It's not you, she tells him silently. It's me. I'm wrong.

"Good dog!" She says aloud. "Good boy."

Chapter 8

1967

Let's Spend The Night Together

B Y SIX O'CLOCK it was dark enough for them to cross from the house to the caravan without Julian's brothers seeing them. Not that the older boys gave a toss. Why would they monitor two sixteen year olds who were joined at the hip?

THE SMALL, ROUNDED caravan had put down roots in a neglected back corner of the garden, where the towering beech trees gave it a canopy of dense shade in summer and sprinkled its roof with red and orange confetti in autumn. Stalks of tall grass, ragwort, nettles and white daisies decorated the rim of the caravan like a cake frill. Ivy hung across the windows; green curtains that swayed when caught by a breeze. At least, this is how Alice would have described it, if asked. Others might have seen a rusty old can with flat tyres, but others were not tiptoeing towards it, hearts thudding with wild excitement and nervy eagerness. Stars spelled The First Time across the glassy sky. The night trembled with a million insects.

Barefoot and wearing ragged jeans, a lace camisole and pearl earrings, Alice set off from the house carrying two folded white sheets, two pillows, two pillowcases, a box of tissues and a tiny sponge bag. Julian led the way through the jungle-garden with a plain tallow candle, a box of matches and a paper bag of green apples. Always the Fruit Bat. Give him an orchard, a wall to climb, a leap down on the other side and he would consume pounds of plums or apples or pears or cherries until Alice felt sick watching him. He ate fruit voraciously, until juice dripped from his chin and elbows. "Don't want to get scurvy," he always said. A night without fruit – even this night – was inconceivable.

INSIDE, JULIAN LIT the candle, held it at an angle so that drops of wax made a melted base, then pressed it on one of the little chipped, veneered shelves that flanked the bed. Alice put her tight-strung nervous energy to active service by unfolding, spreading and smoothing sheets, tucking them in, stuffing pillows into pillow cases. She watched Julian watching her and read wry amusement and deep love. Don't know why you're bothering to play housewife. We're here to make love. Crumpled, tangled sheets, Alice!

"Budge!" Alice said each time he sat down on the half-made bed, sinking deep where the springs had long since given up their bounce. "No, wait!" she chided, when he reached out and pulled her down beside him. His mood was hard to read – like an animal, she thought – waiting with quiet, assured contentment for the kill.

For a long time they lay on their backs, holding hands as they had done for two years in meadows of ripe grass and on beds of beech leaves – with simple, quiet confidence and contentment – but never with this feeling that the world was about to move on its axis. That's what people said, didn't they? They would emerge as different people.

THE PLAN THAT ended with a bag of green apples in a caravan had been plotted with military precision. The date had been calculated by the stars, moon and all ancient calendars as well as with prayers and sacrifices to the gods and goddesses of all religions. Put simply, the sand in the sexual hourglass had run out. Their virginity had moved in with them. What had begun as a whisper had become a refrain, its volume on full and the OFF button nowhere to be found. The Greek chorus sang on until it silenced them.

It was the end of the summer after A levels. Soon, they would go back to school to spend a term doing mock exam papers to get into Oxford or Cambridge. Then a gap year, except it wasn't called that then. Julian would go to Israel to live in a kibbutz and help orphan kids. Alice would work as an untrained assistant in a library and live at home. This was the pause where the first educational treadmill stopped and let them off, before the next one came along and carried them into their university years. For Alice, the onward motion was the default, but for Julian nothing was random. He knew which subject, which college, which university, which career. Nothing would get in his way.

WHICH WAS WHY no detail of this night had been left to chance. The factors that needed to slot together in a perfect pattern had been anticipated and planned with a compulsive attention to detail which would leave no trailing loose ends to trip them. Julian's parents had to be away for the weekend. Alice's parents would be told about a sleep-over with Gillian to tackle holiday homework in the form of Latin translations. Gillian had gleefully agreed to provide the alibi and protect the truth. About bloody time, she'd told them. Some of us got it over with ages ago. But the delicate, spider-web hook upon which everything hung was the pattern of Alice's periods. While she wrote days and dates in a notebook for four months, Julian read everything he could lay his hands on about the sometimes erratic behaviour of female hormones. Alice's hormones behaved themselves in regular twenty-eight day cycles with two days of niggling announcements followed by three days of heavy bleeding and deep pain.

And still Julian worried. Like a terrier with a bit of bloodied rag, he wouldn't let it go. It's supposed to be a big deal for me, not him, Alice pondered. The male chomps at the bit for sex and takes it when offered while the girl hesitates and worries about getting pregnant. We seem to have got it the wrong way round. It's simple for me. I want to give him everything. I want to be his. Was she being naive? Was Julian the one protecting their future?

THE GRAND PLAN has been conceived in Stratford and filled in square by tiny square over the following months. Only once did it hit a land mine that almost tore it to shreds. The argument blew up on a hot, cloudless Saturday. That summer, they cycled for miles, all over Buckinghamshire, Alice behind Julian. They cycled dangerously fast, sometimes racing each other in deadly competition; to feel the whiplash wind on their sunburnt faces and the adrenalin hit of too-fast downhill descents over potholed roads, but most of all to try to shift the little, nagging weights that some killjoy was piling on their young shoulders.

On that day they had cycled down to the Thames and were pushing their bikes along the tow path, looking for a pub with a garden.

"Where are you in your cycle?" Julian asked, when they had parked the bikes and were settled with their glasses of cider and Ploughman's lunches on benches at a rough wooden table.

"What? Not this again," Alice said, taking a large bite of sliced white bread, orange cheddar cheese and Branston pickle. Julian seemed obsessed by the mysteries of the female menstrual cycle while Alice was sick to death of discussing the ordinary, predictable rhythms of her periods. "Just stop, Julian."

"I'll be responsible if you get pregnant, Alice. I can't handle the thought of that."

"No, Julian. We will be responsible. And I'm not going to get pregnant. My God, how many more times? Why bring it up again now? We're having a day out. A day off. Or did you forget to tell me we're heading for the sand dunes after lunch?" she raised her eyebrows. "I thought we'd agreed what we're going to do. We've got the date sorted. Everything's already decided." She chewed on, more concerned about low blood sugar than the bloody cycles of her womb. "My periods have been boringly predictable for three years. Julian, we've had this discussion twenty times."

"What if we've chosen the one month they go haywire?"

"They won't go haywire. And we'll use… you know…"

"Not reliable. A ten per cent failure rate."

"You've looked up the statistics!"

"Alice…" he was deadly serious. "We don't need a baby. Not now. It would be impossible."

They had crashed into this wall so many times, a wall that could build and rebuild itself in seconds before either of them could slam on the brakes. But this time, Alice saw different graffiti painted on it and finally understood the writing.

"You're scared, aren't you, because I could ruin your future?" she shouted, hurling her sandwich at him and watching lumps of bread and cheese hit his neck and slide down his collar. "You're terrified of having a pregnant girlfriend on your hands! My God, just imagine… marriage instead of Oxford, because you'd do the honourable thing, wouldn't you, Julian? You'd marry me and you'd hate me for it and we'd live unhappily ever after. I can read you."

Julian stared at Alice with something she thought looked close to hatred. His mouth pinched into the tight line she knew meant cold fury. As always, he was right and she was wrong. He unfolded his long body from the bench, silently collected his bike and walked away along the tow path, wiping pickle from his face with his free hand. Bull's eye. Alice had hit the spot.

MAYBE IT SHOULD have ended there and then.

BUT SHE RAN after him, clumsily wheeling her bike, her shins scraping against the pedals and bruises collecting like punishments as the wheels ran into her bare calves. It ended with the inevitable collision of bike and girl – a tangle of upside-down handlebars and blood running from cuts where sharp edges had opened up her tender skin. Julian turned and walked back; separated bike and Alice and pulled her to him. They kissed until they were giddy. They agreed a cease-fire. Another long kiss sealed the very precise plan that would soon turn into reality.

Maybe it should have ended then.

But it didn't.

"I CAN SEE Orion," Julian said, lying by Alice and staring out of the caravan's skylight. "Orion follows us around," Alice said. "I think of him as our very own constellation. Our protector."

What happened next was a dance of exquisite nervous-ness and sensuality. He watched her face, his blue eyes not once leaving hers as he pulled her camisole up over her head, undid the buttons on her skirt, and pulled down her white lacy pants bought especially for this night.

"You are beautiful," he whispered, bending to kiss her ear and fold back the loose strands of hair that fell over her breasts.

When it was her turn, his hands remained steady and resolute on her bare shoulders while hers trembled. It took her a long time to undo the tiny buttons on his white shirt and to pull down his jeans and briefs because she kept stopping – a delaying tactic because suddenly she was bashful –

to run her hands over his wide shoulders and his smooth chest. Safe territory. They had never seen each other naked. Not head to toes naked. Alice kept her eyes firmly above his waist while his hardness pressed into her belly. Still holding on to her hand, he leaned over his clothes, deftly extracted a condom from a pocket, and started to roll. Alice let go, dived onto the bed, and pulled the sheet over her blushing face. Julian moved beside her, tracing the mask of her features with his fingertips, moving his hands down and down until he had all of her, a cotton-wrapped mummy of a girl, tight in his grasp. Then he peeled away the sheet. Hey Presto.

"You're beautiful," he said again.

In the next precious, never-to-be-repeated moments all her senses were held in the rhythm of Julian's pulsing movements as, push by gentle push, he broke in and entered. She felt no pain. No pain, but perhaps no pleasure either. It was too much of a wonder, too astonishing, too raw in its newness to offer Alice anything but a stunned awareness that this was it.

AFTERWARDS, THEY LAY on their backs and stared up at Orion. Julian reached for the brown paper bag and took out an apple as others, in other novels, took out a cigarette. His strong teeth left a perfect smile in the green peel and white flesh. Alice leant over him and they ate it between them, one bite each, until only the core remained.

WHEN JULIAN'S BROTHER pushed his bike past the caravan windows the next morning, maybe out of curiosity, maybe for no reason, Alice was at the sink singing *I Got You Babe* very loudly and rubbing the middle section of a sheet in a sink filled with soapy water while cotton fabric pooled around her. Deleting the evidence; spots of blood and dried semen on the white cotton. While she scrubbed, she switched between pop songs and quotes from Lady Macbeth and would associate 'out, damn spot!' with this moment for the rest of her life.

"We got some mud on the sheets… walking around outside in the dark," she said, completely without conviction, when Dave stopped to lean on his handlebars and stare at her with a bit of a leer. Alice's cheeks were red apples, her eyes sparkling and one camisole strap slid down her shoulder.

"Oh yeah."

"Muddy feet," Alice limped on.

"Yeah."

"Bro!" Julian made an appearance from round the back of the caravan and shook his brother's hand. It was a farce but the characters on the stage played on.

"Had fun, young man?" Dave asked, thumping Julian on the back.

"Yeah."

"Good." And on he went, casting a backwards grin as he straddled his bike and rolled away through the forested garden.

LATER, A PARTLY wet sheet flapped on the washing line in the sun.

Alice settled herself with Wuthering Heights on a pile of cushions on the grass and Julian watched her while taking his ancient, ailing bike to bits.

THE SHEET DRIED virgin white, without a trace of evidence.

Chapter 9

2007

Caught In The Act

I T IS ALMOST nine-thirty.

One policeman yawns.

The police woman stretches up her arms.

"DO YOU KNOW what's worrying me, Mrs Green? You really are very good at this. This is quite a haul, and I don't think I'm wrong in wondering if there may be a lot more." The officer surveys the piles of clothes on her bed.

Alice says nothing. Cynic narrows his eyes. He will pin her down yet. He will stick the insect bruising its wings and fighting for life inside the jar.

"How do you do it?" he asks. "How do you manage to take this much without anyone noticing?"

"It's surprisingly easy. I stuff clothes into carrier bags and walk out."

Cynic rubs his hands over his face, a gesture that Alice has come to recognise as frustration. He is perplexed. He does not recognise her in his A-Z of criminals.

"And how long did you say you have been at this?"

"Since April. About three months."

"Nothing before April?"

"No."

They all regard her with varying degrees of disbelief. Cynic keeps talking.

"Now most shop lifters are either drug addicts needing money for their fix – you can spot them a mile off – or they operate in threes and fours and certainly don't bother with this type of merchandise. They want Gucci and Versace and Marc Jacobs. Now you, Mrs Green, don't fit either of these categories." He strokes his chin.

Warm. Warmer. Like a game of Hunt The Thimble.

"You wouldn't attract any attention, would you? I mean, no shop assistant would be suspicious of you."

"I'm in my fifties. I don't attract attention. I'm of no interest to anyone, including my husband."

Without knowing it, Cynic has touched a nerve as naked as a live wire; Alice's visceral sense of diminishment. When did the waves of anonymity close over her head while she struggled and fought for breath? Still waving, just, but close to drowning.

IN HER BOTTOM drawer are two small, beaded clutch bags which belonged to her mother who, before a dance, would have clicked open the catch and dropped in her gold-cased lipstick, fiery red, and a fine lawn handkerchief embroidered, by her own fair hands, with her initials. She would be dressed in a floor-length gown. Blue taffeta or cream lace. Yards and yards of it flowing out in a full skirt. Her mother would pose and admire her reflection in the full length mirror. She loved dressing up. The bags are wrapped in faded tissue paper, and sometimes Alice unwraps them to stare at the intricate embroidery in gold thread, and the hand stitching of hundreds of miniature beads. One bag has a tiny mirror inside.

Out they come and are dumped on the bed with the throwaway buys from Accessorize and Primark.

"Nice. Vintage." Cynic says. "Where did you pinch these?"

Stupid. Stupid. For a moment she cannot bring herself to answer.

"They belonged to my mother." Alice says, brushing tears from her cheeks. How can they compare their old, faded elegance with the high street dross? She can't bear them fingering the precious purses.

They have enough to convict her several times over. They stop, tell her they will take all this stuff with them.

"You'll be coming with us to the station now, Mrs Green," Cynic tells her.

THEY LEAVE HER to struggle out from under the jar while they gather the clothes mountain, their hats, their armour and their weapons.

Chapter 10

1967

Breaking Up Is Hard To Do

THE HEAT HAD been turned up and the academic pressure cooker simmered nicely. In a few weeks, Julian, Alice and Gillian would each sit at a small wooden desk, isolated from one another in a hall of echoes, terror and hope, and be told, "You may start." They will turn to the first page of the first exam; the passport to dreaming spires or flowing Cam. Alice's hands will be icy cold as she scans the questions and tries to recall some of the thousand lines she has learnt by heart from Shakespeare and Shelly and Coleridge. Julian will think, and write, and think. He has prepared nothing in particular and has certainly committed no wild-guess exam answers to memory. He will rely on his ability to argue.

In the weeks leading up to exams that their teachers insisted would determine their futures, Julian and Alice agreed not to see each other after school, apart from traveling home together on the train. But at four-thirty, Alice sometimes found herself standing alone on the platform because Julian had stayed on for an extra tutorial, or a spell in the school library. So he said. Then, at his request, Saturdays were crossed off because he needed, and wanted, to go for long walks by himself. To think, to play with ideas, to be silent. Alice told herself this was all perfectly reasonable and put his apparent withdrawal down to his ambition and determination to get to Oxford. It would pass. He would pass. And get a scholarship.

After the exams were over, there came a moody lull while they all waited for letters inviting them for interviews. Or not.

THEY HAD EXPECTED to feel exuberant with relief. They had planned all-night parties celebrating the full stop at the end of their school years, yet after a few nights of pouring cider down their throats when their maudlin singing and deliberately jarring guitar playing got them thrown out of the pub, the gang met less often and when they did, sometimes the conversation paled to stilted limpness. The buzz faded fast. A poignancy and lethargy crept into their final gatherings and last traipses across the countryside, because each could see the finishing line across a university campus when they would go their separate ways.

On their long walks, which took them through the same beech woods and along the familiar tow paths, there grew, insidiously at first, then tangibly, a tightness and tension between Alice and Julian. Alice perceived this touchiness as a shield which Julian held between them. At waist height, it was a barrier that blocked her hand from slotting itself into his arm and stopped her putting an arm around his hips. At head height, it fended off her insistent and increasingly desperate kisses. The more she clung, the more armour he wore.

ON A SULTRY October afternoon, with the sky threatening a downpour, they picked their way over fallen branches and soggy rotted ferns in their beloved beech woods. When Alice tripped on a buried root, Julian did not turn to help her. When she skidded on a sloping patch of wet grass, he made no move to help her to her feet.

"What's the matter?" she asked.

"Nothing."

"It's not nothing, Julian," she said. "You're moody."

"Preoccupied."

"What with?"

He gave her a withering look. Obvious, isn't it?

"You've been distant recently. You don't seem to love me much anymore." Too much, Alice. Too much. Stop now.

"I'm not distant. Maybe you are."

Alice was dumbstruck. Not for one minute had her feelings for Julian changed. She loved him unconditionally.

"You're passing the buck. I haven't changed," she replied, for once sure that she told the truth. "I love you just as much now as I ever have."

They walked on in silence, Julian taking long strides and staring straight ahead. Alice, trying to keep up. Tension filled the space and kept them apart.

She cracked first. "Julian, stop! Please talk to me. I don't understand what's going on."

"OK," he said, searching out a tree stump and parking himself on it, legs splayed, eyes cast down. Not finding another improvised seat, Alice stood beside him, her hands twisting and wringing her hanky until it was a tight little fabric rope.

She bent to put a hand on his shoulder and murmured, "My Julian…"

"I'm not your Julian," he snapped.

"You were my Julian that night in the caravan."

"Yes, that was the beginning. If there was a beginning. Or maybe it started two years before that. Maybe our night together was the end."

"I'm not interested in your verbal riddles, Julian. Are you saying you had what you wanted from me and now you've lost interest?" Alice shook her head in disbelief.

"Absolutely the opposite."

"What do you mean? You play clever games with words and I just want the simple truth."

"There is no such thing as the simple truth."

"For Christ sake stop messing with words. Just tell me."

"You said 'my Julian.' I'm not."

"I always call you my Julian…it doesn't mean…I didn't mean…"

"I don't think you know what you mean. I don't think you notice what you do or how you behave."

"I love you. And I thought…after our night together…I thought we would be even closer."

"Exactly. And since that night you've behaved as if you own me. That's why I resisted. I said all along that it would change our relationship and make it suffocating."

"Suffocating?" Alice repeated.

"Yes, Alice. Suffocating."

For a long time, the only sounds were their breaths – his

strong and even, hers staccato and strained.

"You thought you could stick us together, didn't you?" he said, finally looking up at her with disdain. "Instead I feel a nagging responsibility, and I don't need that. I love you, Alice, but I want you all the time and I can't have you. I'm torn in two. We can't go backwards to where we were before that night so either we carry on making love and then we get married and then we have kids and we forget about university…"

"Or?" she prompted.

"Or we split. Go our separate ways. Grow up. We find out what life is about because we're only seventeen and we know nothing. You and I have lived in a cocoon for two years and maybe it's time to break open the shell."

"Isn't there a third way? We can be friends and see each other in the holidays and think about marriage at the end of university. If that's what we both want. You don't have to feel trapped by me." Words of desperation. She saw them fall on the loose, stony ground between them and knew he'd already made up his mind.

"It won't work. I don't want to go to university for three or four years with an albatross round my neck."

There. He had said it. Alice listened to his reasoned argument but heard a different truth. He wanted his freedom.

HE NODDED WHEN he stood up, as if to underline his words. He opened his long arms and Alice moved into them. When he bent to rest his head on her hair, he breathed the sighs of an inevitable ending. They stood, their arms around each in a stiff and awkward embrace while the overbearing clouds suddenly turned to pelting, stinging rain. For Julian, the cutting away of Alice was necessary and clean and forever. She, on the other hand, clung by her finger nails to the crumbling rock edge of hope and could not accept that this was the very last chapter. The end.

IN THE WEEKS that followed, Alice's phone calls were answered with curt dismissal. No, he would not talk to her. There was nothing to discuss. Her tearful pleading and increasingly hysterical requests to meet were countered with silence and the click of a phone replaced. When she ambushed him on the tow path and outside his house and threw herself at him, he disentangled himself without saying a word, turned his back and walked away.

How do you carry on when your heart has been torn out? Like a rag doll whose seams had split and opened to expose the softness inside, Alice was completely undone and did not know how to mend herself.

WHEN THE EXAMINATION and interview results came in, Julian, Gillian and Nome had their places at Oxford. Alice and Andrew accepted their second choices of Birmingham and Sussex. Julian set off for Israel while Alice numbly stamped books in her local library.

IN OCTOBER, ALICE packed a single suitcase and set off by train for Birmingham University. On her first night away, her desolation became a nightmare that returned at painfully regular intervals. Trapped in a police station, taking part in an identification parade. As a long line of males slowly walked past her she stared into every face, searching for Julian's but she never found him. The dream haunted her for decades.

INTERVAL

O N THE PAVEMENT, two women who look vaguely similar, like mother and daughter, stand shoulder to shoulder. People returning home after work or walking to the shops in Morningside stare at the police cars and the women and correctly assume a connection. An accident. Perhaps a death.

"When I came back to support you, I wasn't expecting so much sadness," the younger Alice sniffs. "I would be the strong one. You could lean on me."

"You are the strong one. You moved on. Found Cal."

"Only after years of hollowness."

"But you put on a brave face…"

"A veneer. I wasn't invisible, just a lesser version of myself."

"Exactly."

"And you? What's happening now?"

"I'm about to be taken to the police station."

"You must be terrified!"

"To my surprise, I'm not. Can you carry on with the story?"

"Yes of course. The next years are fun. Good luck with

the coppers. I'm here if you need me."

"They can't really hurt me."

"Not like Julian did, you mean."

Chapter 11

2007

One Of Us

STREET LIGHTS BURN yellow in the gloom outside.

The bedroom curtains remain wide open.

"Right, Mrs Green," says Cynic. "We'll make our way to the car now and take you down to the station for formal questioning."

"But you've already questioned me."

"Only informally, Mrs Green. We'll charge you, get a formal statement, ask you a lot more questions, check every one of these stolen items on our computer database, take your finger prints and a DNA sample. Normal procedure. Did you think this was it?"

His smile is cruel.

Well, yes. They would go away and let her eat bread and jam and get some sleep while they stuffed her clothes in a locker at the police station and went for a pint. They would return in the morning or in a week's time. Instead – oh my God – Alice realises that she is about to be escorted down her own gravel drive by four policemen carrying a stolen clothes mountain, in full view of the residents of The Grange, including the Sheriff. She will be bundled into one of the police cars and driven away.

I'm in the wrong film, she thinks, not for the first time, and it's turning into a horror movie.

"May I phone my husband and tell him what's happening?"

"You can."

These days Alice has a different recurring nightmare in which she has to get urgent help following an accident. She reaches for the phone. Sometimes, it's melting and soggy. Sometimes it has no numbers. Sometimes the numbers are jumbled. Most often, she is simply unable to press the right buttons in the right sequence.

Now, in a different kind of nightmare, Alice is unable to manage the speed dial for her husband. She gets her dentist, her sister and the library before she gives in and presses it in full, mouthing each number like a small child doing sums.

"Stephen Green." Not a second's pause. He must have been leaning over the phone.

"It's me," she says quietly. "You can come home now. I'm just leaving."

"Alice...for God's sake. I've been waiting for four hours...what's happening?"

"They're taking me to the police station..."

"They're still there?" Stephen interrupts. She hears shock. Disbelief.

"Yes. Obviously. Or I would have phoned you sooner."

"Right, I'm leaving now..."

"Did you hear what I said? They're taking me to the police station."

No, he hadn't.

"What!" he explodes. "Why?"

"To charge me, I suppose. Come home, Stephen, and take Hunter out. I'll phone you when I can."

Alice is aware of Cynic tapping his foot on the floor, jingling car keys on the end of a finger.

"Alice, have they been in my study?"

This is about me and you're still on about your study.

"No. I have to go." Cross, she hangs up.

"Come along now please, Mrs Green," shouts the unsympathetic officer. "I shall be leaving Constable McBrier here to look at the two computers. She's an expert."

"Computers?" Alice parrots him. Plural. "Why?"

"Because we find all sorts of things. Lists. Emails. Computers can tell us more than humans. Sometimes." He smirks.

"Not my husband's...there's no need..."

"Both computers. We don't know yet that he's not involved."

"But that's outrageous. As if he could be bothered with..."

"Just doing our job, Mrs Green."

Oh my God, Stephen. I'm so sorry. You've been wrong too, but I don't want you drawn into my mess. Not like this. And I've just lied to you and now you're coming home feeling false relief. No chance they'll let me phone you again. Toby was just a teenager when he hacked into your computer and told me things I didn't want to know. Two days ago I would have revelled in the police exposing you and your nastiness. I would have laughed out loud. I would have said you had it coming and about bloody time. Yes, I want you to be caught, and hung out to dry, but alone. Not next to me. Our crimes are separate.

NO TIME NOW because three uniformed police officers, refitted into their black uniforms and hats and add-on weapons, two of them bearing stacks of clothes on green and yellow plastic hangers, are all waiting at the top of the stairs.

"Please..." Alice begs. One last request before the guillotine. "Would you mind putting all those clothes back in the Johnson's dry cleaning bag? It'd make it easier for you to carry."

"You don't want the neighbours to see," replies Cynic. "Well, I can understand that. I'll admit I wouldn't want my neighbours watching this lot being taken out of my house. Okay, put all that stuff into the bag," he tells the other two. Alice gains a stay of execution and five minutes more to comfort her troubled dog, who is whining at her side.

"Thank you," Alice says, and means it. She bends down, holding Hunter tight. "Good boy," she whispers. "You are a good, good boy. I'm sorry you've not been out. Stephen will be home soon to take you for a walk."

At that final W word, Hunter whimpers and cocks his head on one side. Alice can't bear it. "Later, Hunter," she says and for a long moment, while the police look on, she buries her face in his sweet fur and lets bitter tears fall. "Later. You'll go out later."

THIS IS THE worst moment.

SHE ADOPTS A slow, nonchalant walk, a few paces behind the police, and keeps her face composed in an ambiguous smile. She's helping them with their enquiries, isn't she?

When the car door is held open, she nods her thanks and slides into the back seat, as if this is something she does every day. As they drive away, Alice wonders if, for a final touch, she should lift her hand in a queenly wave.

Alice pretends to stare out of the car window, pretends to be absorbed in the scenery of betting shops and Asian fruit stores, until they pull up round the corner from St Leonard's Police Station. The second police car has arrived before them. Creases waits on the pavement. While Alice has clocked the journey at half an hour, it has been a five minute drive from door to door. In they go, through the revolving glass doors.

ALICE HAS BEEN here before. She once found a brown leather wallet on the pavement in Morningside High Street. Concerned that it belonged to an elderly person – so many totter along to M&S from sheltered housing – she got straight back into her car, leaving her own shopping for later, and drove to the police station to hand it in. Alice knows how, with lost and empty lives, molehills of worry grow into mountains. Not that losing a wallet is trivial. The next evening, someone from the station phoned to tell her that the wallet had been safely reunited with its owner.

"She was quite elderly and hugely grateful," the police woman had said. "She wanted me to thank you and to tell you that she is so pleased and reassured to know that there are still some honest people in the world."

Act 2

Oliver

Chapter 12
1968

How Does It feel?

I T WAS FROM a net-curtained, worried, lower-middle class home without books or music, and parents who thought daughters didn't need a university education, that Alice came to the buzzing, bitchy corridors of the English Department of Birmingham University in the late 1960s when David Lodge, Stuart Hall and Richard Hoggart peopled its corridors. In seminars and tutorials, Alice sat mute, blushing and misplaced in the presence of tutors who were almost household names. The silence that had floated with her from a home where words were considered dangerous flurries that could rock boats, made her feel stranded. Alice went to university armed only with politeness and a pleasing smile.

SHE BOARDED THE train to Birmingham University struggling with a leather suitcase full of books and unsettling emotional luggage. Heading north, she sighed her way through each station, imagining the journey as a punishment that pulled her ever further from a hope, a faint dying hope, that he was following her every move and would ask her to come back. Having no sense of direction, she was lost twice over. The train shunted on through cities she had never heard of. A cardboard cutout of the once vibrant Alice traveled on to a place that was only a name. Scooped out and hollow, she stepped off the train into a seething, grubby city centre and looked for a sign to tell her where to go next.

AND SO, WHILE her motor-mouthed peers gathered in the coffee bar or the Union or on a landing somewhere in the Arts block to argue late into the night about Descartes and Sylvia Plath and whether Enoch Powell should be allowed to visit the university, Alice stood alone at a bus stop waiting to catch two buses back to her digs in Small Heath. There, in a small room with a narrow bed, flowery bedspread and matching curtains, Alice read her set texts and despaired. Her grim-faced landlady didn't like her. She gave her a copy of the written rules of the house which allowed Alice a bath on Tuesdays and Saturdays and a cooked breakfast between 7:30 and 8:00 each morning. Alice couldn't stomach sausages, black pudding and baked beans first thing, and asked politely if she could have a reduction in rent in lieu of breakfast.

"It's all part of the package," the landlady said. "You should eat a decent breakfast. You're too thin already. If you don't want it, that's your decision, but the rent is for both."

So Alice scoured corner shop notice boards and queued in the Lodgings Office for somewhere more sympathetic. Only a few weeks had passed but like others billeted in similar quarters, she was desperate to flee stifling suburban lodgings which had all the disadvantages of living at home without any of its compensations.

THE ENGLISH DEPARTMENT was housed in the Arts block; all light and space with open-plan mezzanines and vast landings lit by the natural light of wall-to-ceiling windows. These public spaces allowed solitary Alice to blend with the anonymous crush of paired and grouped students on their way in or out of lectures. But turn around and push open the heavy double doors and there were the dark, labyrinthine corridors of the older building, where doors opened into the tutors' and professors' rooms. Here there was no hiding. At 2pm on Tuesdays, Alice stood outside one of those mighty doors while the butterflies in her stomach knocked themselves unconscious against her rib cage. Her young tutor, Clive Dunn, and his passion for the structure of the novel terrified her. It took courage to knock on his door and push it open. The heads of those assembled swiveled towards her and quickly turned back with barely concealed disdain. Clive Dunn looked straight through her. He sat at one end of his big mahogany table and filled the room with pipe smoke, refusing to break the daunting silence until some articulate bloke with a regional accent made an incisive comment. Then they were off, all but Alice, peeling apart the onion layers of Conrad while Clive Dunn stared ahead with an expression that suggested indifference or loathing. Or maybe he was silently writing his next novel.

ONE DAY, AS she left one of these stomach-churning seminars, an angry, ugly young man appeared at her side and fell into step beside her as she rushed across the campus. She had noticed him staring at her but there was nothing unusual in that. It dawned on her that this at least she could use to her advantage.

"Don't you ever 'ave anything to say?" he asked.

She replied, truthfully, "No. I'd rather listen."

"Aren't you interested in anyfing?"

She considered this question for a while.

"Yeats," she said. "I like Yeats."

"Well, why the fuck don't you talk about Yeats? Try opening your pretty mouf next week."

"Because we're not studying Yeats, we're reading…"

"Never 'eard of comparisons? Still at school doin' what you're told to do, Alice?"

"It's a bit hard to make a link between an Irish poet…"

"Crap!"

Alice was flummoxed.

"Look, Sunshine, next week you 'ave a go at makin' a very minimal contribution so that the rest of us don't 'ave to tolerate you sitting there like left luggage. Okay?"

"I'm not very confident about expressing myself."

"Of course you can bloody express yourself. You know how to open your mouth to flirt, don't you?" His little eyes narrowed.

Alice remembered the two medics she had bumped into outside the refectory at lunch time. Yes, she had batted her eyelids. Yes, she had smiled and chatted to them easily enough, but not about Yeats or Conrad. Another bloke from her tutorial had passed, turned his head and sneered. He must have told the others.

"You're just a fuckin' cock-tease, aren't you? You're pathetic. Don't know what you're doing 'ere."

And with that he peeled away, leaving Alice completely

in agreement with him; that she was indeed pathetic, and a flirt because she was good at that, but knowing too that compared to Julian – and every male she encountered on that campus she compared to Julian – he was nothing.

ONE TO ALICE. And maybe one to the rude student.

ALICE DID NOT master the art of argument or analysis, at least not orally, though she could do a fairly good job on paper and her grades surprised both her and her tutors. For the whole of her first year, Alice sat with her knees clenched under Clive Dunn's table, ashamed and humiliated, unable to form or articulate a single relevant thought fast enough to give it an airing. And once she had established her reputation as the dim blonde, it was hard to peel off the label stuck to her forehead. Her already diminutive intellectual confidence shrank to the size of the button on her cardigan which she twisted feverishly in her fingers throughout each excruciating hour until one day it fell off, coming to a halt right next to her tutor's feet under the table. He ignored it, just as he ignored her, and she didn't have the courage to ask for it back. She felt very, very small. And stupid.

Still, out of the corner of her eye, she scanned the shadows and hidden corners of the campus for Julian. At night, any unexpected knock on her door – now opening into a room in a comfortable hall of residence – would be his hand reaching out to make an entrance and take her in his arms once again. Any envelope promised his apology and an admission of his terrible error. And shouts along the corridor that she was wanted on the phone quickened her heart beat.

TOWARDS THE END of that first year, she discovered the record library where she could borrow an LP and shut herself in a booth with headphones. It was in one of these little transparent boxes that some fellow English students found Alice sobbing her heart out while listening to Beethoven's fifth piano concerto. It had been theirs, especially the incredibly poignant, step-by-held-breath-step Adagio. When discovered, Alice was curled over the little desk, her head on her crossed arms, tears flowing and mascara smeared down her cheeks. For a year she had carried around a balancing scale, with grief and fragile hope set against each other in a delicate equilibrium. During Beethoven's Fifth she dropped the contraption and saw hope roll away as the piano roared to its heart-break crescendo.

Chapter 13

1970

Those Were The Days My Friend

DURING HER SECOND year, a resigned Alice turned her back on the library and her clever, cynical peers whom she failed to impress. More significantly, she let go of the kite string that flew the futile, soul-destroying yearning for a boy who, she now admitted, had left her forever. Without the drag of rope that kept her grounded, she opened her eyes and looked around and noticed other people and other groups on that vast campus. So, do something, she told herself. Move! Kill the self-pity and get out there. Even widows abandon their black garments after a year.

SHE MOVED HER pitch from the library to the student union and then to the coffee shops and beer bars, to observe and listen to people she hadn't even noticed. She mustered the courage to go to events organised by groups committed to politics, athletics, flying planes and eating strawberries at operas, but none captured her imagination. Instead, she was drawn to those on the margins of all these activities; those brave misfits who were clever in ways out of sync with the expectations of tutorials and seminar rooms. Tentatively at first, then with mounting excitement, she found acceptance on the fringes of the campus where wild kids embraced the freedom of the late 60s with beer and sex, drugs and dancing, and the occasional just-in-time essay.

For the sheer fun of it, Alice leapt into the arms – and beds – of sexy long-haired youths because it was a distraction and a pleasure and they were all forever young. She kept a list of them – descriptions not names – in a little black notepad so she wouldn't forget. The one in the black-painted, windowless attic who introduced her to pot and the Velvet Underground. The rich, unhinged one with a coveted sports car who drove her at suicide speed through the city's night, missing cars, buildings and pedestrians by inches until, at a set of red traffic lights, she pushed open the door and got out. The vain one who slept in a sarong because, he said, his erections were too large and frequent to be contained within pajamas; she wanted a partner with a smaller ego. Then there was the short, peculiar one who played Tchykovsky's concertos without the orchestra on the grand piano in the Students' Union. He taught her nothing.

As she laughed through these easily forgotten interludes and briefest of romances, the previously withered Alice blossomed, her petals opening with a hunger for light and growth. Her skirts climbed higher while her hair grew long. This was the era of Twiggy; of blue eyes circled with kohl, left-bank black polo necks, long ragged skirts, bangles, velvet, knee-high boots, Hey Jude, gypsy earrings and bare feet. Alice was, for now, in her element.

No-one worried about labels or fashion or celebrities in

the late sixties. The young women in the Arts departments were free to invent. In her rebellious stage, Alice perfected her own flamboyant style of jagged sewn-together pieces of velvet and lace. She wore pavement-trailing skirts or groin-hugging minis. She saved up for clunky antique rings and stuck paper flowers in her hair.

BUT HER LOVE of clothes did not match her red-zoned finances.

"Have you sent back the form about paying my maintenance?" she had checked with her father a month before leaving for Birmingham.

"No." he replied. "Nor will I."

Alice was flabbergasted. Why hadn't he said?

"But how am I supposed to live?

"I told you...if want to go to university, then go ahead, but I'm not supporting you."

Alice racked her memory but failed to find any recording of the conversation.

"But you have to..."

"I don't have to anything. Women don't need to go to university. Your mother did just fine as a secretary."

"But I got As in all my subjects. You know I want to carry on."

"I don't believe you're especially intelligent, Alice. Never did. And you've decided to study English." He gave the word the weightiness of a fly.

"SO A DEGREE in law or medicine might be acceptable?" she

asked, not knowing whether to hit him or cry.

"Possibly. I'm certainly not paying for you to read books."

"I had no idea…"

"Oh, you certainly did. You know my views on this subject. I suggest you give up the idea now and do something useful."

SO ALICE HAD turned to her mother who had no money of her own and whose occasional, tiny treats were pinched out of her metered housekeeping money.

"Oh dear, well I think I agree with your father," she said after looking around the room in case an answer was hidden there. "Darling, I really don't know what you can do with a degree in English."

"I can teach or work in a library or in publishing…"

"And anyway…" her mother continued, not really listening, "I don't think men really like clever girls."

Damn them, Alice decided. I'll do it on my own if they won't support me.

WITH A VENGEANCE and determination, as each term drew to a close, Alice scoured the newspapers and small ads to find a job – any job – to pay for board, lodgings and books.

She worked as an untrained welder on a factory floor where she went home each evening with a hundred tiny bullet holes in her pants from the sparks that showered her when she pressed the red button. One day, dreamily and silently reciting 'Ode To A Grecian Urn,' she forgot to insert the lower part of the washing up rack and welded the two parts of the machine together causing an electrical break-down. She was sacked.

That autumn, in wellies and a waterproof that wasn't, she stumbled around muddy, rutted, rain-sodden fields picking blackcurrants until her hands, arms and face were the colour of ink. She and her fellow students bent, stood, stretched and bent again until their back and shoulder muscles were an agony of elastic. She dumped clumps of berries – no leaves, no stalks – into a cardboard container which she lugged to the next bush. The scale of payment ranged from derisory to minimal, depending on how many boxes were filled in a day. As dark descended, scratched, soaked students formed a queue at the weighing table clutching towers of filled baskets, trying not to drop one or all of them, which occasionally happened. Alice was twelve or thirteen berries short of the breadline wage every time. Then she caught a stinker of a cold which kept her in bed for a week, and on her return was told she'd been replaced by another disposable student.

One Easter holiday, she stood for eight-hour shifts at a factory production line, poking skinny plastic tubes into the upright cans of furniture polish that raced relentlessly past her. It was like watching Wimbledon – left-right, left-right – only faster, with no breaks between sets. The conveyor belt maintained its relentless speed and when Alice missed the moving targets there were shouts of indignation and anger from the regulars who finished the cans further down the line by pushing the nozzles on top. They were paid piecework so if Alice screwed up, their pay packets were lighter. They already resented the stuck-up students who would escape the hell hole after four or five weeks, and put in a complaint. Too slow for aerosol, Alice found herself demoted to shoe polish. Another conveyor belt. At night she dreamed of ever-moving objects that escaped her grasp. By day, the tins blurred into surreal objects that bounced and jumped on their fairground ride until she had to look at the walls to reset her vision. At the end of the line, another resentful man packed the lidded polish into cardboard boxes. When she hallucinated the tins into ping pong balls one day and failed to catch a single one, he complained to the manager and Alice was sacked.

BUT FOR TWO glorious summers, factories and cold fields gave way to the holiday camp in Bognor Regis where Alice pushed an ice-cream cart by day, and carried a laden tray down the aisles of the cinemas and theatres at night. The choice for punters was a little cardboard tub of vanilla or strawberry which came with a tiny flat wooden spoon, a foil-wrapped choc-ice, or a Mivi; a sickly coating of chemical raspberry over artificial vanilla on a stick.

Those were the days. Those were the nights. Late in the evening, Alice ran from the primary colours and child-like activities after spending the day entertaining punters who paid to live in a hut, eat soggy chips and be whip-lashed into hysterical activity on the fair-ground rides and ballroom dancing sessions and glamorous granny competitions. The students-turned-red-coats and camp slaves used their smiles and fake jollity as cattle-prods to force the campers – Wakey Wakey Campers!! – into seven days of jolly good fun. To the young folk, the campers were sad and desperate while they were bright and beautiful and forever young.

Alice, like others, turned her back on the older generation and danced with her own.

When the campers were safely asleep in their bunks,
Alice and her friends did Cinderella transformations into
their real selves in dark bars and cellars that pumped music
into the night and intoxicated them with the heady fumes of
beer and sex. Ripe hormones bled into the heavy air and
hung there. Alice searched for another body-on-fire. A
kindred spirit. A one night stand. A consuming affair. She
sang along to San Francisco and went dizzy with longing.

Like others in those dark rooms, Alice was drunk on a
sexual yearning that had no target except possibility and, in
the haze of smoke, almost every male was a mysterious rose-
tinted goal. It was a potent time of rock and roll and
freedom. She was young, fizzing with hope and happiness.

And then the sun went down on the summer of love.
Autumn began and the student's good will and effervescent
energy were rinsed down the gutters along with the rain. The
love-ins ceased and people drifted away. For Alice too, it was
nearly time to leave.

But one more drama waited in the wings; a tragi-comedy
about an ice-cream. They allowed Alice one ice-cream a day
free of charge while the sun blazed down and she pushed the
trolley around fairgrounds and amusement halls and dance
floors until she felt faint. At the end of every twelve-hour
shift, after Alice returned from standing in the aisles of the
cinema with her tray of melting goodies, the seedy bloke who
ran the ice-cream parlour counted every coin and every leftover ice-cream. One evening, he accused Alice of eating an
extra choc-ice without paying for it. He called her a slut. She

said it was only a choc-ice; that the wages were an insult and he could afford it. He ripped her blouse and grabbed her breasts. She slapped him across the face. He pushed her hard against the counter and shoved his hand up her skirt. She kneed him in the balls. This was 1969, and Alice had not heard of trade unions or women's' rights or sexual abuse. She was sacked.

The Alice who returned to her studies was more realistic, more resilient, and very cross.

Chapter 14

1970

Pretty Woman

AS HER WAYWARD second year limped towards its ending, Alice took to wandering around the department stores in the city centre, skint and fed-up. Her love of beautiful clothes and her budget resided on different planets, so she had always ransacked expensive designer clothes racks for inspiration and thrown together rough copies on her Singer sewing machine. But as term fizzled out, another motive drove Alice to the fashion floors – to run away from a place where she felt alienated. It's normal, tutors told her and her peers. The last term of the second year is always the low point when the novelty and eagerness of being a fresher has long worn off and the guillotine of finals has not yet come into view. You'll get over it. Final year will be different. But still her friends displayed a sighing listlessness as they rose later and later to avoid the tedium of the days and took their pleasure in the darkness of pubs and clubs in the small hours. Three of Alice's friends walked from the campus never to return. They called over their shoulders that they were off to find work in the real world. With two weeks to go, Alice took the bus to town every morning because she didn't know what else to do.

ONE MORNING, SHE closed her fingers around a wand of black mascara, which she discretely transferred to the pocket of her floor-length black coat. How did that happen? She had never stolen anything in her life, apart from a choc-ice, and that was disputed. But once safely outside, a slow grin spread across Alice's pretty heart-shaped face. Her success brought an adrenalin rush that made her skip with joy. And then, without plotting any of it, she was in Boots and laying a hand over a small pot of blusher before sliding it off the counter. Next, she rolled away a pale-pink lipstick.

Alice had found a way to make her heart beat fast again. Whenever she felt the campus closing in on her, she caught a bus to town and nicked nice little things from big shops. She persuaded herself that these slightly naughty acts of defiance hardly counted as crime. Mistakes, perhaps. Moments of abstraction. Understandable when you were broke. If she was caught – and she took every precaution not to be – the store manager would give her a slap on the wrist and send her away with a caution because Alice was obviously not a thief. Thus reassured, over the next few weeks she promoted herself to black tights and gothic jewellery and silk scarves, and still she felt no heavy hand on her shoulder. Apart from the afterglow of owning pretty new things, the greater satisfaction was getting away with it. She pitted herself against shop managers, store detectives and the staff on the counters and made fools of them all. She knew that there were other students who patrolled the shops like she did, waiting for an opportunity to reach out a hand. She wasn't alone as she circled the make-up counters. A few clumsy ones were caught and found themselves in front of the Head of Department. Alice was either more adept, or just plain lucky. Or maybe her pretty face and ice-blonde hair distracted people from the wicked business of her hands.

Alice danced many a Saturday night away in the Students Union in a short (stolen) white dress worn with no shoes at all, or in her knee-high, laced-up, red suede boots which were bona fide. She danced under lime green strobes, by herself, often on a near-empty floor, because her confidence and natural grace deterred male partners who feared being put to shame beside her. On the union dance floor, with a second rate band banging out a thunderous base through a stack of speakers, Alice turned the tables on the men who made her feel bad in the seminar rooms.

Alice, a slight, bright firefly caught in the red and blue strobes, danced on alone.

THE GIDDY TRIPS to town that left her hot and breathless with excitement stopped as abruptly as they began. The final year came upon her and with it a change of tutorial venue that probably saved her academic life. Away from the brutality of the great sprawling campus and across the busy main road that ran in front of it stood a romantic annex – the Shakespeare Institute – which Alice had never even noticed. It was a baronial pile, a short walk from the main faculty buildings, a place of manicured lawns and paved paths that wound through beds of decadent old-English roses and hummocks of scented lavender. Here, the tutors took afternoon tea and made themselves available for gentle conversation about poems and sonnets. Time was slower. Words were softer. Alice looked lovingly at the arches smothered in lush white roses and the stained glass and window seats with velvet cushions and did a quick chameleon personality change. She belonged here – of course she did – among the flower beds and the wood-panelled rooms and the rarefied atmosphere of a bygone era.

The chief actor on the stage of the Shakespeare Institute was Professor Laurence, a man of immense stature and presence with a large pockmarked face and flowing white locks. Never did any student catch him out of the role which by now, in his long and illustrious career, was less of a mask and more of a full-blown character part. Did he even have another self? Alice would get to the lecture hall early before his weekly lecture and plant herself on the front row, where she waited for an entrance that was never less than dramatic.

Occasionally, Alice caught a glimpse of this mighty figure as she sat reading Wordsworth in the weak sunshine on the lawns of the Institute. He would bow his head as he passed, as he did to all the students who littered the place, and in so doing kept them charmingly at arm's length. None of the in-groups of the English department flowered here. All was formal and old-fashioned. Of course, many students found the act unappealing, but Alice liked her new role of young gentlewoman. She walked at a slower pace and, in the long gauzy skirts and lace camisoles which she now favoured, she could imagine herself the very embodiment of a wan muse for the young dying Keats and the doomed Shelley.

Alice's ripening and mellowing continued with two

serious, insecure students for company, under the timid eye of Dr Lindsay. He was newly appointed and fresh out of university himself where he had completed a doctorate on the pastoral imagery of Shakespeare's sonnets. Alice found in this desperately shy man a patient, gentle mentor. The poet fell in love, unrequited because a tutor-student sexual relationship was the biggest taboo and one for which the man would pay with his career. She freely soaked up his blushing adoration, knowing that nothing was demanded of her in return except her company once a week, and some sharply critical essays upon which her reputation – and his – rested. He offered her extra tutorials, one-to-one, until finally Alice began to pick up the rules of the intellectual game that so far had eluded her.

When her opinions were accepted, even valued, she grew bold and articulate. She became enamoured of subtext and the ocean depths of meaning in romantic poetry, and fell in love not with her tutor but with Keats, Byron and Mansfield.

She had been in love with Yeats for many years. Now he was consigned to Irish history while she drank weak tea from china cups and nibbled wafer biscuits and switched her allegiance to poets with consumption who wrote about the reconciliation of man and nature.

Chapter 15

1970

I Can't Stand The Rain

B UT THEN CAME a beast of a bitter winter, one of the coldest since records began, as they say, and Alice coughed and shivered. In the early evenings, after classes, along the streets of posh Edgbaston, and then along the canal as she made her way on foot back to her grim basement flat with the damp walls and peeling wallpaper, she wheezed and choked in the yeasty damp air, and saw under each street lamp the yellow fog which swirled down to the soggy leaves on the pavement. Being cold became her normal bodily state, a cold too deep to be thawed by the single bar of the electric fire where she crouched as close as she dared without scalding her elbows or setting her long hair on fire. In bed she wore a jumper, hat and gloves.

Once again the stores in town called to her. From the arctic street, she rode in on a current of hot air perfumed with Coty's L'Aimant and 4711. Her hands and feet tingled and thawed. She pulled off her gloves. Occasionally she held out a wrist for a spray of perfume or lingered while a sales assistant persuaded her she was never too young to start caring for her skin.

ALICE WOVE HER way through scarves and gloves, then jumped on the escalator up to the first floor, the warmth rising with her, putting colour back in her cheeks. In the instant of stepping off, her eyes fell on the carousel of trendy, maxi coats of dark brown, positioned in perfect alignment with the top of the escalator. She picked up the scent of real leather. Alice stroked the heavy, deliberately creased fabric and buried her face between the hangers. They were the best thing she had ever seen, with a price tag to match. Alice wanted one. She had taken a few things from John Lewis in her previous incarnation as Bad Girl, but nothing since her transmogrification into Dreamy Nineteenth Century Muse. Until that day, she had trodden on eggshells to make sure she would get away with a gossamer blouse or a string of fake pearls. It had been petty crime and it had stopped as abruptly as it had begun. But on this bitingly cold day, the devil got into her, made her hell bent on owning one of those fabulous floor-length coats.

While she hovered around the carousel, holding up one coat after another, it crossed her mind that the woman on the opposite side was a store detective. The woman kept glancing up and across at Alice instead of being smitten, as Alice was, by the sumptuous feel and smell of the leather. Was it defiance or wishful thinking that made Alice ignore her instincts? In this lunatic mood, she took off her own coat and hung it over her arm, making a display of being too hot. Then she tucked and folded one coat from the carousel under her own while draping two more coats on top. Three leather coats and her own balanced on one bent elbow. A tonnage of coats. At the entrance to the changing rooms, she was shown into the first cubicle, close to a gaggle of assistants who waited to take back the rejects. The store was not very busy. The brief stilted exchange, the lack of smiles and the deliberate way they drew back the cubicle curtain should have set off loud alarm bells, but Alice blocked her ears. Her desire for the coat overruled her usually reliable antennae and desire for self-preservation.

"How many?" asked one of the women.

"Two." A lie.

"Just two?"

"Yes, two."

Alice saw the glance that passed between them but stubbornly ignored it. Flash! Danger! And while she was trying on the coat, the curtain twitched. Someone messing with the curtain and still Alice turned her back on the red warning signs. Flash! Flash! Don't do it! Through the gap, Alice could see the assistants as well as the woman who had been at the carousel. They all waited. Flash! Flash! Flashing red lights! Alice flicked the curtain shut again. And pondered. Better give up on this one and get out of here. The odds were loaded against her. Flash! But a perverse desire to outwit the establishment, and the thought of the tsunami of adrenalin that would follow such a monstrous crime, nudged her to carry on. Or maybe that day she had simply taken leave of her senses. She folded the coat as small as it would go, which wasn't very small at all, and put it into her big carrier bag. However hard she pushed, the coat remained visible. Yet still Alice did not call it a day. By now, having taken so long in the changing cubicle, and with the store women still on watch outside, Alice could hear police sirens wailing. She could have stopped the performance right there, unfolded the coat, returned it to its hanger, and handed three garments into the hands of the waiting women with an apology for getting the number wrong. Miscounting was not a crime. They would know, but they would have to let her go. Instead, she pulled open the curtain, stepped out, handed back two leather coats, and made a bee line for the exit.

OH ALICE, WHAT play did you think you were in? What drama dragged you into its plot? After months of being a diligent, devoted student, whatever turned you, this crazy morning, into an unconvincing, lunatic thief?

QUICK FOOTSTEPS BEHIND her. Running. Catching up with her, but she did not turn. She weaved between stands of clothes, around the carousels, determined to make it to the stairs and out of the store. She could have dropped the bag, done a runner, but she chose to continue even as her odds diminished by the second. Long before she reached the exit, a hand gripped her shoulder and another grabbed her arm and twisted it behind her back.

They meant business. Shoppers pressed back against the counters they had just left to leave a clear pathway for this criminal and her two fierce keepers. Alice's face flushed crimson while she was marched, already a prisoner, through the honest, the rich and the good.

In a small back room she was kept waiting for a long

time until the police arrived. No-one spoke to her or offered her a drink of water. She was despicable. When the police came, she confessed. What else could she do with a full length leather coat, its price tag still attached, on the table in front of her? She wept and said she was sorry, but none of that made a dent in their hard-faced disdain, and soon she was marched off again between two uniformed men, across the second floor – furniture and curtains – down in the lift, across the ground floor, past perfumes and gloves and stationery, watched by goggle-eyed Saturday shoppers, through the main exit and on to the street. When novelists write 'bundled into a police car' that is exactly what happens. They shoved her into the back seat, where she knocked her head against the window. An officer squeezed in beside her, and off they went, a grim and deafening silence filling the car.

THE INTERROGATION WAS long and without mercy. Alice sat in a cold, shabby, bare room for two hours where she watched paint peel while two policemen asked her over and over again what else she had taken, whether she took drugs, whether others were involved. And Alice said No and No and No. When they asked her what she did for a living, Alice took a risk and said she was a model. Please God, don't let them take me away from my chance of a degree, from my poetic tutor who believes in me, from the romantic poets who express emotions which make me faint with admiration. In a way the lie was true because in her spare time Alice posed for a weirdo photographer who dressed her as a cowgirl or a belly dancer and once as Alice in a short blue frock and white socks. He told her she had a beautiful back – a backhanded compliment if ever there was one – and paid her a pittance for standing around in fancy dress while he played David Bailey. The policemen smirked when she said she was a model. Oh yeah? Nudge nudge. Wink wink. That fitted. They were thinking porn. Filth. Tits and bums. A shoplifting porn model pinching stuff for her next fix. It figured.

They told her she would remain in a cell while they searched her home. Did porn models live in damp basement rooms? As long as they didn't notice the stacks of books and essays. Models don't read poetry and plays, do they? And then Alice felt a tiny glimmer of hope, even of victory, because these hard-faced men would not find much. She had worn the few clothes she had stolen, straightaway and in delight, because she had so few. If they were looking for a criminal stash, they would be disappointed. One gold-cased lipstick had barely been used, but hell, even porn models must buy themselves the tools of their trade. And no, she didn't do drugs because she preferred her head clear for reading and writing poetry, so they would find no little bags of white powder or tea-caddies with funny-smelling leaves in them.

THE CELL REMINDED her of a telephone kiosk, only without windows. Just the sliding oblong slat on the door which every half hour or so was rattled back, revealing a pair of expressionless eyes. The whole point was the claustrophobia – to concentrate the mind, to be afraid of never being let out. For the first hour or so, she sat on the bench with her hands in her lap, shocked and shaking from cold and loneliness. Being slight, she found she could just about sit on the bench with her legs bent. When her calves lost all feeling, she tried lying down with her legs up against the wall.

"Get your legs off that wall and sit on the bench," a voice shouted into the slit that reminded Alice of a letter box.

Back to sitting again. And sitting. Of course, just as they intended, scenarios of doom and gloom shook her into a reality she had, until then, studiously avoided.

One, her respectable, law-abiding, nervous parents would find out. They didn't deserve to be told that their daughter was in a police cell after trying to steal a leather coat.

Two, she would be thrown off her degree course. The police would find out that she was a student, not a porn model, and she would be summoned to the Head of Department and told to pack her bags.

OF COURSE, SHE vowed that never, never, never again would she take so much as a pink jelly ring or a striped mint humbug from the Pick 'n Mix counter at Woolworth's without paying for it. Round and round went the policemen's words. Even if they found no evidence of further crimes, she would be charged and appear in court and be punished, but – and here they paused for effect – if she were ever caught again, she would be given a prison sentence. She would go to jail.

UNTHINKABLE. BUT SHE had to think about it. Think, Alice, think. She would live in a concrete-lined cell with hard edges and without bookshelves. White rolls and mince. Barked orders. A militant regime of sitting on a narrow bed and walking brutal corridors and eating in a canteen. No deciding anything for herself. It was while she sat at a graffiti-scarred desk in the company of policemen that Alice understood her freedom was more important than anything else. Freedom to put on her wellies and march along the canal on a rainy day. To stay up half the night reading Wuthering Heights for the fifth time. To walk out of her door at night simply to turn her face to the ghostly light of the moon. Freedom to be herself. Panic surged in hot waves up and down her body until she leant her head on the desk, sick at heart, sick to her stomach. One last image drove her to sobbing despair while the policemen showed not one quiver of emotion: never again would she walk on the lawns of the Shakespeare Institute or sit in an oak-paneled room and talk with passion about sonnets and poems. There, Alice had found her niche and her voice. Please, please don't let her lose them. She promised herself then and there that if she got away with this – this phase of crazy recklessness – she would never risk her freedom again. Not for anything. Not for anyone.

IT WAS 8.30PM when a police woman let her out. Ten hours in the toilet-sized cage. When Alice stood to walk, her knees gave way and the suet-faced woman with pink fleshy arms in short sleeves had to hang on to her until her head stopped spinning. For the past few hours she had been in some limbo-land between nightmare and hallucination. The corridor was hurting-bright and its neon tubes brought tears to her sore eyes. Up some grubby stairs, through a maze of corridors, she was marched back into an identical drab room. The cell had done its job. She felt dead-white through and through. The walls shimmered and vibrated and the policemen faded in and out of focus. Whatever questions they threw at her now would be answered by the brain-stem answer machine. Yes, she said. Yes and Yes. She barely heard the questions. They showed her a pale blue jumper with a label attached, and she said, Yes. They showed her a black t-shirt with a tie-dye panel, and she said, Yes. Nothing else. No, nothing else. They wrote Model in the space on the form headed Occupation, sniggering and sneering, and asked her to sign a statement which she could not see because the words jiggled and jumped off the page. When she had signed her name in shaky letters, they told her she could go. She had been charged with shop lifting. She would receive a letter telling her when to appear in court. She was over eighteen, they said, as she lifted her bag to her shoulder, so no-one else would be informed. She was an adult and bore full responsibility for her actions.

Now get out of here. They didn't say 'Slut' but she heard it. They didn't say 'Whore' but she heard that, too. They did say 'Thief' and 'Shoplifter' and 'Criminal'.

PLEASE LET THERE be no-one who recognises me, Alice prayed, when she walked into court a few weeks later. Her shame was in being visible and accountable, not in having stolen. Guilt passed her by lightly. She was given a hefty fine that far surpassed the cost of leather coat, and had a bellyful of accusing, damning words spat all over her before she fled the court, and ran down the street, and in a day or two miraculously became integrated into her previous life of writing essays and thinking about her third year dissertation.

She sprawled on the lawns of the Shakespeare Institute, reading Kubla Khan, for all the world as if nothing had happened. As if the maverick two months had never been. But Alice clutched a treasure far more valuable than anything she had pinched. Her freedom.

Chapter 16

2007

Subterranean Homesick Blues

A LICE STANDS IN front of a counter above which is a bulletproof glass window.

The woman standing behind nods and cracks jokes with the uniforms.

She opens a side gate.

Into the bowels of the police station they go.

Colditz.

AS THEY ALL stomp down several flights of grubby, dimly lit stairs, Alice gets out her mental clipboard and puts on her novelist's hat. This is her only way of coping. Observe. Do not participate. And strangely, because Hunter is at home and no longer her responsibility, and because her neighbours are now deprived of their voyeuristic excitement, she does feel a bit more relaxed, and quite interested in the inner workings of a police station. It's thirty years since Alice was in a Birmingham police cell, and back then she was too terrified to notice her surroundings.

AT THE BOTTOM of the stairs, Cynic pushes open a door into a neon-lit corridor, the same colour as an outpatients' waiting room, greenish-khaki, with another counter where a female police woman, middle-aged with arms like hams in a short-sleeved white shirt, takes Alice's details while the police disrobe.

Have you been here before?

Okay. Name?

Date and place of birth?

Address?

Telephone number?

Height and weight?

So she is in a hospital. The police woman will ask for a urine sample next and maybe take blood. When Alice says, "Five foot five, and eight and a half stone," the police woman replies, "If only," and laughs a nicotine laugh which turns into a phlegmy cough. She emerges from her booth and frisks Alice, a professional, rapid slide of the hands over the shoulders, down her sides, round her waist, down the outside of the legs and up the inside. Not a hospital then, thinks Alice. An airport.

"How do you stay that size then?" she asks.

"Just the way I'm made."

"Lucky you. Now give me all your belongings. Yes… your coat and bag. You can keep the bottle of water."

"And the nuts? I haven't eaten today."

"Alright, since you're already too thin," the woman says. Almost motherly.

CYNIC EMERGES FROM a side room and stomps past her

carrying the clothes mountain on one arm. He's on his own turf. "I'm going to have to check every one of these thirty odd items on the computer to get a reference number, a possible place of purchase, and a price. It's going to take a very long time," he growls. All this boring late night homework is her fault. The poor sod is stuck with Alice Green, shop lifter, when he could be out on the trail of a juicy murderer. "Go into the interview room and wait with Police Sergeant Allerdyce."

IN THEY GO, and sit on plastic chairs at a table in which many a criminal before her has expressed boredom or futility by scrawling and scratching graffiti on the wooden surface and legs. How did they get knives into here? Alice wonders. Maybe they use their nails. After hours in here under this flickering neon tube, you might resort to scratching your name with your nails to pass a bit of time. The policeman is too young to be a policeman. About sixteen. He sits clouded in embarrassment, apparently as unhappy with his confinement as Alice.

Loud, foul language erupts from the corridor, followed by heavy thumps. Policeman Allerdyce gets up and opens the door. Alice stands and joins him, and sees the doubled-up body of a puny boy of about thirteen who is kicking out and head-butting the air. On either side, she sees the backs of two full-sized policemen. The boys' arms are held in a vice-like grip. He jerks like a wonky puppet.

"Fuck off, bastards! Fucking let go! You fucking bastards." His voice ends in a squeak as the policeman on his right wrenches an arm further behind his back.

"Oww!" roars the boy. "You're fuckin' hurting me!'

"What's going on?" Alice asks.

"Och they'll have just brought him in. Either he's pissed…sorry…drunk. Or he's a druggie, maybe selling. Maybe creating a nuisance. That's mostly what we deal with here."

"They're hurting him," Alice says.

"No' really," Allerdyce shrugs. "What can you do, eh? He's probably one of our regulars."

"Oh dear," Alice says because the two men have wrestled the boy to the floor and are now holding him down, squashing his small face hard into the lino. He's so young.

"You's not supposed to be watching this. Better get back inside."

THEY WAIT SOME more, and some more, until it's stocktaking time.

CYNIC, CREASES AND Allerdyce face Alice over the clothes mountain teetering on the table.

"Right, Mrs Green. I've traced each of these items. I'll read out one question for each item and you need to answer Yes or No."

No preliminaries. The man is bored witless. He would rather be chasing after the man who has been raping university students on the Meadows. He wants opportunities to be tough and cruel and Alice fails to offer the goods. "Right… item one…did you, Mrs Green, steal this pair of shoes from Hobbs, valued at £65?" Item held up for Alice to view.

"Yes."

Item moved to a different pile.

"Item two...did you, Mrs Green, steal this navy blue dress from..."

Yes. Yes. Yes. She has wasted enough of their time. Each piece of clothing passes from Cynic to Creased and still it takes another forty five minutes to reach the last scarf, by which time everyone is knackered.

Cynic takes everything away, and returns with another chair. He sits down, tips it onto the back legs, kneads the loose flesh on his face and sighs loudly.

"Why did you do it?" He sounds almost human.

"I honestly don't know. I've been under a lot of strain recently. I think I was defusing anger."

"What kind of strain?" Creases asks. "Financial problems? There's a lot of people panicking out there what with the bankers and businesses going belly up..."

Nah. Cynic waves away his colleague's chatter. Way off beam.

"How long have you been married, Mrs Green?"

"About a hundred years."

No-one laughs.

"Our records say you've been married to Professor Green for twenty-four years."

"Your records are correct."

"Has your husband done something to upset you, Mrs Green?"

He does know something. He's on the case. He suspects Stephen – fine – but there's no connection. The two of them are separate. What they have done is separate. Out of nowhere, tears well up. If she's going to sink, she wants to go down alone.

For a long time the uniforms sit and look at the walls while Alice battles to gain control of a sorrow that sticks in her throat like fish hooks. She can't swallow. She can't speak. Cynic gets up and leaves, with a nod to Creases to do something with the distraught woman.

Leave it, Alice. There's nothing you can do for Stephen. And anyway, why give him the benefit of a single thought? Deal with what you have to here. Leave Stephen's iceberg to float a bit longer, its venom hiding beneath the surface.

"Look…the normal procedure with someone who's pinched this much stuff is to detain them but since you've cooperated with us…" Creases is saying, "we've decided not to keep you in a cell overnight."

A stone drops into the well of Alice's stomach.

Wake up, Alice. You have come within an inch of spending a night in a police cell, where you would've had to face your demons. Time to pull your head out of the sand.

"We just need to do fingerprints and DNA and then you can go home," Creases is saying. "I'll take you to the technicians' room." He stares hard at Alice. "This has been an unusual case…to be honest we're all still a bit puzzled."

Me too.

Me too.

Act 3

Oliver

Chapter 17

1971

Talking About My Generation

THE STUDENT COFFEE bar, two hundred yards down from the refectory, was the place where the gregarious, the hungry, the lonely, and the caffeine-depleted students gathered to moan about essays and deadlines and exams. They scanned the crowd, antennae waving towards a chat-up opportunity, a one night stand or a potential soul mate.

THAT DAY, ALICE noticed an older man in front of her in the queue with his empty tray resting on the rails. Alice stared at his back in an absent-minded sort of way as they shuffled past doughnuts and ham rolls, but then he turned. Blue eyes in a crumpled face held hers and Alice did not look away. A spark. She felt her face flush and saw that he saw because his lips curled lopsidedly. No more than a twitch. Ted Hughes, Alice sighed to herself. Or Heathcliff. This lecturer – for surely that was what he was – had strayed in here for a coffee and a bun en-route to his room from the nearby campus book shop. The assumption took no detective work because a bulging carrier bag hung painfully from the fingers of one hand. Perhaps to everyone else he looked the cliché of the clever but absent-minded professor, whose thought processes and neural connections depended on fingers raked through a nest of curly grey hair. But another look revealed his worn splendour, his lived-in skin, and the years of experience filtered and analysed in a brilliant mind. Unlike his skinny, preening and self-conscious juniors, he was absolutely sure of himself and carried his heavily built body with a quiet arrogance. Did the other young women see him as Alice did? Or did they see a fifty-something wrinkled university teacher, past his prime and far too old to be worthy of their nubile attentions?

In those days it was de rigour for students to ignore staff. Alice remembered her very first evening when all the freshers had gathered and an English Professor, arriving in their midst, had been invisible to everyone except Alice who piped up, 'Hello, Professor Brown' in a lone little voice that had echoed across the marble-clad hall. Her social gaffe sparked sneers and convulsed giggles from her smart-arsed peers. Alice was not street wise. She was not canny. She was gauche and unworldly. But that was two years ago.

THE OLDER MAN'S restless eyes again found Alice's, perhaps because she was staring so hard at him, as she did when something or someone interested her. Was it because the place was crowded that they ended up carrying their trays of drinks and buns to the same coffee-stained table, where they sized each other up and acknowledged an immediate, mutual attraction?

"What subject?" he asked, biting into his croissant.

Nothing original there.

"English."

"Year?"

"Final."

"You look too young."

Cliché.

"I'm trying to make up my mind about my dissertation topic," Alice said between sips, ignoring the compliment. She could feel her cheeks glow pink and not from the hot coffee.

"So…what do you think you'll do?" Another bite of croissant.

"The sexual imagery in Shakespeare's tragedies."

She waited for the raised eyebrow. The dismissive smile.

"Good choice. A limited area of study, so lots of scope for original ideas. From my own experience, students take on too much and get their knickers in a twist. Should be fun, too."

Alice fell in love then and there. He approved of her chosen topic. He hadn't laughed. He hadn't used the terms boring or passé.

"There are layers and layers of meaning…" Alice began earnestly. "That's what I love about Shakespeare. You can be grabbed by the plot and characters, especially on stage, or you can read it slowly and find contradictory or teasing meanings below the surface which makes you question your first interpretation."

"Subtext. It's quite a hot topic at the moment, isn't it? In sociology, we're interested in what people don't say as much as what they do. Body language tells a quite a different story from the spoken word…"

THAT MORNING, HE showed Alice the tip of a vast iceberg of cultural and artistic knowledge, which left her swimming around him in tiny waves of awe. A very faint voice warned *Julian* but she ignored it. This man was so easy to talk to. They both liked Janacek, especially Taras Bulba. They both raved about Jules et Jim. He asked her if she went to the student film house and left that dangling for later. With a wave of his hand around the crowd of students in the cafe, he told her about his own research into group dynamics. He didn't shout at her as if he were in the lecture hall, but talked to her intimately and quietly, as if her opinion mattered.

"You know, you can very quickly identify the student alpha groups, and the next layer in terms of popularity, and then, of course, the loners. If you look around this cafe you'll see students grouped in a kind of hierarchy because most individuals know exactly where they stand in the pecking order. And then within each group, the leaders shine like super-bright stars, and there are those who are content to bask in reflected glory. It's called the halo effect. He paused and looked at her. "You have a halo effect right now. The sun is shining on your hair, do you know? It's gold and silver and very lovely."

And instead of throwing the compliment back in his face, as she would have done with someone of her own age, thinking it a pathetic come-on, Alice blushed and smiled and said, "Thank you."

He stood up. "I have a lecture to give in half an hour. I must go."

Perhaps he saw the disappointment in her eyes because he added, "But would you like to meet up again? I've enjoyed talking to you about poetry. It's a welcome change from group dynamics and pecking order."

Was he teasing her?

ON THAT FIRST chance collision in the student coffee house they did not stray outside the boundaries of animated intellectual conversation, although the subtext was certainly there. In his compliments, in the way he looked at her, in the way his knee pressed against hers just once under the table, and in the brief touch of his hand on hers when he got up to leave.

IF CHALLENGED, SHE would have denied it, but Alice was smitten. Until now, she had taken her pick and no-one had turned her down. After Julian, she had always been the one to finish a relationship. But each new flame, when compared to Julian, flickered out. Perhaps the instant attraction of Oliver was that he couldn't be compared. He was a different species altogether.

THE FOLLOWING MORNING, Alice woke with butterflies in her stomach when she recalled the chance meeting in the cafe. Her appetite grew eccentric; she lived on a huge chocolate gâteaux for three days and then roasted parsnips for the next week. She walked into lamp posts and somehow couldn't get through doors without banging and bruising her knees and elbows.

OLIVER PHONED ALICE a week later and invited her to a

Truffaut film at the University Film House, and Alice's heart sang. They sat close together on a hard bench among dozens of other film buffs and when, afterwards, Oliver talked perceptively about the film, Alice managed only wild stabs at intelligent meanings because her attention during the film had been distracted by the male presence at her side. Bulky and broad shouldered, he smelt of expensive after-shave (very subtle) and good clean sweat (more pronounced) and pheromones (overwhelming). They agreed to meet in the Botanics the following weekend where, on a dreich Autumnal day, they squelched around the Japanese gardens and topiary displays and the hothouses while discussing Hardy's late tragic characters.

BACK IN HER basement flat, her feet sodden and worms of mud oozing through the holes of her now-leaking red boots, Alice pressed, as a memento, a single purple five-fingered leaf, picked up from the pavement on her way home, between the pages of Dostoyevsky's Crime and Punishment. A man in his autumnal years, she thought. How certain. How reassuring.

OVER THE NEXT three or four weeks, Oliver and Alice met often in the tiny, crowded Druckers in the town centre; one of the first places in those far-off days to serve real ground coffee. Here, the cakes were very fine – light concoctions of chocolate and coffee and almond – and the conversations rising from the other tables were very loud. No-one could possibly overhear them. They couldn't even hear themselves and took to sign language and lip-reading. Oliver took her hand in his and kept it. Under the table, he pressed his thigh against hers. He held out a forkful of his honeyed baklava and she fed him sticky apple strudel. They licked crumbs off the same spoon. Oliver dipped a finger into the froth of Alice's creamy cappuccino while she, unbidden, parted her lips to lick his offering.

Afterwards they would walk along the canal, Oliver's arm heavy on Alice's slight shoulders, while she reveled in the loose tumble of thoughts and arguments that came so easily in his reassuring presence. At last, here was someone with whom she needed no mask and no pretense. They talked often about the role of a muse in the life of an artist or writer, and Oliver said that researchers and scientists needed muses too, implying that this would be Alice's role in his own work.

She was comfortable with him. And, of course, in love.

INTERVAL

"HANG ON, ALICE. You're painting this episode…this interlude…as a romantic courtship. Let's stick to the facts."

This time Alice didn't jump in surprise. She was getting used to her older self managing to extricate herself from whatever she was doing with the police and appear at her side. It was a trick they shared. "So what's your take on it thirty years on?

"Well, how long was it from the coffee bar conversation to Oliver getting you between the sheets? Five weeks?"

"Getting us between the sheets."

"OK. And it's so damn obvious why you fell for him. It's almost funny."

"Well?"

"Well… there you were going out with young men and immediately getting out your clipboard stamped with Julian's template and of course they all fell short."

"He was a hard act to follow."

"I agree. Julian was exceptional and you fell in love with him at a tender, impressionable age. You were imprinted on him. Hooked. Like the ducklings described by Conrad

Lorenz. He says that if the first creature they see at a critical stage early in their development is not the mother duck but, say, a collie dog, they follow the collie dog. Fixed. Forever. Biology!"

Alice smiled. "I'm not sure about the theory, but I was imprinted on Julian."

"Then along came Oliver and you were stuck for a comparison. Different categories. Different boxes. Late-middle-aged, heavily built, wild grey hair, sexually experienced, a womanizer, cynical…"

"I haven't come to cynical yet."

"You will soon."

"Stop. Don't give away the plot. And now you've explained the attraction, please go away and let me continue."

"I will, but it wasn't by chance, was it, that the first man to hold you – in both senses – was nothing like Julian."

Young Alice sighed. "I'd looked and failed to find another Julian. Oliver came along and filled the void. I don't regret it."

Chapter 18

1971

Love Is Just A Four Letter Word

FROM THE START, Oliver had been open and honest with Alice. He told her he was a married man, aged fifty-eight, with three almost grown-up children. There had been no cover-up or deceit. He had laid his cards on the table at their fourth meeting, over the vanilla cheesecakes, when it was clear to both of them that they couldn't keep their hands off one another. The fact that even a hint of a sexual relationship between a lecturer and a student would spell disaster for his career persuaded Alice that he must be very serious indeed. Would he risk so much otherwise? He told her that although the passion had long drained away from his marriage, he still loved his wife and would never leave her. Alice heard honesty and faithfulness and was grateful. What she didn't hear was sexual greed. What she didn't see was an older man wanting both the security and convenience of a wife as well as the ripe sweetness of a young girl. Alice was seduced by power and status. And pretty words. Joni Mitchell's *The Last Time I Saw Richard* played on, and on, and still Alice did not make the connection.

He proposed a contract, to exist in their psyches, so there wouldn't be any emotional muddle or recriminations. Although they had not yet made love, he suggested that perhaps they would want uncomplicated sex as well as good conversation over good coffee and good cakes. They would not fall in love. They would not take their relationship too seriously. Neither of them would pine for the other, nor apply pressure for anything more demanding or more encompassing than passionate trysts. Alice swallowed the caveats and constraints along with a mouthful of almond tart covered in frothy cream because she was in her third year, on the home stretch, with finals looming and a dissertation to be completed, and so persuaded herself that this kind of arrangement would suit her perfectly because she did not have space in her life for a complicated relationship. How mature this arrangement was. Like the man.

She signed the contract on the imaginary dotted line and was grateful for this older man's clarity.

IT WOULD BE untrue to suggest that Alice was misled.

SHE HAD STEPPED lightly into lots of fleeting affairs, but Mechanical Engineers and Geography students displayed a pitiful lack of erotic skills. Even the alpha males of the five-starred Medical School seemed unable to transfer their knowledge of anatomy to love making. Their repertoire was as limited as their peers' as they mauled her breasts and flicked her bare nipples with hurtful fingernails and kneaded the flesh of her bum as if they were making bread. Most kissed with wet goldfish lips pursed into a round O, eyes squeezed tight. In bed, the young men came so quickly that Alice barely had time to get her knickers off.

So Alice already knew that she needed someone older and wiser. At least, that's what she told herself.

ONE NIGHT, ALICE and Oliver lingered in the pub long after everyone else from the Poetry Society had dissected 'The Wasteland' and left. They held hands until intelligent conversation dwindled to half-formed sentences and sighs, and remained while huffy waitresses banged chairs on top of tables and brushed the floor right under their feet.

"Are you closing?" Alice asked; the first to be embarrassed into animation.

"Only an hour ago," the waitress snorted, giving Oliver a filthy look.

Very slowly, he retrieved his pipe from his jacket pocket and puffed the thing into a red glow before he deigned to move. When he got up, he indicated that the timing was purely his decision, and Alice felt a thrill at being the companion of someone so sure of himself that he was immune to criticism and impervious to trivial rules and regulations.

Outside in the warm, dark wind, Oliver pulled Alice close inside his thick blanket of a coat, and kissed her. It was a kiss of exquisite loveliness. A kiss that was full and sensuous. Slow and tender. Molasses and treacle and tobacco. He kissed her until the world was spinning faster on its axis and the stars were shining more brightly in the night sky while Alice laughed at the silly and inadequate verbal clichés that popped up like cartoon bubbles. She had not known that such kisses existed. Even Julian's kisses…. no, don't go there. It was like sinking deep into a pool of silken water, and down she went, kissing him back and wanting more.

Silly, impressionable Alice. Blind, butterfly infested Alice. Yearning, aroused Alice. She swooned and clung to him right there on the pavement while the traffic roared past and hoots of laughter and lewd words from vans and lorries bounced off the magic circle she had spun around them.

"YOU KNOW WHAT kisses lead to," Oliver said, a couple of days later when they were walking along the canal in a fine drizzle from a slate-grey sky.

"Yes," she replied, as their lips met.

"I'm a very good lover."

Did he say that? Or did she imagine it? She couldn't be sure either way since her ear was pressed hard against the fuzzy lapel of his coat. He undid the three big buttons on her shiny yellow PVC mac, worked his way round to her shoulders and pressed his thumbs into all the tender places with their tight little knots of tension. Those assured hands then moved to circle her waist, measuring its circumference, and curved down over her slim hips, then softly, slowly, inch by inch, they caressed upwards again until they held her breasts. Certain. Skilled. When he finally let go of Alice, he stepped back and laughed as if he had just overdosed on pleasure. Alice laughed too. Somehow they found themselves walking towards Alice's bed-sit.

IN HER BASEMENT room, he drew the curtains against the rain and Peeping Toms, then without pause flung off his wet coat, unbuttoned his shirt, and unzipped his trousers. He bent to peel off his pants and socks. Alice suppressed a small pang of disappointment because in her fantasies she had envisaged undressing him slowly and with kisses, whereas he was already heading for the bed while she had yet to remove her wet, plastic Mac. Shut up, she chastised herself. He knows what he's doing.

Alice was shooing away the thought that without his clothes this alpha male was stripped of a layer of dignity and gravitas when he grabbed her by the waist, pulled her down on the bed and peeled off her jeans and knickers. Half-shy, half-appalled, half-shell-shocked, Alice successfully hushed her gremlins and with swooning gratitude handed over her body to a man whose sexual expertise were so much greater and more magnificent than hers. She had a brief moment to register surprise that he didn't stop to look at her. And to wonder why, like others before him, he didn't run his fingers through her golden hair or stare into her youthful blue eyes. She had been worried that he would find her lacking. If he wanted full breasts and a ripe peach of a bum, she would disappoint with her tomboy body of long limbs and narrow hips. Into the room floated more lyrics by Joni Mitchell as Oliver tugged Alice's velvet waistcoat and tie-dye T-shirt over her head and snapped apart the hooks of her bra. Heavens, he was adept. Alice lay down while Joni sang on.

Except that he didn't seem to be doing any gazing at all. Had he noticed the golden birthmark on her ankle? Had he admired the slightness of her wrists and ankles? Did he know

127

the colour of her eyes?

Alice looked at the naked Oliver; a focal-male triangle of strong shoulders and a barrel chest tapering to a nonexistent, almost caved-in bum, the whole amply protected on the outside by an animal coat of wiry grey hair which was rough and resistant to her touch. She thought of pan-scourers and Brillo pads. She thought terriers. His prominent red nipples poked through the curly covering on his chest, harder and more sexy than her own flat, pale, moons.

"DO YOU CRY out at orgasm?" he asked, biting her earlobe.

"Wait and see," she improvised.

"Do you reach orgasm easily?"

Alice had no idea. With whom to make the comparison? Why was he asking?

"Do you have clitoral or vaginal orgasms?"

Even more clueless.

What is this? Alice thought, glancing through her curtain of hair at this man who, instead of muttering sweet nothings, was asking questions from a medical questionnaire. Is he writing up this encounter in his sociology note book? Perhaps I'm just one of his experiments. I'm data.

"Ever tried a threesome?"

Why doesn't he shut the fuck up and hold me and make love to me?

Oliver rolled on to his back and laughed a hoarse, smoker's laugh while Alice wrinkled her pretty nose, propped herself up on one elbow and for the first time since they had arrived back in her flat, stared straight at him. Properly. Where was the Oliver of the seductive sweet-talk and sugar-dusted cakes? The older academic of their enticing discussions? She was just considering how to do a runner, eyeing the door and contemplating a rapid, naked exit, when he rolled close to her, kissed her beautifully on the lips and whispered, "You're lovely." And Alice relaxed and banished the bad thoughts.

Except a tiny little niggling one: He didn't say that to every woman he bedded, did he?

He explored her body with knowing, probing fingers and sweet mutterings and, like a detective softly brushing a crime scene for clues, he licked his way down her torso to his end goal. Alice suppressed a giggle. Then fingers and tongue were inside, massaging and rubbing and moaning.

"You're so wet. Do you always get this wet? Oh my God."

Wasn't she supposed to do the moaning? Stunned into complete silence by this man who now lay with his head between her thighs, Alice added a few little sighs of her own so that he didn't feel he was singing solo, but his excavations gave her not the slightest pleasure. Making a last valiant effort at self-delusion, she told herself that she was being naive and narrow-minded. This is how mature, knowledgeable men make made love, she told herself. Just go with the flow. Relax, Alice. For God's sake.

After more burrowing and groaning, Oliver emerged to kiss her stickily on her lips.

"Did you orgasm?" he asked.

"Yes. Thank you," she lied.

"Help me come," he whispered.

"How?"

No young stud had ever made such a request. Up to now, she had experienced penises like concrete bananas which were quickly thrust inside her followed by instant release, but against her thigh lay something flaccid.

"I'm too old for this. I'm sorry," he said.

Lust made way for pity. Clear vision replaced mind-numbing sensuality. Alice felt sorry for this man because he was no longer young. Or sexy. Or able to keep an erection.

On his back again, Oliver seized his cock, took Alice's hand and held it inside his, and so began a frantic and finger-crushing – Alice had not removed her lumpy rings – up and down, up and down, upanddownandupanddown, accompanied by single expletives fired like verbal bullets towards the ceiling.

"Fuck!"

"O!"

"O FUCK!"

"O GOD! I'm coming."

"I'm coming."

About bloody fucking time, Alice thought, wishing she was anywhere but in bed with an older man for whom making love was reduced to sad, aided wanking. And when he finally exploded, he dipped his fingers in the pool of semen on his hairy chest and licked them one by one.

"Salty," he announced.

"Protein," he said.

"Lovely," he said.

"Do you know, I used to wank into a glass of water and drink it? Very nourishing."

Alice did not want to know.

She did not want to be here.

Alice backtracked fast, rearranging her observations and memories and desires in the light of this recent experience and deciding that given a choice, she preferred after all the frantic, clumsy orgasms of sweat-soaked, skinny-ribbed male medical and mech. eng. students. How could this gorgeous older man of exquisitely fine words and beautiful kisses morph into such a pathetic old bloke?

Alice felt sullied and stupid. Duped and disgusted for allowing herself to be led down the primrose path. You idiot, Alice. You silly, naive idiot!

Chapter 19
1971

It's A Man's World

I T WAS HER own fault. The only comment this man had made was that she was lovely and any male could manage that. She might as well have been a blowup doll for all the notice he took of her. How many women had he taken to bed and used for his own gratification? She decided to harvest some knowledge from this sad situation.

He had lit his pipe now and was puff-puffing smoke all over her.

"Look, you've been straight with me I know. You've told me you've had lovers before…but how many?" she blurted.

"What's up, Poppet? Worried? Don't be."

"I'm not worried at all, I just want to know."

He laughed again.

"A long time ago, I came to the conclusion that monogamy is all wrong for the males of the species. I've been married for more than twenty-five years and I miss a good, zip-less fuck; isn't that what Erica Jong calls it? You should know. You're the English student. I still fuck my wife, but it's boring and sex within marriage…at least after the first randy six months or so of kitchen tables and bathroom floors…is no different from eating or drinking. A good fuck is like a good cup of coffee. Same kind of thing…just another appetite. Having affairs doesn't hurt anyone…"

"Your wife?" Alice interrupted.

"I've never told her and I never shall. What she doesn't know can't hurt her. I'll never leave her. There have been women who have asked me to, but I've never led them on or deceived them. I've always made a contract with them first so we both knew where we stood and there were no misapprehensions."

Bully for you.

"So how many?"

"Oh… a lot. I'm fifty-eight, Alice. Old to you no doubt, but sex, well, it's essential and it's as gorgeous as ever."

But you're hopeless at it, Alice almost said. Yes, you! The great Don Giovanni (ha ha again) is lousy at lovemaking. Sex? What you do is wanking in the almost irrelevant company of a female. Any female.

"Were any of your affairs serious?" she pursued. She might as well pick his brains while he was there.

"Some. One of my muses did grow too fond of me…she wanted all of me…she wanted to marry me, so I had to walk away."

OK. Faithful with a bit on the side. Security with added excitement.

"One night stands?" Alice pursued.

"Yes. One of the perks of academic life is the conference circuit. We yak all day and fuck all night."

He sat up, blowing clouds of smoke into Alice's hair

while she tried to get to grips with an experience that was sad and limp. The next question came unbidden.

"Do you ever visit prostitutes?"

"Yes."

"That's awful…"

Alice saw vermillion. Her hackles rose.

"You don't approve? I thought you'd be more enlightened than that. They're lovely, warm women," he said, as if appraising ripe fruit on a stall.

"I'm not criticising the women!" Alice said fiercely, sitting up and pulling on her knickers. "I'm criticising you. And if you think I'm going to buy into that Happy Hooker story, you must be joking. They do it because they have no choice. Prostitution is the last option for a woman. Either they're stuck in a poverty trap, or they're drug addicts. They sell their bodies as a desperate last resort because they need the money to survive! It is a horrible, degrading, dehumanizing way of life. Prostitution is a violation of a woman's soul and sexuality and don't you ever kid yourself otherwise."

"Wow, Poppet! This is getting a bit heavy. Hold on…"

"You go out and buy a woman's body like you would buy a packet of cigarettes or a can of beer. You are robbing her of her humanity. Her dignity. You reduce her to a sex object and you think she enjoys it."

"You're wrong, actually. The woman I go to is a good friend. She's lovely, we talk about all kinds of things. I'm fond of her, and she's very, very good."

"Spare me the details. She tells you what you want to hear because you pay her…how much?"

"What?"

"How much do you pay her?"

"Sixty-five pounds. She gives twenty to the owner."

"For how long?"

"What is this? An inquest?"

"I want to know. I've never met a man who uses prostitutes."

"Half an hour."

"You pay sixty-five quid for half an hour's sex with…"

"I told you, she's very good. She wouldn't get paid unless she…"

"Don't kid yourself, Oliver. She's a professional sex-worker whose scary, repulsive job is to have sex with men like you and make them think it's all good clean fun. She services you. Like a car going for its MOT. Nothing more."

"Hey…calm down. What's all this about, then? We need to talk about this."

"I don't think there's anything else to discuss," Alice replied from inside her T-shirt.

Was she being fair, or was she reacting badly because she had discovered that hers was just another in a long line of female bodies and, judging by his tepid sexual response, not one that even turned him on. She had offered this older man her youth and in return he had barely looked at her. It nagged at her. Tomorrow, or the next day, he would remember almost nothing about her body. She would blend into his composite picture of dozens of women, her edges blurred to accommodate other females with larger or smaller breasts, rounder or heavier hips, dark or auburn or grey hair. This beautiful, powerful man had managed to make her feel insignificant. And dirty.

He dressed quickly and in silence, not bothering to wash the semen from his legs and chest, before bending down to her dressing-table mirror and combing his fingers through his mad grey hair. He put on his trench coat, tied the belt loosely, and waved at her with a trill of his fingers. As his footsteps retreated up the basement steps, Alice understood that for him the excitement had been in the chase rather than the kill, whereas she had hoped for a new life, not death, at the end of the pursuit. It had been, for him, just another trivial game.

HIS JADED INDIFFERENCE left her hopelessly sad. Sitting on the bed with her T-shirt on back-to-front and her jeans still in a tangle on the floor, she experienced a loss out of all proportion to the event. While her mind rebuked her for her silliness – after all it was just an affair that had petered out before it had begun – her heart told her otherwise. Was she someone so bland and vapid, physically and intellectually, that a sexually obsessed, middle-aged Casanova had failed to make love to her.

SHE STOOD NAKED for a long time in front of her full length mirror, and, coolly considering her reflection, concluded that her body was really rather ordinary. When she looked at herself sideways, she saw a flattish chest, long lean legs, straight lines. Alice imagined an exam question which would ask: find an image to describe Alice Green as a lover and justify your choice of words. It would have to be a small pink blancmange, she decided. Even though she didn't wobble very much. And with that assessment, she forgot the many young lovers who had been eager to possess her. She twisted their hungry kissing and desperate love-making into a new explanation; they were in a permanent state of hormonal over-dosing and it wasn't her they wanted to fuck, it was any female of any shape, size, or religious denomination. Alice forgot to factor in their sighing gratitude and moony stares. She crossed out their protestations of love and adoration. She obliterated the way they followed her around the campus pleading for one more chance.

DURING THE DAYS that followed the basement bedroom scene, Oliver's attitude and ineptitude were recast by Alice into a failure on her part to engage with him. To the nagging worry that her body was lacking was added the deeper pain that her mind held no lure or interest. Her thoughts were anodyne. He had hood-winked her into thinking that her views on Coleridge interested him. If she were an attraction in a fairground, she'd be the candy floss stall, not the big dipper or the dodgem cars. It had been a long time since the ugly student had told her she had nothing worthwhile to say. Maybe he was right.

For Oliver, she had been almost invisible.

And of course he didn't remember the colour of her eyes.

Chapter 20

2007

Under My Thumb

FOUR FLICKERING NEON tubes of the 1950s kitchen variety cast a green hue on what looks like a hospital sluice room with a sink, a few pigeon holes, and torn posters hanging lop-sided off the wall. The guys in here are wearing white T-shirts and black trousers. They are more relaxed, Alice thinks, because this is the final fence in the obstacle course. Endgame. The victim has gone through the torture chambers and emerges here in a colder but brighter light. Only formalities remain.

The two men, one with red hair, look first at Alice, then at the young guy in uniform.

"This her?"

"Yeah. Mrs Green."

They stare at her. Alice smiles politely and reads their thoughts.

"This shouldn't take long, then. Fingerprints first. Over to that machine there."

Alice doesn't miss the amused raised eyebrows and the 'search me' look exchanged between the pair. Ginger presses a few buttons, gets up the menu, presses Start, and there on the screen is a hand shape drawn by a child.

"OK, left hand," says Ginger. "Place your index finger in the space there…press hard on the plate…"

A red light comes on.

"Och…it's playing up. Technology, eh?"

"What's up?" asks the sidekick.

"Search me. I can't get a reading."

"Let me try. You're not computer literate!"

"And you are?"

The jokes and banter continue. Alice can follow some of what they say, and smiles in appropriate places, but their accents defeat her.

"Try her thumb," suggests Ginger.

"Why?"

"Maybe her thumb's got a print."

"Why?"

Ginger slaps Sidekick on his shoulder and pushes him to one side.

Alice puts her thumb on the plate, presses hard, Ginger squashes it harder, rolling it from side to side for good measure.

A red light comes on.

Both men start laughing.

"Go and get the chief," Ginger says.

Don't bother, thinks Alice. I have no finger prints. I don't exist.

WHEN CYNIC LEANS his bulk against the door jamb, Alice can see 'Not you again!' pasted into his mean eyes.

"What's wrong?"

"She's not got any finger prints."

"Of course she's bloody got finger prints."

"We're no' joking. The computer won't give a reading," Ginger replies.

"Then use bloody ink," he says between clenched teeth, each word separated by a big space.

"Did he say ink? I've not used ink for about fifty years."

"You's weren't born then," says his sidekick.

"Well, use it now, son." Cynic says. Without humour.

AFTER A LOT of rolling of fingers on an ink-soaked slab, Ginger and Alice are smeared with black and Ginger's T-shirt looks ruined. They wash at the sink with Day-Glo orange washing up liquid that doesn't remove the stains. They dry their hands on paper towels.

"Right. Over here next." Ginger is collecting cotton buds and a polythene bag.

Now what?

"Open your mouth. I need your DNA."

On autopilot, Alice obeys, but as the policeman rolls a cotton bud around the inside of her mouth, she stiffens. She twists her head, resisting this probing of her mouth, but the policeman only pushes the probe deeper, scraping the back of her cheeks until she gags. The search and the arrest have been ignominious, but by maintaining a grim amusement she has come through. This forced entry of her mouth feels like an assault. It is too intimate. In a hospital or at the dentist, fine, but not here, in a grotty room with a couple of lads in T-shirts.

The most intimate and unique part of herself has been violated, stolen, taken without her consent. She watches in silence as Ginger drops the swab into a little plastic bag, seals it, and writes her name on it. The essence of Alice Green, captured and contained in a jiffy bag. The men, perhaps sensing what she feels, do not throw jokes into the silence.

"You can go now."

Alice jumps. She hadn't noticed Cynic back in the door-way. Does he relish her discomfort? Can he even put himself in her shoes?

"Right. Follow me back up to reception. I just have to remind you that you have been formally charged and your case will go to court."

Alice says nothing. They retrace their steps, past the cubicle with the sliding windows where Alice is handed her coat and bag, up the stairs into Reception where the clock says twenty minutes past midnight. Beyond the revolving doors, the night is black and the street empty.

"I'm afraid you won't be able to phone your husband now, Mrs Green." Cynic says. "We'll call a taxi to take you home."

"I don't want to phone him." Alice does not bother to ask why they won't let her.

"Actually, Mrs Green, we need to talk to your husband too."

There is a glimmer of triumph in his dead eyes.

"What? He hasn't done anything. I told you back in the flat that this has nothing to do with him. He knows nothing about it."

"You told us all sorts of things back in the flat." He twists the knife and enjoys the feel of it. "I can't say any more at the moment, I'm afraid."

What more is there to tell?

"He will be appalled."

"Any husband would be."

THE MAN HAS managed a human comment, thinks Alice. He has formed words into a sentence beyond the ring fence of police-speak. But he's wrong. Most husbands might be appalled, but she can think of one husband in particular who would have picked her up from this police station with a wicked, comradely grin. He would have teased her mercilessly; there would have been no disdain from the moral high ground. They would have laughed and celebrated over a bottle of cheap Chianti.

Chapter 21
1971

Get Up, Stand Up

IN APRIL THE students, who were both politically well versed and vociferously active, were in a state of hysterical fervour verging on hatred as they anticipated a visit to the campus by Enoch Powell shortly after his 'Rivers of Blood' speech. In the Students' Union, the Marxists and the agitators, the egoists and the oddballs, and even those who preferred to spend their days peacefully reading and writing in the library, had come together to orchestrate a noisy, forceful and hostile protest. Students deserted lectures and tutorials in droves to write pamphlets and make posters and to stir up the few remaining students who dared show apathy. The campus became a political hotbed. Students and lecturers gave heated speeches and waited like lions for the kill.

The Powell Protest Room in the Students' Union was an explosion of stinky sandwich wrappers, polystyrene cups stained with coffee dregs, fag ends, abandoned clothing (some never to be reclaimed), books, and art materials strewn across and below a huge table. Alice wandered in one day because she was passing, and because she felt a twinge of curiosity and conscience. Within an hour, she was stripped to her T-shirt and red in the face with the effort of colouring huge letters on a banner. Since the banner had been spread out across the floor, the only way to work was to shuffle about on her bum. The motley crew of streetwise students, many of whom were proudly from the working classes and had lived on council estates all their lives, fascinated her. Maybe their accents were a bit exaggerated, but their fervour was not.

Overseeing the proceedings that afternoon was a tall, thin, pale-faced lad called Cal who looked as if he had been up all night and had not eaten in weeks. Bounding around the room like a cat, he leapt between groups and individuals with a cigarette pressed between his fingers, giving advice and encouragement with his motor-mouth and his infectious, wicked grin. He talked ten to the dozen, taking on anyone who wanted to challenge his rabid left-wing views.

"Hi," he said to Alice during a brief pause in his restless pacing. "Who're you?"

And when Alice really looked at him, she saw black curls falling on skinny but wide shoulders and eyes as blue as cornflowers. She felt his palpable, racing energy.

"Haven't met you before, have I?" Cal said, and received an imaginary gold star from Alice for his ability to distinguish her from the dozens of other blonde students who must have passed across his territory. "Good to have you join us. What subject?"

"English. And you?"

"Politics and Philosophy. Final year."

"Me too."

"You've deserted swatting then? For our good cause? The

vibes here are amazing, don't you think? We're going to have a massive protest when Powell shows his fucking face next week. How dare he turn up?"

"Individual right to speak?" Alice suggested, putting down her crayon while he beamed his ferocious energy on her.

"Difficult one. I agree in principle… everyone should have the right to free speech… but what if the viewpoint voiced is damaging or discriminatory or inflammatory?"

Alice considered this. "I don't know," she replied. "Free speech or muzzling? Maybe you allow everyone their say but we have the freedom to respond and react as we choose, if necessary by voting with our feet."

"Exactly. So…if someone gives public vent to racial stereotyping… as Powell has done on several occasions…"

"Yeah…egged on by our labour government, don't forget." Another student shouted from across the other side of the table. "I'm Adam, by the way. Pleased to meet you."

Alice nodded and found herself in the midst of a quick-fire debate as articulate students hurled their arguments around the table.

"Yeah well, I'm going to play devil's advocate here…" called a crop-haired young woman with a pierced nose. "Just for practice, you understand. I've heard people say he was simply airing the concerns of his constituents. Isn't that what a MP is supposed to do? Duty to his constituents and his conscience come before loyalty to his party or his own career. Aren't these commendable qualities? Isn't this what we want from our politicians?"

Articulate stuff, Alice thought. Envious.

"I can answer that." Cal replied in his rapid, breathy way;

words tumbling out in his hurry to express himself. "Powell's speech wasn't balanced or neutral. It reeked of racial hatred and incitement to racial hatred. He called black kids 'wide-grinning piccaninnies.' He wasn't even subtle. The way he linked crime and fecklessness to colour was playing straight into the hands of anyone frightened by someone from another culture or with a different coloured skin. Immigrants are dangerous, right? Crude stuff, man."

"I suppose he touched a deep racial nerve in our society," Alice said quietly, surprising herself at having something to say, something she believed in too.

"Dead right, he did. He knew what he was doing all right." Cal grinned at her. "Spot on the money there, Alice."

"I suppose, too, the racists now feel free to crawl out of the woodwork because they're no longer ashamed of their secret fears and thoughts. Someone in authority has expressed what they have been thinking for years so now it's OK for them to shed their inhibitions and admit that they want to keep the country white and British."

Cal looked at her admiringly, then bobbed down to squat beside her.

"Hey, where have you been all my life, sweetheart?" he asked. "Good to have you aboard. What are you doing tonight?"

Alice laughed, thinking he was joking, but he put his arm on hers. "No, I'm serious. I'm going to pack up here about eight… been at it since nine this morning. Want to come for a drink?"

AT A STROKE, Oliver was obliterated and replaced by gangly,

mouthy, high-energy Cal. Afterwards, but never at the time, Alice would ask herself why Cal had picked her when he could have had any number of beauties more articulate and radical and restless than her. The answer she gave herself was that she, Alice, represented some kind of secure anchorage for him. An alter-ego. Cal, untamed, flamboyant, and sometimes out of control, needed on the other end of his psychological seesaw someone who was calm and quiet and grounded. He needed Alice.

A WEEK LATER Powell is battling his way inch by inch across a Birmingham University campus heaving and seething with students and staff who block his path every inch of the way while at his side, his bodyguards and protectors and supporters try to nudge him forwards. Waiting on the library steps, Cal and Alice stand in a crowd of yelling, heckling students, their hands closed tight around their eggs.

"Now'" shouts Cal as Powell comes within hurling distance.

Alice raises her fist. Others aim. Cal's egg falls short, but Alice's egg hits the lapel of his dark suit and for a few seconds the bits of shell and yellow goo hang there, an obscenity, before yielding to gravity. Powell has the presence of mind not to react. Head held high, he continues on his embattled, hate-filled way, as if there were no egg yolk dripping down the front of his immaculate suit.

"Bull's eye!" shouts an overwrought Cal. He hugs Alice and yells, "Marry me!"

And in the heat of this heightened political moment, Alice says, "I might."

Chapter 22

1971

Talking About The Revolution

ALICE SOMETIMES CONSIDERS herself unworthy of the charismatic Cal as she accompanies him all over the campus, to meetings in smoke-filled rooms, to the pub for more persuasion and debate, to students' rooms where arguments rage into the night. She watches in admiration as he charms people into donating funds, voting for his cause, backing his latest ambitious scheme. He manages to be everywhere, and all things to all people. So it surprises no-one when, sometime after the Powell protest, he stands for President of the Students' Guild and wins by a handsome margin. This is what he has been working towards, and from now on, Cal's days and many of his nights are consumed with NUS politics, students' rights, committees, boards, and conferences. He is a sleek, political athlete of an animal freed into his natural territory, bounding across factions and disputes with ceaseless energy. He is superb.

When she has time, Alice acts as his secretary and help-mate, remaining in his shadow because that is where she is most useful. When he is not busy with individuals and groups, their evenings are spent stuffing leaflets into envelopes or delivering pamphlets to all the students in all the halls of residence. Alice feels no resentment about the time Cal spends on student politics because she is preoccupied and busy herself, finishing her dissertation and studying for finals. Unlike Cal who will wing it, she has to memorise hundreds of quotations and prepare dozens of dummy exam answers after doing her research on which questions come up most frequently because she knows that she cannot think on her feet, nor can she produce fresh and cogent arguments under the pressure of exam conditions. She does not trust herself to invent, and so she learns by rote. Her head is choc-a-block with Blake and Camus and Jane Austin and Byron and Stanislavsky and Grotowski. Please God, let these subjects appear in the papers when at last she sits down in her chair, at her desk, and the examiner says: "You may now turn over and begin."

Just occasionally, Alice and Cal manage to clear a whole evening for themselves. On these treasured occasions, Alice gets ready with meticulous attention to detail. Beginning in the late afternoon, while Cal is still caught up in meetings which may or may not finish on time, Alice showers and washes her hair because she wants to smell sweet for her lover. She shaves her legs even though the soft, fair down is barely visible, and shaves under her arms. She attacks the soles of her feet that are as hard and dry as a Massai warrior's from going barefoot all summer. Out of the shower, she rubs body lotion over her already smooth limbs and tummy and bum. While her hair is pulled back in a towel-turban, Alice plucks the fine, unwanted hairs beneath her brows and uses a flat disc of emery paper to banish unwanted facial fuzz. From a little square packet, she squeezes a mud mask over her face, and settles on her bed to listen to Neil Young until the paste is hard and cracking. Then warm water splashed on silky skin and more unguents and moisturisers. Alice's hair is as straight and fine as sewing cotton, but with skill and mousse and artifice and a lot of twisting of strands round her fingers under the heat of her hair dryer, she concocts a wavy mass that she pulls up into a deliberately messy-looking knot, pulling free a few tendrils to fall artfully about her pretty face. This face, without make-up, Alice considers to be a pale full moon without any distinguishable features, and so she sets to work to pencil in her eyebrows, and paint liquid black lines on upper and lower eye lids, and to thicken her pale lashes with layer upon layer of black mascara. After all, this is the era of Jean Shrimpton and Veruschka and Marianne Faithful with their ghost eyes rimmed in black. Once, when washing her hair in the grim Victorian vault that houses the student baths, a girl from one of Alice's tutorial groups saw her without make-up and didn't recognise her. Alice is clever enough to make the best of what she has, and is lucky enough to fit the fashion template of her day.

The preparations for Cal's arrival continue in the depths of Alice's wardrobe where she considers a denim mini skirt or jeans with a black polo neck sweater. Chameleon-like, Alice can adapt her appearance to her surroundings. Since meeting Cal, the floaty frocks have been neglected for black jeans and black tops and, worn with irony of course, a beret. Through the piercings in her ears, she pulls big silver hoops, and finally pins a fabric rose in her hair. Alice is beautiful enough. She puts a Leonard Cohen LP on the turntable, and hums along to 'Suzanne' while reheating the Bolognese sauce and laying the table. She lights candles, arranges the flowers she nicked from the park, turns off the lights, and waits. And waits.

Cal crashes into Alice's basement flat at about nine thirty. Having recognised his two-at-a-time footsteps pounding down the basement steps, she quickly rechecks her appearance in the mirror to make sure that all is picture-perfect for his arrival. Cal falls in the door, in mid-sentence, wearing the jeans he has pulled on every day for the past fortnight and a sweaty old Che Guevara T-shirt. Unshaven, hair a greasy clump of black curls, eyes baggy from chronic lack of sleep, he puts his arms round Alice while telling her something which sounds urgent and important, but she can only half-hear the words because his mouth is buried in her hair.

"….and he actually wanted to put it to a vote…but I said it was a foregone conclusion so a complete waste of time and resources…" Cal, having withdrawn his face, continues his monologue, until Alice gently takes his face in both her hands before releasing one to cover his mouth. She raises an eyebrow. Gives him a wry smile.

"Sorry." He pushes the word out through her fingers.

"Try and find the off switch," Alice whispers in his ear.

"Difficult. I might find it if we go to bed though," and already he is dragging her into the alcove where they have moved the mattress and covered it with an Indian bedspread.

"What about supper?"

"After."

BUT 'AFTER' NEVER comes because Cal is pulling off Alice's

clothes, and grabbing a fistful of hair, wrecking her artfully arranged knot, and smudging her mascara by kissing her eyelids. And after he has made love with an animal energy which leaves her limp and trembling, he passes out. Alice gently extracts her numb arm from under his dead weight, and goes to the bathroom to wipe away the rest of her smeared make-up and pull a comb through the ragged, snarled hair. Emerging fresh and shiny from her second shower of the day, she changes into her cami top, sweat shirt and pull-on pajama trousers, and while Cal sleeps, dead to the world, Alice settles herself against his spent body, the complete and very heavy works of Shakespeare propped up on her knees, and begins reading his twentieth sonnet.

> Whoever hath her wish, thou hast thy Will,
>
> And Will to boot, and Will in overplus.
>
> More than enough am I that vex thee still,
>
> To thy sweet will making addition thus.

Hmm, thinks Alice…sexually graphic and teasing and egotistical. As she reads on, she realises that a homosexual love is being hinted at here. She knows of very few people who have challenged Shakespeare's sexuality, yet here is an opening for an interesting hypothesis. There may be more if she searches. I might be able to work that into a proposal for a doctoral thesis, she thinks.

With Cal and Will beside her, Alice thus decides her future and signs away the next three years of her life.

IN THE EARLY hours, when Cal stirs just enough to announce

that he is starving, Alice pads back to the kitchen, warms up the Bolognese sauce and brings to bed two big bowls of sweet-smelling pasta topped with grated orange cheddar which they eat propped up against the pillows.

A blob of red sauce stains the white sheet.

Chapter 23

1972

Killer Queen

AFTER THE AGONIES of finals in which Cal managed an upper-second having done no work whatsoever, and Alice scraped a first after filling every corner and crevice of her mind with quotations that would haunt her for the rest of her life, Cal threw himself body and soul into local politics while spending the early hours of every morning stomping along the seedy streets of Hall Green as a temporary postman. He felt it appropriate that he should experience real work like the working classes he revered and so delivered his post with enthusiasm and bonhomie. Alice, on the other hand, with her excellent degree and a glowing final reference, was granted a studentship and settled calmly and gratefully to preparatory reading before finally deciding on the subject of her doctorate. The poetic and platonic tutor of her successful third year agreed to be her supervisor. Alice was in heaven.

When she told Cal that she was going to write about the subtext and sexual imagery of Shakespeare's sonnets, instead of getting a hug and congratulations, she brought down on her innocent head a bucket-full of scorn and derision.

"My God, Alice, you might as well write another mean-ingless book about the lives of the Brontës for all the relevance it has to today's society!" Cal shouted over the background din of a noisy Italian restaurant in Selly Oak. Fishing nets filled with straw-bottomed Chianti bottles and coloured red and green glass balls hung from the ceiling. More Chianti bottles on red check tablecloths dribbled wax from candles lit night after night when students ate their white over-boiled spaghetti topped with a thin, fatty, meat-flavoured sauce.

"As a matter of fact, I would love to study the lives of the Brontes," Alice retorted, not cowed by the opinionated Cal on her own intellectual territory. "They were incredible women who wrote epic works of fiction, despite the constraints of the society they were born into. I find them fascinating and they are absolutely relevant today. Our first feminists. But anyway, you know perfectly well I want to write about poetry and drama."

"Then why not the political metaphors of Samuel Beck-ett?"

"Everyone's studying Beckett, and anyway, apart from Godot, I'm not very moved by his plays," she replied evenly. Too evenly. What a damn cheek, she thought, offering me a random alternative subject. If I were to suggest that he support one local council policy rather than another, he would crucify me.

"Or Brecht's use of drama as propaganda?" Cal blun-dered on with the help of too much rough wine.

"Oh do shut up!" Alice exploded. "I don't want to write about any of the twentieth century playwrights, thank you,

Cal! Not Brecht nor Beckett, nor Pinter nor Wesker nor…"

"OK, something broader in scope," Cal interrupted, slurring scope, oblivious to Alice's fury, and used to holding the floor with his arguments. He was talking so loudly that half the diners were now staring at him and wondering how his sweet pale companion would hold her own against the onslaught. "What about… the theatre as a forum for political ideas?"

"Excuse me?" Alice's voice was ice. "May I not choose my own thesis subject? I have a first class degree in English, I do know what interests me, and I have spent the last three months discussing my options with my supervisor, so just for once, get off my turf and shut your big fucking mouth."

A small cheer and clapping broke out from the tables near them, and Cal, turning round to confront his hidden audience, actually blushed.

"Christ, I'm sorry," he conceded, silenced by the feisty outburst from his beloved, and the obvious support for her from the other spaghetti eaters. "I'm knackered, Alice. I'm sorry." His words slurred.

But Alice would not be placated. She slammed a pound note on the red-stained paper table-cloth, scraped back her chair and stood to leave. As she wove in and around the packed restaurant, she was greeted with more clapping and yelling and the stamping of feet.

"Well done that girl!" someone shouted.

"Forty love to the poetess!"

"Dump the arrogant bastard!" a male student said, trying to grab her leg as she brushed past him. "Come out with me instead, darling."

AT THE TIME, the significance of that ridiculous argument was not noted by either of them, but it marked the moment when the first small crack opened up in the landscape of their emotional geography. Cal plunged further into student politics with a commitment verging on mania, while Alice spent her days at the same desk in the university library, staring out at the green grass and watching the sun move from left to right across the sky while she made notes for a thesis which would, three years later, win the George Cadbury Award for its perceptive, original and sensitive stance on the sexual subtext of the sonnets.

The crack widened, but they were both too preoccupied to see it.

INTERVAL

"YOU'RE BACK!" ALICE says, noting the older woman watching her with wry sympathy. "How did you get out of the police station?"

"How did you visit me in the first place?" Alice retorts. "You look wretched and we need to talk because I no longer know who's supporting who."

"We're kind of supporting each other."

"That wasn't the plan. You came to help me because I've been arrested for shoplifting and – to put it bluntly – I've lost the plot. We're trying to find the fault line where it all caved in. I'm hearing that Julian was your soul mate and he still holds you in thrall and influences your moves. While searching for his replacement you plunged into two rather stupid affairs. That's all they were, weren't they? Compared with how you felt about him?"

"Oliver turned out to be a red herring. A case of a silly girl's mistaken identity. But not Cal. I went to him with my eyes open."

"No wonder Cal filled the space vacated by Oliver. His charisma and energy spun you round so fast you became dizzy. I'm watching you on his roller coaster ride and see you clinging on tight. You're getting breathless, Alice."

"He's exciting. He's lightning quick. Never a dull moment. I admire his passion and commitment."

"But does he care more for you or for his politics?"

"I don't see it as one or the other. He has enough energy for both. Anyway, I join in less and less because I have my own passion."

"Exactly."

"You sound resigned."

"I am."

"Oh dear," Alice sighs. "Please carry on and be quick. I need to know."

"OK. Fasten your seat-belt. It may be a bumpy ride."

"And when you've caught up, I'll be there. I'll have heard the whole story, so maybe I can help. Be objective."

"Thank you. See you later, then."

"Where are you now?"

"I'm sitting in the foyer of the police station. They've let me go even though I've been charged. But Stephen is about to appear."

"Who's Stephen?"

"Ah… that's another chapter."

Chapter 24
1972

Revolution

A LICE AND CAL tied the knot one Monday morning in a
Birmingham registry office with khaki walls. A wedding
in a church was obviously out of the question because they
were both atheists, and to spend a pile of money, which they
didn't have, on just one day conflicted with every capitalist
idea they held. Alice sang Joni's *My Old Man* as she pulled on
a mini dress and new calf-length white boots. Not for them
the bourgeois route to union. On that they agreed. Cal had
only suggested it, grudgingly and against his principles,
because he was thinking about putting himself forward as the
youngest ever Labour candidate for Birmingham Selly Oak
and even in those liberal days, a wife was an asset whereas a
mistress was not. The word 'partner' had not yet been
invented except to mean someone you worked with.

Cal deemed it very right-on to tell none of their relatives
or friends about the marriage, so they accosted two somewhat
astonished passers-by to be their witnesses. Alice gave her
agreement to all of this because she was still in love with Cal,
and because her involvement with Shakespeare's sexual

identity and the possible hints of homosexuality in Sonnet Twenty, had been so absolute that the brief arrangements for matrimony and the service itself pretty much passed her by.

Groomed fast by Cal, she had become a free spirit, unfettered and unworried by convention or tradition, sure of herself and of her own intellectual abilities. In fact, as Cal retreated from the intimacies of their daily life together into the waiting arms and red beating heart of the Labour Party, she began to wonder if she needed him at all. As a husband or as a lover. He certainly showed diminishing signs of needing her as he travelled the country with his propaganda.

CAL HAD NOT been home for weeks. These days he was semi-resident in London, staying on the sofas of committed friends and colleagues, and barely finding a moment to phone Alice to tell her of his whereabouts. Or so he said. It was true that he was kept there by his passionate involvement in the planning of a huge rally which would march to the US Embassy in Grosvenor Square to protest against the US war against Vietnam, but it was also true that another kind of involvement kept him there long after the march that ended in calamity.

Ten thousand protesters rallied peacefully in Trafalgar Square but came up against a police barricade outside the embassy which, depending on the media report you believe, either clashed with a vicious, stone-throwing rent-a-mob or turned its brutal force on peaceful demonstrators. Cal was there, though not one of the eighty-six people who were injured, nor one of the two hundred thousand who were arrested. He instead marched hand in hand with a beautiful

French student from LSE, whose political views were as fevered as his own and whose tumbling black hair and brown cat-eyes achieved the almost inconceivable feat of distracting him from the intensity and single-mindedness of his purpose that day.

WHEN THE END came, it was as swift as the opening moves. Cal did not hang about.

"I'm sorry, Alice, there is something I have to tell you," he spoke to her from a pay-phone in a pub, shouting against the background noise of animated conversation, the tinkling of glasses and the thumping beat from a juke box. "I've met someone else."

A long silence.

"Did you hear what I said, Alice? I've met someone."

"Which means…"

"Which means I don't think you and I are going to make it. I'm sorry, Alice. We're too different. I should have seen it sooner. You disappeared into your ivory tower and I want to be a part of society… to change society…"

"Spare me the excuses," she said, deathly quiet.

"They aren't excuses. Nathalie is passionate about all the same causes. We have so much in common. I feel that I've found a soul mate."

"Then stay with her," Alice said, and put down the receiver.

ALICE WEPT FOR half a day then retreated into resigned, reflective silence. She packed her meagre belongings and her many books into boxes collected from the local off license, and moved out of Cal's flat and out of Cal's life. She continued to sit in the same chair in the library. She began divorce proceedings on the grounds of his adultery which he did not contest, and soon she had another piece of paper from the city hall.

Act 4

Stephen

Chapter 25

1974

Get Back To Where You Once Belonged

AFTER SHE HAD finished her thesis, and still stung from Cal's easy rejection, Alice had applied for the first post for which she was qualified. What the welcoming arms of the interviewing committee did not reveal was that no-one else wanted the job of librarian in Handsworth's Soho Road. Cal would have snorted with laughter at Alice's naivety. He would have crucified her for her sense of dislocation. He might have left her for The Scarlet Woman but she still sensed his scathing presence at her side.

"For god's sake, Alice, you can't just walk across the barricades into their world armed with good intentions," he would have warned. "All very nice of you to bus yourself in to stamp their books and tempt them with carefully chosen outward-facing covers, but you're doing them no favours. Didn't you consider that they might prefer a black face behind the counter stamping their books?"

But none of them are qualified to do the job. Not yet. It's early days in the game of multicultural Britain.

"You haven't the first fucking clue about black immigrant culture, have you? You don't belong in their ghetto, do you? Have you ever walked their streets and looked into their faces? The anger and resentment that boils just beneath a thin veneer of politeness could melt the tarmac! And you think they want your books?"

At least I will try. I won't consign them to illiteracy.

"Have you forgotten what Enoch said, Alice? Or was that just a bit of playtime away from your ivory tower? You never really thought about what we were doing, did you? Were you ever serious about political change?"

No, I was never a political animal like you, Cal, but I have read a thousand novels and can imagine myself in other people's shoes and feel something of their despair.

"They'll resent you, Alice. Don't even think about kidding yourself otherwise. You're irrelevant."

Ah but you're not here, Cal, to make me tear up my application form and point me in a more appropriate direction.

Alice did not know that she was doomed before she began. Looking back, she had perhaps imagined the library as a safe, calm little island of serenity in the sea of social unrest that spilled around its foundations. Conscious of the need to be politically correct, careful never to appear patronising, she stood behind her counter like a white wooden doll with a stiff painted smile and eyes wiped clean of emotion. She stamped the books of her black clients and willed them to accept her on their territory, as she was inviting them into hers. She set up a crèche so that young mothers – and many of the young mothers in Handsworth were children themselves – could spend some time in the library, but it stayed empty. She made beautiful posters advertising a creative writing group, but when she opened the doors for the first session, there were no takers. She prepared a multimedia talk on African American writers that attracted maybe three huddled, silent people who came in, Alice suspected, only to shelter from the wind and rain.

All of this would come to pass, but not yet. Not in the 1970s when white and black did not know if they were blending together or encircling themselves with barbed wire and shatterproof glass to defend their roots. Black librarians would arrive later and walk with sure, confident steps in the tracks they already knew because this was the place from which they came. Alice was a well-meaning but useless onion in a colourful begonia patch of first and second generation immigrants.

When Alice saw the advert for the post of head librarian in the Education Faculty at Birmingham University, she knew the job was hers. It was inconceivable that it could go to anyone else because no-one could want it as fiercely as she did. She would run into the familiar, sheltering arms of her Alma Mater and tear the brief, crazy Cal years from the diary of her life.

THE DAY SHE left Handsworth, she felt only relief that the sad sham was over. When she wrapped her small hand around the polished brass handle of the library on the university campus and pushed open the heavy wooden door, she felt that she had come home. She breathed in the smell of teak oil. A smile hovered on her lips as she walked softly into the hushed, rarified atmosphere where dedicated students worked hard to become teachers. She understood from that moment, that slowly and tentatively, the bud of her heart which was so tight-curled that it hurt, would unfold and blossom in the warmth of this academic sanctuary.

THE EDUCATION FACULTY was tucked away in one corner of the campus, down a rolling hill and across a stretch of grass, as if it were an afterthought. Students came here after their degrees to train to be teachers or to coast for a year while they decided what to do. Mature students, exhausted after too long at the chalk face, found an oasis here while they studied for a Masters degree course or settled down to a few sheltered years of writing a doctoral thesis.

For Alice, this place was already familiar. During the years when she had worked on her thesis, when Cal was away or distracted, she had sometimes slipped in, not to tune in to its radical, intellectual buzz about new models of education but because the small library offered a welcome escape from the brutal multi-storey block. She loved the wood-paneled walls and little private alcoves which smelt of beeswax. She would climb the stairs to the gallery where she could sit and study while feeling she was in the upper tier of a theatre, looking down on the audience of students and lecturers who came to borrow books.

Balmy autumn days ticked over with a healing monotony as Alice settled into her new job. She put a deposit on an attic conversion in a ramshackle detached Victorian house in a tree-lined road in Edgbaston. How bloody middle-class, Cal would have howled, referring to the area and the mortgage. The house was ungentrified but imposing, its old walls smothered in ivy. It had a vast south-facing garden, patches of which were sometimes adopted by a new resident with a short-lived enthusiasm for home-grown vegetables. Through its cycles of care and neglect, it gave Alice joy on a clear night to look out and watch the sun go down behind what was once an orchard.

In the big flat on the first floor were five male medical students who worked hard and played harder, and had an arrogance that comes from an expensive education. Alice didn't mind the rowdy parties because only the faintest notes of Led Zeppelin and low-volume words of the Rolling Stones reached her windows under the eaves. When they apologised the following day, sincere and hung-over, she hid her tolerance behind a curt nod.

After a number of years, a reclusive, food-loving philoso-pher and fellow lecturer in the same faculty moved into the flat on the floor below hers. From his kitchen wafted the dark crimson wine smell of coq-au-vin and cassoulet, the green slivers of lemon grass long before the masses had discovered Thai cuisine, the sweet bitterness of roasted red peppers and purple aubergines, and the velvet scent of a hot chocolate pudding. This man was an artist in the kitchen, yet the meals he prepared were eaten, as far as Alice could tell from the lack of footsteps below, in solitude.

Sometimes late at night, when Alice lay stretched out on the sofa, dreaming or lost in a novel, the haunting notes of a Chopin cello sonata or a Bach prelude would interrupt her reading and make her put down her book. Not only was the man an artist in the kitchen but a magician when he picked up his cello. Some nights he played jazz with quickstep, syncopated rhythms, but more often his chosen repertoire came from the most melancholy music of the Romantic period and was played with heartfelt angst and solemnity. One night he played the whole of the Dvorak concerto, without the orchestra of course, and at its brilliant finale Alice leapt to her feet and clapped and stamped her feet on the floorboards in tearful appreciation.

Chapter 26

1984

Help!

I T WAS WITH an unexpected little twist in her stomach that Alice saw the cellist-chef-philosopher swing open the door of the library. Head down, shoulders hunched, he headed for the section that housed works on logic. During the twenty minutes or so that he spent randomly removing and replacing books, Alice kept a sly watch out of the corner of her eye. Mostly she saw his back in his black polo neck sweater, and the red curly hair that brushed his collar.

Without taking her eyes off him, Alice mused on the snippets of gossip about Stephen that she had picked up from the Masters degree students. They were a small, comradely band of experienced teachers who either needed a further degree to up their chances of a Head Teacher's post, or were studying because they were desperate for some role reversal and a chance to learn. And then there was Emma – beautiful, bright, and clearly not confined to a career in the classroom. She had served her statutory year in a single-sex school where her pupils adored and admired her, and copied her hair and clothes because at twenty-something she had more style than the most outrageously inventive of them. For a year she did her very best to interest them in everything from Silvia Plath to Germaine Greer, but teaching fourteen year olds was not her life's destination.

A few days previously, Alice had chanced on this normally jolly group of men and women hunched round a low table on the first floor concourse. Except on this occasion they were far from jolly. They had just emerged from one of Stephen's incomprehensible but compulsory seminars and they were red-faced and fuming.

"Oh, Alice!" Emma called. "I'm glad we caught you. Would you mind joining us for a moment? We're in a right mess and you might be able to help."

If I had your looks and confidence, thought Alice, I don't think I would ever be in a mess, but she recognised another woman's plight and was gratified to be consulted.

"Of course." she replied, smiling, and sat down beside her.

Each yearly intake usually revealed one exotic bird and this year Emma sat on the highest perch while the more common species fluttered around her. Alice, in her library uniform of white blouse and beige slacks, useful for climbing up the ladder to retrieve books from the top shelf, caught the comparison briefly and quickly before swatting it.

"Can you please suggest an idiot's guide to philosophy, because apart from Tom here who did it at university, we are utterly lost and have to sit a bloody exam in six weeks."

"Have you told Stephen?" Alice asked, feigning ignorance. She knew Stephen's reputation from previous years. This had happened before.

"Him!" Emma said with venom. "He's the whole bloody problem. You can't even get eye contact, never mind understand anything about philosophy, and it's hard enough without him making it totally elitist and opaque. He prepares nothing, gives us no notes, and couldn't give a damn whether we learn or not. He hates teaching."

"I can try and find some books for you," Alice said, before repeating, "but you really should tell Stephen that you can't understand his teaching because it's his responsibility to help you."

"We have!" exploded Moira, who was prone to panic, and could sometimes be found weeping quietly in the library after a particularly difficult day. A touchy-feely woman in her fifties with people-related skills, she had an excellent reputation as a teacher of children with special needs.

"That man," continued Emma, "is the worst tutor I have ever had. He wanders in and without looking at us begins midstream without even telling us what he is going to talk about."

"It's bad," added Robert, a quiet, young geography teacher. "I sit there week after week, two hours at a time, and I'm none the wiser."

"I think I can help you," Alice said, secretly amused that these intelligent grown-ups were in such a spin. It happened every year. "You do know, don't you, that all the previous exam questions are available in the library…"

"Where?" interrupted Molly.

"…and you'll see that the questions don't change much because Stephen teaches the same course every year."

"Hurray! I bet he even sets the same damn questions!"

Emma announced in triumph.

"So, what I suggest is that you concentrate on a practical solution. I'll show you the past years' exams, and you can take it from there."

"Brilliant!" Tom said. "Look, we can each prepare one past question. Surely we can manage that? Then I'll photocopy them, hand them round and we can all learn them. Off by heart if necessary. If we get stuck on any particularly tricky theories or whatever, we can do a combined attack." Tom beamed at everyone. "Thank you so much, Alice. You've just saved our lives." He grinned at her.

Alice smiled back. "Okay? Now you can all stop worrying."

"Is this legal, by the way?" Molly asked.

"Well, I know nothing about it. I didn't have this discussion with you. I've been in the library all morning," Alice smiled. "Of course it's legal or the papers wouldn't be in the library."

Tom and Robert and quiet Andrew smiled their appreciation. Molly squeezed Alice's arm.

"And if he gets six identical exam papers, serves him fucking well right," Emma added, as they gathered their things and trooped down the stairs. "And if he fails any one of us, I'll put in a formal complaint about his teaching. And more…if necessary."

Tom stopped dead in his tracks, collided with Alice and stared back at Emma. Open-mouthed.

"No, you dimwits, of course he hasn't, but if he fails any of us, I might pop up to see him by myself and come out all weepy. Most men are dumb enough to fall for it…"

"Er…could you withdraw that last generalisation?" Tom asked mildly.

Emma barged on. "He's certainly not gay. I would have picked that up immediately. I think I could just about tolerate a red-haired hand on my shoulder without screaming if it saved us all from failure." She shuddered.

What bloody arrogance! thought Alice. Does Stephen really deserve this? Should she warn him about a possible primed sex bomb?

"I prefer Plan A," Tom said, raising an eyebrow at Emma. "Come on, you lot. Into the library. We'll share out some exam questions. Don't look so worried, Moira. I'll help you. I'll pick an easy one for you." He gave her a friendly wink.

LATE THAT EVENING, Tom, Moira and Robert were still huddled over text books, scribbling in their big notepads but Emma had left, trailing faint musky perfume, a long lacy hem, a whiff of sarcasm and disdain.

Chapter 27

1984

Paint It Black

THIS RECENT LITTLE rebellion played in Alice's mind as she gazed at the back of Stephen's black polo neck sweater and decided that if Emma laid temptation at his door, he would probably prefer death by jumping from his window than physical contact with the scheming siren. Right now he appeared to be physically stuck between the book shelves. Like an actor stranded on stage without an exit, he could neither bring himself to leave nor could he stay any longer pretending to read without the sham being obvious to everyone else in the library. Not that any of the students were interested in a grumpy hermit of a lecturer. Alice noticed a blush spreading towards his face from his already pinkish neck, at which point she knew that she had to rescue him. As she emerged from behind her desk and started to walk towards him, he managed to squeeze his way out and began to march, head down, towards her desk carrying a book. They collided halfway.

"Do you want to borrow that book?"

"I want to borrow this book."

A collision of words, too.

"Sorry, I need to get back to my desk."

"Sorry, I'm in your way."

A duet.

Followed by a dance.

First a jump to the left, then a step to the right.

"Follow me." Alice instructed.

In single file they returned to the comfort zone of card extraction and date stamping and the handing over of the chosen tome. Stephen stared at the floor while Alice used exaggerated hand and arm movements, like a mime artist, as if she had never stamped a book before in her life. She thought this man looked like one of the walking dead and was wondering how she could breathe life back into him, like one would a drowned body, when the corpse revived, lifted his head, and spoke.

"I wonder... I've been meaning to ask you...would like to come down and have dinner with me one evening?" Alice could see from the colour in his cheeks and a muscle working away in his jaw that this sentence had cost him half a day's energy.

"Yes, I'd love to," she replied. "It's not that far from my place to yours, is it?"

"No. Actually we live in the same..." He caught her teasing smile and turned russet. "Well, yes, of course we do. Live in the same house. I see you sometimes."

"And I smell your wonderful cooking and hear your cello. They both drift up..."

"Oh I'm sorry..."

"Not at all. Both much appreciated. Your playing is

beautiful."

"I'm very much an amateur."

"An excellent one."

"I don't practice enough."

By now a small queue had formed at Alice's desk. It was her turn to blush.

"Please excuse me. We'll have to continue this conversation over dinner."

"Oh…of course…" he said, rushing towards the doors where he cracked an elbow getting through the gap. Alice stamped the books of the students who waited in line and realised that they had not decided on a day for dinner and that he had left his book behind.

THAT EVENING ALICE walked home with a light heart and smiled to herself as the gentlest of breezes carried the familiar smell of malt. For Alice, Birmingham would always be drizzle, fog, canals, red brick, and the smell of breweries in tree-lined avenues. In the dusk, she wound her way through Edgbaston where the houses were large and rambling and well-spaced, until she was in the territory of the huge Victorian properties once owned by the Calthorpe family and not sold off to industry, like many others in the city. Edgbaston was quintessentially English, yet saved from the banal by the canopies of old trees, the cricket ground, and the recent splitting up of the houses into flats as more and more lecturers and students moved into the area to save it from the property developers' gentrification. Arriving under a yellow circle of foggy lamp light, Alice trod hard on the cornflake leaves and kicked and scattered them for the sheer fun of watching the gold and flame colours floating and air-born. Silly, she told herself. Don't be silly and foolish. He's just a lonely man who got stuck in a book shelf. Apart from some long-lasting and light-hearted male friendships which were sustained by visits to art galleries and the student film house, and a couple of brief affairs which did not touch her heart, she had managed to avoid getting her knickers in a twist. You are in your thirties, she reminded herself. Settled, sensible and content. Julian and Oliver and Cal are just old leaves, like those swirling around your feet, pressed between the pages of a book. They no longer trouble you.

BACK IN HER flat, though, she checked the clock every few minutes and became preoccupied with choosing the best time to take the forgotten book downstairs to Stephen. As if it mattered. Instead of curling up on her pale sofa with the paper and a glass of white wine, she monitored the silence, and then the familiar sounds from below. She waited for the first treacle kick of frying onions, a smell so vivid that she could imagine them blackening at their papery edges, or the sweet-tart smell of courgettes glistening in a pan of olive oil. But tonight the air was empty. What was wrong?

At eight o'clock, wearied by her self-imposed vigilance and unable to concentrate on the Channel 4 news, Alice jumped up and made a dash for the back stairs that had once led to and from the servants' quarters; now the only way down from her attic flat. The medics, on the other hand, in the drawing room apartment on the first floor, leapt down the steps of the great, ornate wooden staircase that curled round to the grand entrance hall below. One night, aroused from sleep by a series of unusually loud thumps and bangs, Alice put on her dressing gown, exited at the back, crept round to the front entrance and peeped through the letterbox of the main door. Waiting in a line at the top of the staircase a queue of young men apparently waited to make their descent on skis. The one in front was already leaning forward, as if about to scream down the ski jump in the Alps, while the others shouted, "Go go go GO GO!" Oh well, if they break their bones they will know what to do, she thought. She withdrew sharply, before she sustained a serious injury herself, because the skier at the top was already hurtling off the first step in a crazy descent and zig-zagging across the two wide landings before crashing to a terrifying, skidding halt a few inches from the front door. If one of them went through it, a lot of rather beautiful, irreplaceable old stained glass would become mountains of multi-coloured shards and she didn't want flying fragments embedded in her flesh, even if a medical student was at hand to remove them. Alice had crept back to bed, a smile playing on her lips. She forgave them their novel adrenalin sport because of course they needed a way to unwind after practicing colonoscopies and sinus surgery.

SILENCE REIGNED ON this particular evening when Alice reached the modest landing on the second floor, with its small window overlooking the garden and orchard. It was likely that none of the medics were back yet. No matter how many times Alice passed the entrance to Stephen's flat, she never failed to smile because the door, painted the deepest, glossiest black, said GREEN. This appealed to her sense of humour and so she was standing there staring at the name plate and grinning inanely when the black door opened and Dr Green stepped out. They seemed destined to collide.

"I've just popped down because you left your book in the library…"

"Oh Alice… I was about to come up because I stupidly left my book…"

Then they stalled.

"You're not cooking tonight?" Alice asked, to break the silence, and held out the book which Stephen took.

"Oh…after you told me about the smells wafting up from my kitchen I realised how intrusive my cooking must be so…I'm having bread and cheese tonight.'"

How thoughtful.

"In fact, would you like to come in and join me?" A pause. "Or maybe you've eaten?"

"I haven't eaten. I'd love to join you."

"Then come in. I'm sorry it's only bread and cheese. And excuse the mess."

He turned and led the way past cream and ivory toned walls hung with framed black and white photographs of film stars from the 1950s. Ahead of his time, Stephen had transformed a bog-standard, one-bedroomed, lino-floored and floral-wall-papered flat in a Victorian house into an open space of light and grace. Alice trod across honey-coloured, sanded floors with old Turkish rugs scattered in places where their rich maroons and reds caught the light, past more pale walls hung with Japanese prints, into a room twice the size of hers lit by big windows at the front. Like an illustration in a house-and-garden magazine, it was immaculate, more art gallery than home, but fabulously beautiful. A wooden ladder reached a platform which stretched across the whole of one side of the room, its thick mattress hidden by a cream bedspread and huge oriental cushions. A bespoke bookcase fronted this perfect mezzanine, and Alice saw with awe that the books were colour-coded, grouped in whites and creams, then greens and blues, then reds, rather than sorted by author's initial or the Dewey classification she herself was used to.

"Do you sleep up there?" Curiosity overcame politeness.

"Sometimes. I knocked down a wall across here when I moved in six years ago. It used to be two poky little rooms. There's a bedroom too but sometimes if I'm reading late, I lie up there and nod off."

"It's beautiful," Alice said, and then she saw the cello, with chair and music stand, in the window. "And your cello…"

"Yes. The light is good there. Come on through. The kitchen's in here. It's quite small, but it's functional."

Alice wandered after him, past a bamboo screen, into a marvel of fitted wooden cupboards, terra-cotta tiled work surfaces, a big white butler's sink, a knife rack holding a terrifying array of chopping instruments, and gleaming copper-bottomed pans hanging from hooks in the ceiling. Orchids in white pots bent gracefully under the weight of velvet petals – and this was before they could be bought for five quid from Ikea. At the breakfast bar, another novelty, sat a wooden platter where three moist cheeses were melting sideways, and inside a raffia basket snuggled an assortment of crusty rolls and crisp, salted biscuits. In a pink ceramic bowl were black olives, and next to them an opened bottle of Sauvignon and about a dozen blue irises in a white vase. Alice stared. It was like a painting.

"My kitchen is under your lounge," he said abjectly.

"But I don't want you to stop cooking and live on bread and cheese, for Heaven's sake!" Alice said. "It was meant as a compliment. I'm a boring, inadequate cook but I love eating so my pleasure comes vicariously from the exotic smells of your casseroles and cakes."

Stephen blushed. "Would you like some cheese and wine? I'll cook for you another evening."

"I'd love some," Alice replied, as she sat and helped herself to a piece of bread and an olive.

THUS THE BLACK-CLAD lecturer with a reputation for being an unpleasant, grumpy sod who was rotten to students, revealed to Alice a soul that was sensitive to colour and light and sound and taste. His awkwardness was shyness, and his scowling rudeness probably his way of hiding clumsy social skills. At least, this is what Alice concluded as they talked easily about the department and her work in the library over a ripe Brie de Meaux, a sharp Beaufort, and a creamy round goat's cheese whose centre was almost liquid, all washed down with wine that tasted like tart apples and lychees. Stephen told Alice that he had wanted to be a musician, but had proved not brilliant enough for a career as a solo cellist. He decided, therefore, that music would have to be his hobby because he didn't have the temperament to play popular classics or impossibly difficult modern compositions, night after night, in an orchestra where fragile and ferocious egos bumped elbows. He had settled finally on a degree in philosophy at Oxford. Alice heard longing and disappointment.

When they had finished eating, and when Stephen had washed and dried the plates and put everything away in the cupboards (he had waved aside Alice's offers of assistance), he moved without comment to the seat in the window and began tuning his cello with slow, caressing, vibrato strokes, starting with the exquisite heartache of the top string and ending with the profound melancholy of the base. Alice burst into tears. This man poured into his tuning a greater emotional intensity than many a soloist managed during an entire performance of the Bach sonatas.

Under the bewitching spell of his playing, Alice imagined fine veins of tenderness and passion running beneath his thin skin. He was not rude at all but guarded and defended against a harsh and hurtful world.

Did Alice fall in love that night with a man or a cello?

Chapter 28

1984

We Don't Need No Education

ALICE FOUND HERSELF glancing at the clock or the library door. She forgot appointments and left a trail of papers and belongings all over the building. Preoccupied with decidedly non-literary matters, she stared right through a sighing student who had been standing at her desk for goodness knows how long. For Christ's sake, Alice, she told herself crossly, one meal of bread and cheese and one short cello recital and you've regressed to wayward adolescence. She was preoccupied with the mismatch between the reputation of the lecturer whose behaviour suggested a complete disregard for his students and the man who could make a lemon soufflé that sent bittersweet, mouth-watering steam curling up to her window and who could reduce her to tears by tuning his cello. Oh come on, Alice! It is quite possible to be a lousy lecturer and still have positive attributes. People's characters do contain contradictions. Stop making a drama out of the man's existence.

But the questions rumbled on. And on. Perhaps he hated his work. Perhaps he was happy only away from the campus,

on his own territory. Teaching was an art and not everyone
had the gift. On the other hand, Stephen did not have the
excuse, as others did, of being buried in a research project
that absorbed all his mental and emotional energy. Those
sorts wandered around the campus with their coats buttoned
up all wrong, their jumpers on back to front, and with
expressions of abstraction or lunacy on their faces. Some
talked to themselves. After much deliberation, Alice came to
the conclusion that Stephen was a redundant, sad spare part
in the Education Faculty. He had been there for seven years –
during a time of rapid intellectual and political changes,
which had neither moved nor touched him. She felt sorry for
him.

Still wondering about her newest friend, Alice watched
with wry amusement as the Masters degree students
organised themselves with admirable efficiency into an exam
preparation machine. She'd seen it all before, but this bunch
were unusually tough and determined and made no pretence
about what they were doing. They sat at a low coffee table on
one of the landings and handed around stapled stacks of
papers and openly discussed their prepared answers. Stephen
had to walk right past them on his way to and from his office.
He ignored them, not raising his eyes from the floor. He
must have known what they were doing.

"Wanker!" Emma muttered, loud enough to be heard.

WHILE ALICE AND Stephen pretended to hardly know one
another at work, they had slipped into the habit of meeting
up once or twice a week in his flat after hours. She had
invited him up to hers for a drink once, a few days after their

bread-and-cheese supper together, and although he had made no comment, she read his restlessness as discomfort with her mismatched chairs and offence at the old ladies' wallpaper she had meant to replace. Perhaps he was affronted by her old cream sofa whose every rip and stain she knew by heart. Perhaps he correctly judged her wine glasses to be the cheapest; the white wine not as skilfully chosen as his; the nibbles and snacks to have been shaken from packets and not extracted from a hot oven. Even her John Lewis bowls, white with a navy rim, seemed suddenly not good enough. When he stood in her doorway to take his leave, and looked with a worried frown at her jumble-sale of a room, she saw through his eyes a living space without harmony or visual pleasure. Perhaps I should smarten the place up, she told herself. Make a bit more effort. But when Stephen showed no inclination to return to her eerie, preferring to invite her down to his, Alice forgot her good intentions and continued to live comfortably and cheerfully immune to her home's aesthetic failings.

Soon, the unspoken agreement was that on Wednesday and Friday evenings, she would trip down the back stairs to knock on the glossy black door and be met with a nod and a small smile. He made no extravagant gestures, but he left little gifts on her door mat if he arrived home before her – a dew-damp, string-tied bunch of violets, a box of the best Belgian chocolate, a perfect white stone. Sometimes there were postcards – reproductions of works of art or sculpture from various museums he had visited. These she framed, and hung in the corridor so that he would be greeted with something that pleased his eye if ever he deigned to cross her threshold again.

His meals were infallibly delicate and delicious. Duck breasts in a port and orange sauce, white fish cooked in wine with tiny shallots, a tray of roasted parsnips baked with parmesan and served with his own crusty rolls and a perfectly dressed salad. She sensed his pleasure in the preparation of these meals, and knew that he would cook much the same thing for himself if he were alone. Aiming for perfection came naturally to him. She could swear with her hand on her heart that this man would never sit down to a takeaway pizza. He'd rather starve.

"YOU'RE A VERY unusual man," she commented one evening, perhaps having drunk a little too much of his apricot-scented Chablis.

"How?" He was succinct. Like satisfying equations, his sentences expressed only what he wished to impart and no more.

"Well…your flat is beautiful and tidy…you cook like a dream…and you play the cello."

"And what is unusual with that?"

"Well, I have never met a man who lives like you… with such attention to detail. Most men aren't even house-trained. They leave wet towels in heaps, litter the place with stinky socks, and don't know where the Hoover lives. They certainly don't care about the colour of the tea-towels. In fact…the only men I know who live like this, who have such excellent taste are gay."

"Are you asking me if I am?"

"Oh, no! It's none of my business." Alice blundered. "I was just making a point."

They were sitting side by side at his breakfast bar. Some soft crumbs from the honey and digestive biscuit base of an almond cheesecake had fallen from her plate on to the wooden surface. She had licked her finger and was dabbing at the crumbs when he took her hand, got up, and pulled her gently off her stool.

"I'm not gay," he said, amused.

STEPHEN LED HER, with crumbs still stuck to her fingertips, into a room whose door had always been closed. His bedroom. In the doorway, Alice gasped at its Zen perfection. A very low, black bed covered by a white duvet cover and four perfectly plumped white pillows stood on wooden floorboards. He made his bed? Sliding, slatted doors, painted the same matt black hid, she presumed, all his matching black clothes. In the large window were blinds made of bamboo and paper which were stopped by white string exactly halfway down. Beneath the window, three white orchids in three white pots were all in flower. Next to them, a clothes stand. Through a part-open door, Alice could see a small shower-room tiled floor to ceiling in white with a glass wash bowl on a wooden stand. The towels were white, black and sea-green.

He's in the wrong profession, she thought. He's missed his vocation. He should have gone into interior design if he couldn't be a cellist. A man who can create a room as gorgeous as this must be bored witless teaching the basics of philosophy to recalcitrant students. And how could they possibly read him when so few of them made it into his study and saw his pale blue Chinese rug, his wall hangings and his forest of exotic plants which he propagated himself in tiny, empty yoghurt pots. He chose to teach in a bare classroom as if to protect not just himself but his surroundings.

Stephen smiled at her distraction.

"Alice," he said. "Alice, come back."

He held her at arms' length and looked into her eyes.

"Will you let me make love to you?"

"Yes," she sighed.

Like the closing cadence of a Bach sonata, this was the inevitable, irresistible finale. It had been held at tempting tipping point over weeks as Alice and Stephen had danced in polite, yearning circles around one another, not wanting to upend the precarious balance between friendship and possible love. For Alice, these were the closing lines of one novel and perhaps the opening ones of another.

"Yes," she said again, unequivocal and certain.

It had been a long, long time, but Alice's mind had not erased previous occasions and she was surprised at this man's delicacy. To undo her bra, Stephen twirled her round, undid the hook, and carefully peeled the straps down her arms. For a long moment he looked at her breasts. Still watching her, he slid down her pants. Each act of undressing was deliberate yet delicate, like the slow movement of a Brahms partita. Finally she stood in front of him. He took a deep breath. Exhaled. He placed a gentle, soft kiss on her lips.

"Beautiful."

Alice blushed.

"Inside and out. There's a harmony about you."

Alice heard the truth in this quiet assessment of her.

"You are complete," he said. "Quiet and complete."

"You make me sound boring."

"Not at all. Enduring. Your beauty will endure."

Turning from her, Stephen moved to the corner of the room and removed his clothes, placing jeans and shirt and pants on the stand. Then he turned and walked with slow, barefoot steps towards her. He folded back the white duvet, and pulled her with him into the whiteness of cool, ironed cotton.

If lovemaking was graded on the Richter scale, that first uniting of their bodies would not have reached gale or hurricane force. Perhaps a three, or a four at its climax, but what it lacked in intensity, it made up for, on his part, in sweet sensuality and consideration. *What care he takes*, thought Alice. *He sees me. He sees every detail.*

And as if he had heard her thoughts, he said, "I'm counting your freckles. Seventeen across your nose and twenty-nine and still counting on your shoulders. I want to store you in my memory so that I can revisit you when you aren't here. Alice, I consider myself very fortunate that you have wandered into my life."

"But there have been others, surely?"

"A few. Nothing lasted. I had almost stopped searching…"

"What were you searching for?"

"Someone like you."

They were silent. She stroked the red-gold hairs on his pale body.

"What about you? What's a nice girl like you doing all alone?"'

"Oh, a long story. Several stories, actually. I'm quite

content. I love my work. I enjoy the freedom of living alone."

Stephen was not fooled. "Did someone hurt you?"

"Yes, someone broke my heart a very long time ago. Then it happened a second time. But it seems to have mended. The only lasting effect is that I feel less than I was before. My edges are blurred."

"I can understand that."

"I don't want to be hurt again. I'm at ease the way things are. I like living on my own..." Alice repeated, as if to persuade herself.

"So do I."

They looked at each other and laughed.

"So why don't we just go back to our own flats and carry on as before?" Alice asked.

"Because I don't want to spend the rest of my life alone. Because you have unsettled me."

"I think about you a lot," Alice admitted. "I try not to, but you intrude at the most inappropriate moments. At work..."

They kissed and kissed again.

"HERE'S A SUGGESTION," Stephen said, stroking her hair and wrapping a strand around his finger. "Your hair is so many colours... gold and yellow and amber and brown. How about you move down here for a week? Let's call it an experiment."

"It's a deal," Alice replied. "And at the end of the week, if you feel that I have intruded into your well-ordered life, or that I am surplus to requirements, then I will pack my bag without resentment or bitterness, and walk back up the stairs."

"You are so sensible." Was he teasing her?

"Boring?" Alice suggested, smiling.

"Impeccable," he replied. "My impeccable Alice."

Chapter 29

1985

Come Together

IN THAT HONEYMOON period, Alice sometimes forgot the arrangements, walked straight past the black door named Green and up to the floor above where she would laugh and do an about-turn back to Stephen's flat.

The week together had passed so smoothly that they agreed to extend it to a fortnight, and now they were in their second month of clandestine cohabitation with neither having raised the possibility of separating. It remained a delicious secret which they agreed not to share. They couldn't hide the happiness that glowed on their faces, but if anyone in the Education department assumed anything, it was that Alice Connor had found herself a new man, and that Stephen Green had found himself a woman, but no-one thought of connecting the two events. They continued to arrive for work at different times, and Alice left later than Stephen, as she always had done, enjoying an hour of solitude in her own space after everyone else had gone.

ALICE'S ROUTINE was not much different except that she had

easy company over her glass of iced wine. After eating Stephen's delicious meal and helping to clear up – because Stephen could not tolerate dirty plates and pans in the sink – her evenings continued much as before. She lay on the sofa reading a novel or looking at articles she had printed out during the day. At the weekends they watched a film or a documentary on TV. Stephen worked at his desk after their meal, his back towards the room, though what he did Alice had no idea, since he resolutely left his university work at its door. At the exact moment when dusk darkened the flat, Stephen clicked on his spotlight and shuffled his belongings into perfect, pristine order. Pencils were sharpened, rubbers lined up in order of size, and papers were tapped to line up the edges and held with a paper clip, colour-coded according to subject.

THEY WERE SEPARATE but together, until the moment when the sun finally slid below the horizon and Stephen moved to the chair in the window. The vibrato glide of bow over strings became Alice's signal to put down her book and to gaze with awe at this man's absolute concentration on the emotional truth of the music; a nightly gift that often, to his alarm, made her cry. Afterwards, Stephen took Alice by the hand and led her to his room (yes, it was still his room) and into the white sheets of his bed, where he wiped her tears and chided her gently for being so emotional. It was a bit of a conundrum, Alice felt, that a man who mined the depths of passion with his playing, preferred the rest of his life to remain tepid and undisturbed.

BECAUSE HER PASSIONATE outbreaks disturbed him, Alice learned to hide her tears and soon managed not to cry even when Stephen played those famous opening bars of the first movement of the Elgar concerto, recently reinterpreted as a work of almost unbearable poignancy by Jacqueline du Pré. Alice worked hard to achieve an atmosphere of suitable calmness, reassuring herself that a quiet mood was a good thing. Not that Alice was ever volatile. Stephen had told her that she was bombproof. If Alice needed to sob her heart out at a passage in a novel rather his music, she took herself away to the bathroom where she wept into a wad of tissues to silence her sobs, or she went down into the garden where she buried her face in the Gloire de Dijon roses and let her tears soak the soil.

ALICE'S TEMPORARY SOJOURN on the floor below became a more or less permanent arrangement. She didn't bother to move her possessions. Her blind-spot with aesthetics and her untidiness were still endearing rather than annoying, and Stephen's perfectionism did not yet grate. Looking back, she would ask how much of herself she had absent-mindedly left upstairs in the muddle and comfort of her own flat. Had she effaced herself in her keenness to fit into Stephen's perfectly ordered living space? Then, in love with the man and his music, it didn't bother her to turn herself into an apricot-white picture that matched the apricot-white walls, but one day she would wonder where her own warm, clashing colours had gone.

If she had been allowed only one word to describe this period of her life, she would have chosen content. And so it continued, until about a year later, when Alice, climbing the stairs after work, noted the absence of taste-bud teasing aromas sliding through he cracks of the black door. Inside, Stephen was not in the kitchen slicing something with a Sabatier knife, but pacing the living room with a folded newspaper in his hand. She knew not to pre-empt, so continued the coming-home routine. She stacked her books and papers neatly (one of many small rules) on the table in her corner of the room then changed into her beloved 501s and an old T-shirt. She slapped cold water on her face to wash away the day's irritations.

"Drink?" she asked, picking two fragile long-stemmed glasses from the cupboard.

"Please. There's a Pinot in the fridge. Let's sit down for a moment."

"Don't we always?" Alice joked.

"I mean…let's sit down and talk." Stephen was not amused.

Alice poured wine so pale it looked almost green, cooled to a frosty iciness. It tasted very dry but delicately fruity. Gooseberries and apple and maybe lemon.

"I've been thinking." He wasn't one to beat about the bush. "It's a waste of money keeping on your flat."

"Of course. I've been thinking the same, but I didn't want to push you into anything…" Intuition told Alice that this was subplot; the opening lines to the main drama. She could read Stephen pretty well by now. She sipped and waited and sipped.

"Alice…"

Her name hung between them, heavy with significance.

She knew to stay silent.

"Alice…there is an academic post I'd like to apply for." He spread the Times Literary Education Supplement in front of them. "It's in a philosophy department."

Alice noted the word 'a' not 'the'. Not here then. Not Birmingham.

"In Edinburgh."

Birthplace of Robert Burns, Robert Louis Stevenson and Arthur Conan Doyle. A literary city.

"It would get me out of the bloody Education department where I am a total irrelevance."

Alice still said nothing. She did not say that she loved the Education department.

"But it would mean you giving up your job and I know how much that means to you."

Alice put that verbal hand grenade to one side and concentrated on the idea of a fresh start for this man she loved who had his back against a hard brick wall.

"You need to leave. I watch you creeping ground the margins of the building, like a wretched ghost, while I'm thriving at its centre."

"I don't think I can get through another academic year here, Alice. I've thought about pulling out altogether. While you've had your feet up, absorbed in your novels, I've been considering other options. Looking at other jobs. I even thought about teaching cello to private pupils."

Was he criticising her? "I didn't know…"

"There's no reason why you should have known."

But Alice had, at least, suspected. After the exams, she had surreptitiously watched Stephen marking the Masters papers, knowing how anxiously the group of students waited for their results. She had seen him skim through the pile of answers and scribble a murderous mark on each one. Surely Tom had done better than that, she wondered, as Stephen scratched 53% with enough venom to tear the paper. And he had failed Moira by two marks, forcing her to resit. Surely he could spare her that. Alice gasped when she saw Stephen give Emma a mark low enough to prevent her from getting the Distinction everyone expected of her. And then it had turned very, very nasty. Emma had put in a formal complaint about Stephen's teaching of the course and his marking of the exam papers. With her reputation as a hard-working, gifted student, she knew it would be taken very seriously.

"What does she bloody expect?" Stephen had fumed. "They all learned the same answers and regurgitated them. Emma's paper was mediocre at best."

So he did know about the conspiracy. What he didn't know was that Alice had been party to it.

"She got over 90% in every other paper," Alice had replied.

"That doesn't concern me. I'm not remarking her paper."

But after a summons to the dean of the faculty, Stephen had his elbow twisted very hard. The balance of power had shifted and the good old days of docile students were gone. They knew their rights and would take action to correct perceived injustice. Stephen could not slap down the students he despised with insulting marks, nor would he survive in this new climate of accountability. It was the watershed.

"If this offers you a new start, then you should take it." Alice finally gave her reply, staring into her wine and blinking back tears. The two envisaged scenarios were equally distressing: either he would leave without her and she would move back upstairs, or she would give up a job she loved with all her heart and go with him. For a few long moments she considered them both and did not know which was worse.

"Will you come with me?" Stephen asked, taking her hand and kissing her lightly. "I'm asking you to marry me, Alice."

Alice's fear and anxiety dissolved. It could be so much worse. Edinburgh is a literary city. A place of galleries and museums. There may be possibilities and openings for me too. And there will be even better compensations, she told herself. Little compensations with russet curls like Stephen who will want bedtime stories.... *The Wind In The Willows* and *Dr Seuss* and *Charlie and The Chocolate Factory...* all the books I loved as a child. Where has all this come from? What have I not been admitting even to myself? What a sentimental idiot I am, sitting here with a grin on my face when I've just been told I have to leave my adored library.

"Alice? Alice, come back."

"Mmm?" She'd moved on to books for older children. *The Secret Garden* and *Stig Of The Dump* and *Lord Of The Rings...*

"Alice. You haven't told me if you'll marry me," Stephen said, taking the glass out of her hand and gently turning her head so that she had to look into his hazel eyes. He kissed her on her lips.

"I thought we were married already," she replied.

Chapter 30

1986

Windy City

"OVER THERE, ALICE, that's Arthur's Seat."
Stephen became unusually talkative and upbeat as he pointed out monuments and architecture. In overdrive. It wasn't hard to hear his plea that she accept and love the windy city, as he already did after his brief trips to reconnoitre and cross the threshold of his new department. Confidence nudged aside trepidation. She saw that Stephen was accepted and welcomed, and he, soaking up the appreciation, was content.

ALICE HAD WORKED out her remaining time at the library while Stephen made his preliminary sorties up north. This was her first trip and her mood sank like a sponge cake taken too soon from the oven. From the passenger seat, she saw grey and more grey. She saw Morningside High Street where elderly ladies in sensible shoes and tweed skirts were shopping at the butcher's, the fishmonger and the ironmonger. Not a boutique or coffee shop in sight. No Druckers. Alice smiled to herself. What a long time ago that was, and why on earth was she thinking about it now? Oh heavens! At five months pregnant and very emotional, she did not want to be dragged away from the rambling red-brick house where the yellow fog and the smell of the brewery lingered around the lamp posts.

STEPHEN DROVE ALONG the cobbled streets of Marchmont, where the Victorian tenements loomed up, blocking the sun. Like barracks, Alice thought. Prisons. Some of the facades had been sandblasted back to their original warm oatmeal colour, but others waited, barricaded behind scaffolding for restoration or remained blackened by time. The sky hung low, threatening rain. The East wind blew. Cars bumped along the cobbles. Women clutching the hands of small children battled along the pavements. Umbrellas blew inside out. Hems were whipped up. Alice felt depressed and intimidated.

"We can probably find a flat here," Stephen was saying. "It's affordable. Just."

"It's grim," Alice replied. "No green. No foliage. No carpet of leaves."

"But famous. The tenements of Edinburgh."

"I don't want to live in one."

"In the Old Town…you'll see that in a minute…the tenements are ten or eleven stories high and look down on Princes Street gardens. They date back to the 15th century…"

But Alice wasn't listening. This was not her kind of city. The immense scale felt cold and dour and inhospitable. And imposing. Why couldn't Steven have got himself a job in Bristol or Exeter or York? She wanted a semicircle of

Georgian houses with pretty gardens and little shops selling homemade jam and patchwork bedspreads. She would shrivel and die here. She would be obliterated by the wind.

"Lots of people react like you the first time they see Edinburgh. It is monumental, but you'll get used to it."

ON THEY WENT, along one of several artery roads that ran to Princes Street. Stephen saw how Alice clenched her hands together, willing the car to stop. He saw her worried brow and her down-turned mouth. He understood that she was overwhelmed by the massive presence of the city. His initial awe had mellowed with each visit into appreciation of the blackened military castle, the plain Georgian architecture, the complete lack of anything bijou or frivolous or chocolate box. Edinburgh could never be called pretty, and Alice was seeing it for the first time, while blown off course not just by the wind but by a storm of hormones.

"This is the Mound, Alice. In a minute you'll get an amazing view."

As they inched their way down the traffic-logged descent towards Princes Street, the sun came out and for a few perfectly timed moments Alice saw a different city, one lit by streamers of clear, cool light. To their left stood the castle, its ramparts grey now rather than funereal black. Further ahead, glimpses of the Forth peeped seductively between tall buildings, although even in the sun, the water remained a foggy, navy blue. The view was stunning. But it was only a tease, and when the clouds closed, so did her certainty that this city would never be home.

Alice looked down on the famous Princes Street and saw

a high street writ large but transplanted from any place in Britain. Debenhams and BHS. Dorothy Perkins and Boots. Samuel's and Mothercare. She couldn't imagine anyone walking the length of this noisy, traffic-burdened, litter-blown street for pleasure. Alice appreciated little circular routes for her occasional shopping trips. She liked curling narrow streets with small pavement cafes and shops that held surprises. She loved the back streets of Selly Oak.

They drove down Hanover Street, eventually found a parking bay, and walked back up the steep hill, buffeted by the wind, Stephen towing Alice. He stopped outside black railings with steep, worn steps leading below pavement level. Not very promising, Alice thought, but Stephen smiled as he helped her down. Inside, she saw yellow walls pinned with posters and plain pine tables and a self-service counter with beautiful, ceramic bowls of at least ten different salads and wicked, creamy puddings. On the blackboard, the day's specials were written up: spinach and lentil lasagne or stuffed, roasted aubergines with spicy tomato sauce.

"Henderson's," Stephen whispered as they took a tray each and joined the queue. "They brought me here when I came for my interview. An Edinburgh institution."

Alice breathed out fully and deeply for the first time since they had arrived. She inhaled the yeasty scent of freshly baked bread and the blackening burn of roasting vegetables and the temptation of dark coffee. This was nice. She could cope with this. The relaxed, veggie atmosphere complimented the food which, when they carried it on trays to a table and tucked in, was fresh and delicious. After their main courses, they went back for a chocolate mousse and a trifle, which they shared.

"OK, my sweetheart, we'd better get down to work," Stephen said, after he rose for a second time to fetch coffee.

Alice nodded as she took the property pages from her basket and spread them over the table. Not knowing Gorgie from Bruntsfield, or Westerhailles from Church Hill, Alice was flummoxed. Place names without places attached. Sounds without images.

"Actually", Stephen said, "it's not as difficult as it looks because we can rule out most of it."

Alice looked at him expectantly.

"We don't want to live in the suburbs, so that gets rid of about half of what's in here." He ran his fingers round the inner margins of the city. "Basically, we can afford something in Marchmont or Bruntsfield. Or we just might find something in the New Town."

"I don't like Marchmont," Alice said.

"From the outside. But the interiors will surprise you, Alice. I had a meal with a colleague who lived in a south facing one with stunning views to the Pentlands."

"Fine, but we'll end up with one that stares into the flats opposite and has no light." Alice knew she was being negative.

"We'll avoid those."

"Oh good." Sarcastic, too.

"People sand the floors and gentrify them. They're the same period as our house in Edgbaston. Victorian."

"Our house isn't a flat in a tenement that's five stories high and about a hundred long." And sour.

"Alice, I promise you I'll create a home you love."

"I want to look out on to trees and have lots of light.

Like where we are now."

"I know." He paused. "I promise, I will give you all of that."

Chapter 31

2007

No Direction Home

THE CLOCK FACE slides in and out of focus. Its second hand shudders slowly round, each jump onwards taking a supreme mechanical effort. The ticking is too loud and deliberately painful. The walls up here in the foyer have developed dancing spots wherever Alice moves her eyes. The stains on the red plastic bench wobble into liquid amoeba shapes.

"Shall I call you a taxi?" asks the policeman.

"No, thank you. Just let me sit here for a few minutes. I'm feeling a bit shaky." Alice replies.

"Nae problem."

Half a thought takes shape but evaporates before caught in speech. Concentrate, she tells herself. One last effort and you can get out of here. She mentally places one word deliberately in front of another, but like a house built out of very thin playing cards, they keep collapsing. She rehearses her sentences until they stick together and form a plan. She will walk to a cheap hotel and stay the night. Tomorrow, she will go back to the flat while Stephen is at work. She will collect Hunter, the car, her books and a few other things. The sequence keeps slipping away before she reaches the end, so she has to start all over again. Step one. Step two. Step three.

She will leave Stephen. He will undoubtedly leave her when he finds out about this, anyway. In his eyes Alice will be a contaminated wife. Shoddy goods. He will not even stoop to ask her why she did it. His worry will be for himself, for her shame leaking out all over him, leaving him ruined too. What if the local hacks have a barren day when Alice Green stands up in court? What if this sordid little story is splashed all over the local rags? He will be terrified of the scandal reaching the university grapevine, where someone is always waiting to stab you in the back because your publications are more highly rated than theirs or because there are currently three candidates for a coveted post in the Royal Society. Professor Stephen Green, internationally renowned philosopher, with a wife who pinched clothes from Marks & Spencer, would be crossed off the list. Would he have to resign?

TEN PAST ONE. There's a persistent buzzing which might be the clock or the lights or neither. It's shock, Alice tells herself, and exhaustion. Not unlike coming round from an anesthetic when things have no clear edges and sounds fade and boom and fade again.

"Are you OK?" asks the police guy. "You look pale."

"Not really."

"Aye, it's a bit of an ordeal."

The walls shimmer. Squares and circles of over-bright

light bounce off the glass doors and remain as after-images – lime green turning to magenta. Alice wants dark glasses and a glass of ice cold water.

And a magician's conjuring trick to clothe her again with invisibility.

INTERVAL

"SO CAL LEAVES me, I marry a grumpy lecturer with a compulsive-obsessive personality disorder who's disliked by everyone but you, and I have to up sticks to a city I hate. Great!" Alice has slumped on the sticky bench. She tugs at her hair and tries to hide her distress because she's here to be strong for her middle-aged self. She's still coming to terms with the flash-forward that narrated her separation from Cal.

"That's much too quick. You've just compressed years into moments. Lots of water under the bridge."

"Nasty, dangerous currents of water."

"No...just water that trickles downstream before it hits the rapids."

"That's not how it sounds, the way you're telling it."

"In the beginning I was happy with Stephen."

"But didn't you see warning lights? His insane tidiness and his need to control?"

"It didn't bother me. When I peeled away the onion layers, I found a complex man who was sensitive and unfulfilled. A man who cooked the lightest, crispiest meringues and then played Schmann and Bach.

"So in you flew like a Fairy Godmother and saved him."

"No, Alice. We fell in love. And the new job saved him."

"So what went wrong?"

Alice sighed. "You'll get the abridged version or this will be as long as *War and Peace*. We got married, moved to Edinburgh and Stephen embarked on another Grand Designs project because the only place we could afford was a Dickensian tenement flat. I despaired, but Stephen rolled up his sleeves after work and created another place of beauty. And we had Toby."

"I have a son!"

"Yes."

"It doesn't sound bad enough for shoplifting."

"Not yet. The messy stuff comes later. I must have turned my head very, very slowly. I looked away."

"From what?"

Alice ignores the question. "You know, I think we adapted to the men we loved. Like chameleons. I gave up my beloved job at the library to fit in with Stephen's plans. I don't see any of them changing to fit in with us. We are the accommodating gender."

"Not with Julian. I was myself with Julian."

"And he left you."

Young Alice turns away. The splinter is still stuck in her flesh. A cactus spike that long ago penetrated too deep to be removed. "But nearly all women do that. Men run on their treadmills, wearing blinkers, and we spin plates on poles around them. But not all of us end up stealing stuff. I don't understand."

"Nor do I. I told you that right at the start. Perhaps it

was my fault and I'm leading you down the garden path trying to pin the blame on Stephen and the others."

"Shouldering the blame is like a leitmotif through this story. We're pretty hard on ourselves."

"Exactly. And maybe we are to blame, and the men are peripheral."

"Unless we were pushed into a corner."

"Well, we've been in three corners so far, so there's only one to go."

Alice giggled. "Sounds like a boxing ring. How many rounds have we gone? And when can we get out?"

"I'm coming to that."

"Does something dreadful happen? Better warn me."

"There were times when I was made to feel small. I lost an inch here and an inch there and never did grow back to my former height."

"I'm not very convinced. Everyone gets knocked down, and they manage to bounce back. Like those wobbly toys?"

"Not everyone. They fake recovery and carry on."

"Did you?"

"Yes. I suppose so."

"When did you take the knocks with Stephen?"

"I have a few sharp images of scenes that might be tipping points. There're only postcards. I'll tell you about them and you can judge their significance."

Chapter 32
1986

In My Life

Snapshot 1

HERE WE ARE in our Edinburgh flat for the first time. Our solicitor jumped the gun and put in a quick, low bid so I didn't even see it before we bought it. I'm five months pregnant with Toby and my hormones are running riot. I hate the flat. I've waddled from room to room and burst into tears. Stephen tells me to go and look out of the window.

WITH A HELPFUL shove from Stephen, Alice hauled herself from the soggy brown velour sofa, walked to the bay window and stared out. The uninterrupted views sweeping south to the Pentlands surprised and restored her. She imagined the sun tracking from left to right, lighting the rooms from morning until dusk. Her sobs subsided as she returned and sank down beside him.

"Another thing…" Stephen continued, taking Alice's hand, and pointing behind them. "…that's a stud wall. I'll take it down and the light from the bay window will reach into the kitchen so you'll have north and south light. And the two back bedrooms aren't too bad. Just cosmetic jobs."

"But I won't be able to help you. I'm a great big plum pudding. I can't get through doorways, never mind up a ladder."

"I like plum puddings," he said, kissing her. "And you don't need to help me. I've done it before and I'll willingly do it again. This flat has potential. The other places we looked at were beyond help."

"The layers of lino…"

"Rip it all out. Sand the floors. They're original pine and in good nick. I've looked."

"The tiny bathroom?"

"Make it a feature. Mirrors and chrome. Alice, look at me," Stephen wrapped his arms around her great girth and cupped her damp, pink-cheeked face. "This place will be cutting edge… the most desirable tenement flat in March-mont."

For a while they sat quietly, staring at the red ball of a sun slipping below the window sill and burning round green afterimages on the walls and the furniture when they looked away. Alice planned the nursery. Sunshine yellow, she thought. Stephen considered which plants would flourish in the window, in square, matt black pots. Orchids. Phalaenopsis and cymbidium.

Why did she not rejoice in her husband's insight and enthusiasm?

What made Alice break the harmony?

"I'm worried about you taking this on at the same time as starting a new job," Alice said.

"It will be fine. They're easing me in. My teaching load is quite light for the first two terms," Stephen replied. End of subject.

"Oh Stephen, you will put in more effort this time and not upset people, won't you?" If she could have sucked back the words and chewed and swallowed them, she would have. Alice had never mentioned Stephen's problems, nor his sad exit from the Education department.

"I think you'd better not say any more, Alice." Stephen's mood could shift frighteningly fast. "That's below the belt. Why are you bringing it up now?"

"Because it was awful. You upset the students every year and I had to sort them out…"

"You had to sort them out!"

"Yes, as a matter of fact, I did. Every year. They came to me for books and help and sympathy."

"I suppose you taught them remedial philosophy? It was none of your bloody business to get involved with my students." The muscle in his jaw clenched.

"Don't be silly." Alice had stepped off a precipice and was in free fall. No branches to help her scramble back up and start again with tact and gentleness. Wrong time. Wrong place.

"This is news to me, Alice. Why the hell are you telling me this now?"

Because I'm anxious and upset, Alice thought, but said nothing to the man who gripped the arms of the sofa and stared ahead like a maniac.

"It's no good pretending. The whole department knew how you treated your students. I just want to say that now is your chance to start again, and I don't want anything to distract you from it."

It was out. Shut up, Alice! she told herself. For God's sake, shut up. You idiot, Alice Green.

"You patronising bitch!"

Alice winced as if he had hit her.

"That's not how I meant it." She reached out for one of his white-knuckled hands.

He pulled it away.

"Oh. I see," he said, placing each word on an ice block. "You talked about me behind my back in the staff room while living with me as my lover. Well, that's very nice to know. Thank you."

"It wasn't like that at all…"

"I trusted you, Alice."

"And you had reason to trust me. Stephen, I'm sorry. I shouldn't have said any of that. Can we just forget it?" Alice pleaded.

"Forget it? That would be convenient for you, wouldn't it?"

"It was stupid and inconsiderate of me…"

"It was cruel, Alice."

"Let's get out of here," Stephen said with a cool deliberation that was more intimidating than any outburst. He was already in the hall, rattling the keys, his mouth a pinched line. Alice heard the jangling of the keys as he waited, his back to her, beside the door. Her nerves, wound to the highest C, jangled in sympathy.

From the start of their descent of the eighty-six worn tenement stairs until late that night when Alice turned off her bedside light, he had thrown silent daggers of bitterness at her.

ALICE REPLAYED THE scene until the roll of film frayed at the edges. She replayed it, changed her opening lines to a mild rebuke, followed the rebuke with a quick withdrawal of her barbed words, and ended it with a quiet resolution. But the scene somersaulted back to its original format; she would have to live with it. Why had she chosen that moment to hit him with the worst she had? She reached out to touch him with her apologies, but there was no answering acceptance.

Snapshot 2

STEPHEN, OUT OF practical necessity, thawed out. You can't ask your wife to get quotes from removals men and fetch cardboard boxes from the off license if you aren't speaking to her. Besides, his enthusiasm for the new project leaked out of tiny cracks in the carapace he had built from his fury and disappointment. Off guard, he released excited sentences about kitchen work surfaces made of granite, and marble in the shower. He bought glossy hardback decor books and returned from Homebase with little strips of paint colours. He turned to Alice and asked her which of the ten soft greys she preferred and she admitted she couldn't see a great deal of difference.

"WHAT SIZE VAN do you want me to order?" she asked him one evening when she was still walking on crushed glass.

"Middle sized. We've not got that much."

"You'd be surprised. It's not the big items that take up

the space, it's the books and the stuff in kitchen drawers and bedside tables."

"We don't have any bedside tables."

"It was a turn of phrase."

"Okay, well let's be more specific," Stephen replied, listing the furniture in his flat.

"And my stuff from upstairs." Alice added.

A second's silence.

"You said you'd sold your furniture with the flat?"

"Most. Not all. There's my old sofa and some pictures and my books."

"Not the sofa."

"Oh. I thought it might be useful. That drawing room is enormous.'

"But it doesn't match this one.'

"Oh." Alice said again.

"What pictures?'

"The Klee poster."

"The studenty one with the ripped edges?"

"I like it."

"What else, the dust-covered cat soap in the basket on the bathroom shelf?'

"Oh don't be horrible! Of course I don't want the cat soap. But I'll roll up the Klee poster and bring it."

"I'd rather you didn't."

The sparring wasn't serious but beneath the banter, Alice heard a critical inflexibility. "Bloody decor police," she said, only half in jest.

"Bloody knickknack collector."

"Oh that is so untrue!"

They were laughing, but inadequacy crawled under Alice's skin.

"Look, Stephen, the next home belongs to both of us. I don't want to be the lodger in your abode. Done that. And just you wait until our baby is born. You'll live in chaos for at least ten years."

Stephen came over and put his arms around her hard belly.

"Listen, young man, you have be a tidy person with exquisite taste. Do you hear?"

"She is a creative, messy monster who will crayon all over your pale walls and leave a trail of toys from the door to the attic."

"There isn't an attic."

"You are so bloody literal."

TWO MORE EVENINGS to go. Stephen cooked asparagus spears and trout with flaking pink flesh followed by a perfect vanilla soufflé. Afterwards, he wiped the kitchen surface and unfolded a sheet of thick paper which he spread and anchored with the heavy salt and pepper grinders. It showed the new flat, drawn to scale with neatly written comments.

"Drawing Room," Alice read from the plans. "Cream/very pale beige/red oriental rugs/lots of big plants. OK, I'll buy that. Master Bedroom... why not Mistress Bedroom?"

"Because you're my wife."

Alice smiled. "Monochrome. White. Black. Maybe turquoise. That's exactly the same as here."

"Don't you like our bedroom?"

"Very much. Okay, on we go. Nursery, blues and greens? Oh Stephen, I told you I wanted yellow so her room looks sunny even on grey days in that grey city."

"Negotiable," Stephen smiled. This was the decoy.

"What's this? Study-Stephen. Study-Alice. I don't need a study. We need the second bedroom as a guest room."

"Alright. One objection at a time. I thought you might be offended if I didn't give you a room of your own. You'd quote Virginia Woolf at me. Next objection, easily answered. We never have guests."

"We will when the baby is born. Your mother. My parents."

"I hate people staying," he said on cue.

"But Stephen, can't I have a desk in your study? I'd like to try to write…"

Stephen cut in. "I need to be alone when I work. Sorry, Alice. This is the only thing I insist on. In the evenings you'll be on the sofa with your feet up after running around all day after our child. I'll buy you a chrome lamp with a dimmer switch because I don't want you to hurt your precious eyes."

Bugger dimmer switches, thought Alice.

"What colours for the baby's bedroom?" she asked, pasting over her upset.

"You can choose," he replied, magnanimous.

"Yellow. Sunshine yellow."

He kissed her. "I hate yellow, but I bow to your maternal instincts."

Snapshot 3

TERM HAD STARTED and the students were drifting back. It

was Stephen's first official day in the office as he called it, and Alice was looking out for him, trying to conceal herself on one side of the bay window behind the pine shutter, a wife worrying about her husband's first day at work as if he were a child starting school.

FROM HER VANTAGE point, Alice spotted him immediately, walking along the road with his heavy black rucksack. Instead of the previous head-down, frowning, self-absorbed shuffle that his students had cruelly mimed behind his back, he had a spring in his step and even nodded to people he passed.

Alice's heart beat so hard she had to sit down. This can't be doing my unborn child much good, she chided herself. What a ridiculous state to get into. But the voices from the past whispered in her ears. The ghosts in the corridors and concourses would not shut up. Emma kept shaking her head, rolling her eyes and mouthing insults.

"Hi!" he shouted. "I'm home!" He was hamming it up and his acting gave her pleasure.

"Welcome back!" she said, stepping into the hall to greet him, pretending that she'd been deeply absorbed in something.

"How are you two?" He hugged her hard.

"We're very well, thank you," she replied, keeping her voice calm.

"Be back in a minute then."

Stephen always went straight into his study to place his rucksack on its designated place beside his desk. Of course Alice couldn't see the invisible chalk mark on the floor, but it was there because every evening the rucksack stood in the exact same circle. He returned to the hall to remove his jacket and hang it on its peg. Alice smiled at this super-house-trained man who did not dump his bag by the front door or throw his coat over the sofa. His fastidiousness still amused her.

"So what's it like? Tell me." Alice called as his rituals continued.

"They've given me a big room on the top floor, facing south. An ivory tower in a vertical department. There's just one post-doc up there with me. Not met him yet. You know what the tenements are like… winding narrow stairs where you can't stop to have a conversation because it blocks other people going up and down. The coffee room seems to be the only meeting place and that's in the basement."

Alice murmured her pleasure and heard what he didn't say. Stephen wouldn't be going down six flights of tenement stairs to the coffee room to chat. She heard his delight at his officially designated isolation.

"And the walk to work is glorious. Across the Meadows. Twenty minutes today. Fifteen minutes once I'm fit. Great way to unwind."

"Coming or going?" Alice teased.

"Oh going, of course, after trying to get some sleep next to a beached whale," he teased back.

"Oh Stephen, I've told you to move into the spare room-"

"Shh. I like whales."

Wow, he was in a good mood. He had been complaining a lot lately about her disturbing his sleep.

"When does your teaching start?"

"They've been good to me. All I've got is one tutorial a

week with some post-grads and maybe I'll pick up a couple of doctorate students once they've decided on their topics. The people I've bumped into seem nice enough. I think I'll buy a coffee machine for my room."

Ha. Knew it.

Snapshot 4

AN EIGHT MONTHS pregnant Alice climbed the eighty four stairs to inspect her husband's eerie so that she could imagine him there. Since she'd been climbing tenement stairs at home, the exertion brought on neither a heart attack nor premature labour, but she was puffed and had to sit down before she could speak. She looked around. Stephen had had to accept a green dirt-proof carpet and pale blue walls, but in the window dark rubber plants were already flourishing and on the wall were Edinburgh Fringe posters. His books were in alphabetical order on the shelves. His desk was almost bare – papers in a neat stack and pens in a white jug – except for a bulky grey computer and clunky keyboard.

"Wow!" Alice said. "New toy too."

"My magic machine. How did we manage without them?"

"Easily."

"I do everything on it. No more memos, no more letters in longhand for secretaries to type. It's all email now. Of course there are a few old dinosaurs who are complaining… but this is the way forward. As for the internet, it's like a Pandora's box."

"Wow!" Alice said again, not really listening.

Stephen turned back to his computer, his hands poised

over the keyboard; a signal for her to go.

A bit premature, she thought. His dismissal of her, not the baby.

He turned his head briefly to give Alice a kiss on the cheek as she bent over him.

"I can see you might get addicted to your new toy," she said.

"I already am."

SO HE DID tell her. The signs were already there but in lower case, not big capital letters. And Alice looked straight past them.

Chapter 33
1987

This Woman's Work

TWO MONTHS LATER, by working very late every night, Stephen had finished sanding and varnishing the floors; and a little boy called Toby became the new occupant of the nursery with the yellow ceiling and the pine floor boards that glowed golden even when the sun didn't shine. Stephen had spent one evening up a ladder sticking glow-in-the-dark stars on the high ceiling. He pasted a frieze of animals at dado height – tasteful, not Woolworth's – and hung a mobile of glass birds that jingled softly if the window was open. There were no plastic toys. For his newborn child, Stephen bought smooth eggs in grained wood and floppy animals made of linen and velvet and silk.

ALICE EXPERIENCED THE pull of the thread that stretched with strength and flexibility between her heart and his, and connected them across day and night, across rooms and streets and cities. She forgot to read the book reviews and for a long, unnoticed time, her pile of novels languished. Every morning, she woke with joy, knowing she would be greeted with a big gummy smile and wet, open-mouthed kisses on her cheeks.

She was a natural. Alice pushed Toby in his pram on the Meadows and, quietly content, played with balloons and bubbles and balls. Alice the woman absorbed into Alice the mother. It did not escape Stephen's attention that she left the house clutching her child with a vague smile and absent expression, having forgotten to comb her hair. He watched her pull on the same corduroy trousers – because she couldn't fit into her jeans – and then a shapeless old jumper. He wondered at the power of biology and bonding, and left her to it. He told himself that he felt no resentment about this short, precious stage in her life and that it was just a matter of time before he would get his other Alice back. Meanwhile, he shut the door to his study more often.

He was a good father. At the weekend, partly to make Alice take a break, and partly because it gave him pleasure, he wandered from room to room in one of the museums or art galleries, softly talking to Toby about line and colour and shape. Or he put him in the little chair he had attached to his bike, and trundled him all over Edinburgh, pointing out rare architectural features while Toby cooed at a cat or a dog.

THE RESTORATION AND gentrification of the flat continued more slowly. While Alice splashed Toby in the bath and fed him mashed broccoli cheese and sang him to sleep, Stephen was up the ladder holding the impossibly heavy nozzle of an industrial wallpaper stripper that puffed steam and buzzed in a tone more mellow than the brutal floor sander.

"Why don't you give it a rest?" Alice asked one evening

after putting Toby to bed.

"Because I'd rather get it done while Toby is tiny. This ugliness depresses me."

The first is an excuse, thought Alice. The second is the truth.

"How can you even think of being depressed when we have this little fellow?" she asked.

"It's a manageable depressed. If I leave it, it will be a dangerous depressed. And it stays in a quite separate compartment from my feelings for my son."

"I don't have compartments any more," Alice noted.

"That's how it should be. You're a devoted mother."

"I still enjoy reading," Alice replied feebly, not wanting to be rubbed out altogether and redrawn in purely maternal colours, but her husband spoke the truth. These days she flicked through the same magazines she had once despised and lost interest several chapters into a novel.

"One day, I might even get back to my writing."

"Good."

Was Stephen listening? Sometimes she felt they were losing touch with one another, he absorbed in his work and his restoration, she absorbed in her son. She did not worry. Alice had read enough books on motherhood to know that this single-minded focus on one's child, especially a first child, was natural. Other mothers she spoke to described themselves as milk-bars or play-machines. And all of them said they were too tired for sex. Too tired for anything.

One day she would emerge from her chrysalis. One day Stephen would stop decorating the bloody flat and play his cello again and would reawaken in her the once intense longing for his body. Fugue and counter fugue.

BUT ALICE ACKNOWLEDGED that her dreams were a long way off. One night Stephen took a crowbar to the black range and the kitchen crumbled into piles of plaster and rubble. Only Stephen's study was a no-go area, sealed with tape against the dust that thickened the air in every other room and made Alice's eyes red and sore. For six months, Alice warmed up meals on a two-burner electric mini stove and Toby learnt to crawl through an obstacle course of bricks and tools and wiring and dirt. His feet and hands and face were permanently black. When Alice found him eating coal dust and bits of peeled-off wall paper, she consoled herself that this unusual diet would strengthen his immune system. Later, he learnt to haul himself up to a standing position by clinging to the tops of the cherry wood units and shiny white appliances that stood randomly around the room like a modern art installation.

Stephen fulfilled his promise of creating a space that was pale and light-filled. Three years after moving in, the rabbit warren of dark, depressing rooms they had argued about while sitting on the brown velour sofa had been obliterated. Alice had long considered it finished and perfect, but Stephen still visited expensive lighting shops and bought kitchen gadgets. Last time, Alice had seen only the end result. Now she witnessed the process, and his need to perfect every last detail.

BUT, FINALLY, STEPHEN saw its completeness and locked his

decorating equipment in one of the big storage cupboards in the hall. Aesthetic harmony and pale, light surfaces prevailed. He should have been relieved and satisfied, Alice thought, but with the flat finished, he floundered. In the evenings, Alice watched him wandering from room to room, unable to settle to anything, as if searching for some leftover that still needed his attention. He would pick up an academic paper. Put it down again. Pick up a book. Turn on the television. Turn it off again.

"Why don't you play your cello?" Alice asked.

"I don't know."

"I miss it. Why don't you get it out and try?"

"I don't know," he said again. "It's as if there isn't space for it anymore."

"But the bay window is huge—"

"No, no, no... not physical space, emotional space. Life's already too full. It would be a squeeze."

"Is that our fault? Toby and me?"

"Of course not. It's nobody's fault. It's just how things are. We're a busy couple with one full-time breadwinner, one devoted mummy, and a wonderful little boy who absorbs a lot of our energy."

"I'm sorry if I've stopped you playing..." Alice continued, appalled that despite her husband's assurances, it might be her fault.

"You haven't, sweetheart. It's not you."

"Is it the mess, the toys? I can clear everything away in the evenings..."

"No, Alice. Listen. It's something inside me and nothing to do with you. I can't find the energy for music. Or the will.

Not at the moment."

"Will you in the future?"

No reply.

ONE NIGHT AFTER dinner, Stephen walked into his study and began taking all the books off his bookshelves. Alice could see him as she went backwards and forwards, sorting things out for the morning. Stephen looked absorbed and hummed to himself. The next time Alice looked in, all the orange Penguin paperbacks books were back on one shelf in a block, and on a later trip from room to room she saw the bound academic journals, all red-spined, had been placed neatly beside them. At midnight, he called her in.

"What do you think?"

Alice saw a rainbow of books, colour-coded from hot to cool.

"Wow!"

"Pretty, huh?"

"What made you do that?"

"I didn't like the random colours. The blocks work better. I had my books like this in the Birmingham flat."

"It was one of the first things I noticed. I was a librarian then, remember?"

She had to admit that it was attractive – the mauves and purples huddled in a small space, the white spines stretching for a whole length of a shelf, with the black-spined books a dramatic contrast next to them.

"But how will you find anything?" Alice asked.

"I know them all by the colour of their spines."

THAT NIGHT IN bed, Alice turned to stare at her sleeping husband and wondered why he had felt the need to colour-code his books. It seemed rather a waste of energy. Books were to be read, not used as decoration. She shrugged her shoulders in a non-physical kind of way because she didn't want to wake him, and turned over. It takes all sorts, she thought. It's not hurting anyone. Stop worrying, Alice.

THE NEXT EVENING, Alice spotted Stephen struggling home with arms weighted down by expensive looking carrier bags.

"Heavy!" he gasped when she opened the door to him.

"What?" Alice asked, after he had put his bags down and Toby had been passed to his father for a welcome home cuddle.

"Folders and files and pencils and rubbers. Can't resist stationery."

"Me neither." But not in those quantities. I'd feel guilty splurging on a couple of new notebooks. Now what, husband of mine?

"What's it for?"

"Organising," he said, and threw his son in the air.

AFTER SUPPER, STEPHEN settled to giving his study the complete work over. Files and folders were tipped onto the floor, and papers and documents disappeared into new green and purple plastic folders, and black box files. The next evening heralded more of the same. And the next. He's re-organising his life, Alice thought, and left him to it. Maybe it symbolised the new start. His contentment in the new

232

department. She understood, in a way. Every time the foetus of a new poem stirred inside her, she would treat herself to a new notebook and some shiny pencils. It was a ritual. A rite of passage from one piece of writing to another.

ONE DAY, WHILE Stephan was at work, she decided on a whim to have a look around his newly preened study. Usually she didn't bother, partly because her comfort zones of kitchen and lounge and nursery kept her fully occupied, and partly because she regarded any kind of prying into another person's privacy as intolerable. What she saw shocked and then alarmed her. Absolutely no clutter. Nothing out of place. On his desk, the pencils were all sharpened to a piercing point and the rubbers lined up according to size. Paperclips of different sizes lay in three shallow pots: purple, green, black. The papers on his desk had been perfectly aligned and stacked so that not one sheet broke the exact squaring of the piles. Only one photograph of Alice and Toby broke the horizontal order, positioned at a slight angle under the dust-less poise lamp.

Alice felt the room recoiling from her presence; she messed up its purity and symmetry. Her striped blue jumper clashed with the colour scheme. A bit scary, she thought. Stephen had always been tidy, but this immaculate Homes and Gardens perfection worried her. She would order some books from the local library on obsessive and compulsive behaviour, just to reassure herself of course, not because she thought for one moment that Stephen was crazy or ill. He'd just got carried away. He'd finished the flat and this was his swan song.

AFTER CREATING A room that satisfied his every artistic need, Stephen made the next inevitable move of disappearing inside it. Once in his study, he was lost to the outside world, and had to be summoned back and reminded that outside his closed door was a family who needed and loved him. Sometimes the evening hours passed very slowly.

Don't go, Alice pleaded silently, watching his back retreating cross the hall. Spend an evening with me like we used to, apart but together. Don't leave me behind, Stephen, as if I'm no longer relevant. This mothering is not so intense and all-absorbing now, and the space you once inhabited feels hollow.

BUT ALICE GREEN wouldn't dream of nagging her husband or trying to pull him away from what he needed to do. If he found her boring, it was probably her own fault. Since Toby's birth, she hadn't put much effort into their relationship either, diverting her tide of her love and attention to her growing son. And just look at her – pounds heavier, slack bum in jogging trousers, hair pulled back in a ponytail and not a scrape of lipstick. Time passed, Toby grew, but Alice stalled.

Chapter 34

1993

Separate Lives

TOBY GRADUATED TO the second back bedroom. Stephen had built him a platform bed with a shiny red fireman's pole made from a piece of scaffolding found in a skip and carried home one evening. Nothing as ordinary as a ladder for Stephen's child. Instead of climbing out of bed, Toby slid down the pole and landed, bump, on the shiny floorboards. Beneath the bed hid a play area where the self-absorbed little boy contentedly spent hours building farms out of Lego and rolling his lorries and trucks around the floor with appropriate, accompanying noises. Like the rest of the flat, Toby's room was colour-themed – mainly red with splashes of yellow. The masterpiece was a Gauguin-like painted tropical rain forest filled with birds; a theatrical scene which appeared when his shutters were closed every night. Yes, Stephen had been a perfectionist, as always, in creating this small boy's habitat, but he had got it right. Toby loved this space, inhabited by worlds of his own making. Placid and calm as a baby, he had grown to be an engaging little boy whose inner life was rich enough to keep him happily occupied for hours. Alice would peer round his bedroom door very quietly, not wanting to disturb him. He would be sitting on the floor, or on his knees, totally absorbed, as he moved Lego men and small plastic animals into different places while keeping up a nonstop commentary.

THEN – AND IT came as a shock to both parents because time had done a runner – it was time for Toby to start school and all three walked forward into the inevitable next act of their lives. For Stephen perhaps, the transition was the least jarring, since he was not at home during the day. Toby managed without crisis. Alice grieved for the passing of those early years of hugs and sweetness, when she and Toby had been almost inseparable and yet contentedly apart, two people occupying the same space but never crashing into each other. Alice had been blessed with a child with whom she dove-tailed in peaceful harmony. She wept during the first days when a child-shaped space occupied the places where Toby should have been, and an eerie silence engulfed the flat. But gradually one routine was replaced by another, and Alice eventually accepted that she would survive the separation.

THE PRIMARY SCHOOL railings, where mums gathered to collect their offspring, were today's water-coolers. A place for talk and sympathy. The mums who were juggling part-time work with mothering looked grey and drained. Others, with two or three small children, were dazed. At the school gate, these women (for they were all mums) turned to one another and with brave self-parody, they told how they were clinging to life by their finger nails.

"I'm still wearing my nightie under my coat," one whispered. Alice giggled and squeezed the woman's hand. "I understand," she replied. Others laughed in sympathy. The black humour continued to roll:

"Last night's supper is still on the table."

"Do you go into a room and stop dead because you have no idea why you've gone there and have to go back to base and start again?"

"The other night I tried to switch on the TV with the mobile."

"I tried to switch off the dog with the TV remote when he was barking!"

They believed her because when you're this shattered, anything is possible.

"Please tell me how I get through another four hours before bedtime?" one grey-faced mum asked with a sigh. "I mean my bedtime. I've been up five nights running with the youngest. He keeps coughing."

They stared with varying degrees of envy as the dewy au-pairs arrived in second cars to collect the offspring of well-paid, working mums who had not stepped off the treadmill. The devoted earth mothers said they wouldn't swap places with the working ones even if they could. Why lose these precious years? Others secretly nursed feelings of nostalgia for a former freedom and a time when they had felt purposeful and valued.

In this public place, women spilled their intimate thoughts because at home no-one listened. Ten years down the matrimonial line, more often than not, the romance and the passion had evaporated. They said that their husbands were tethered by strong tent pegs to work because of the mortgage and the council tax and the People Carrier and the cost of children. Many of the fathers, like Stephen, worked late into the evenings and over the weekends. Some were absent even when they were at home. A few of the more attractive, energetic mothers found lovers and pretended they didn't care. Some enrolled in art classes and sang in choirs. Others, like Alice, played a waiting game, finding joy and fulfillment in nurturing a child.

IT WILL COME right, they reassured themselves. It's just a difficult phase. All marriages have rocky patches. All we have to do is wait. But Alice watched and listened and came to a different conclusion.

OK, ALICE GREEN, she said, time to pull yourself together. You will make an effort to become a reasonably presentable woman, even though you are approaching forty. It must be possible in this era of eternal youth. Someone who looks like a bag lady may be taken out one evening along with the rubbish and left for recycling. The council probably has a big black bin for unwanted, out-of-date wives. Do something about it before it's too late. Go and find the previous incarnation of yourself – the confident, fulfilled one – wherever you left her. Search her out and stand her up again. Do it now!

SO ALICE TOOK her first tentative steps back into her writing and escaped, like her small son, into a parallel universe of her own creation. Once she'd seen Toby safely through the school gates, she returned to do the domestic chores on autopilot, tidying up only to placate her husband. She prepared something for supper because Stephen no longer had time to cook. And then Alice made a beeline for her typewriter, settling with a sigh of almost physical pleasure because there was no-one to interrupt her or disapprove of her or make her feel like the bad fairy at the christening. House rules were broken. She carried in her mugs of coffee and left rings on her desk and ate her lunch while typing so that crumbs and bits of cheese fell into the keys and onto the polished floor. She put on the radio and sang. She got up and wandered about as often as she pleased without someone sighing and asking her to keep still and be quiet.

AT HER DESK, hours flew just as years had done. The buzzer outside the door to the communal stair infallibly made her jump and stare at her watch in disbelief. Toby was home already. Her son, feeling proud and grown-up, walked home from the primary school located all of a hundred yards away with no roads to cross, with a friend who lived in the same street. But his arrival invariably interrupted Alice's thoughts at a point when a character or a plot line had finally appeared to her as ghosts on the blank page, just out of sight and in danger of being lost if she did not catch them. Stay, she called over her shoulder, as she jumped up to welcome her son. Don't go and vanish on me. I'll be back. I need you.

MONTHS AFTERWARDS, OR maybe years, Alice woke one day with a sure, cruel knowledge that she had utterly lost her way. In another life, there had been a sign-posted path which she had followed, knowing its twists and turns, and its sudden clearings where clumps of wild flowers brought her to a standstill and made her breathe deeply, glad to be alive. The woman who daily walked that path had been confident in her work and confident in herself. Lately, not only had the bluebells and forget-me-nots disappeared from view, she couldn't even find the path. And where was Stephen? Hadn't he once walked along that path with her?

Chapter 35
1998

The Sound Of Silence

B OTH WORKED ON computers at home now; Alice on a grey Amstrad word processor rescued from Stephen's department when their computing equipment had been upgraded, Stephen on an iMac G3.

"Just look, Alice," he had gloated, catalogue spread out like a child at Christmas choosing what he wanted Santa to bring, "they come in Blueberry, Strawberry, Tangerine, Grape and Lime."

"Blueberry," said Alice, without looking. He would decide.

"Or Grape."

He had come home with a Lime because, he said, it made him smile. Excited, even feverish, Alice thought, he pulled the parts from the box to assemble them, then rearranged the furniture so that the computer had centre stage and became the first thing that caught your eye when the door opened. Soon a lime green mouse-mat and mouse sat next to the new toy. He even bought a packet of luminous green pencils. The computer took up more and more of his life. Alice thought of his room as a big-mouthed vacuum that sucked him in every evening. Whoosh! His chair held him with an invisible suction pad. His fingertips had grown magnets with such a powerful attraction to the keyboard that they kept them tap-tapping long after his wife and son were asleep.

In contrast, Alice's computer was an ugly, obstinate and wayward brute, perhaps because it had to sit in close proximity to the shiny, pretty one. It regularly died or swallowed her writing, never to regurgitate it, and its mysterious workings appeared independent of her mouse movements and key strokes. Were they even connected? Since she hadn't a clue how computers worked and because she was reluctant to interrupt Stephen when he was frowning over his own rapid key strokes, her writing went untouched for days until she judged Stephen's mood benign enough for her to bother him. Then, with somewhat bad grace, he would kick-start The Bugger as he called it.

"You brought the damn thing home for me," she said, grieved.

"But you must learn to use it," he replied. "Do you want to go back to your electric typewriter?"

"I might well."

No-one suggested that maybe Alice would like a new, shiny computer in a cheerful shade of tangerine.

IN THE EVENINGS, she and Stephen ate a simple meal (long gone were the days of salmon and almonds in filigree pastry and ice-cold white wine), read the paper or watched the seven o'clock news, and then Stephen would exit into his study.

Alice cleared up, made an inventory of things to do, put on a wash, ironed Stephen's shirts, packed Toby's lunch box, wrote a letter to the parents' committee, checked Toby was not still reading. Collapsed. More often than not she was too weary to sit at her desk, but there were times when the ghost of an idea appeared to her and she rushed to catch hold of it. She typed loudly partly because she was in a mad hurry – her inspiration didn't hang around.

"Can't you be quieter?" Stephen sighed, as he often did these days.

"Sorry. It's just how I type."

"Have you any idea what a racket you make?"

"No more than you…"

"Rubbish."

It was his stock reply to anything he disagreed with. It was also the full stop at the end of any disagreement with her. Alice took her hands from the keyboard. She had been trying to resolve a gap in a plot line when he'd interrupted her.

"And please pick up those piles of books and papers. I can't get to my desk without falling over your stuff. And the coffee mugs, Alice. How about returning them to the kitchen?"

Alice jumped. A metaphor escaped before it had taken shape. She dragged her glance from the screen.

"You're in a good mood," she said, more cross than ironic.

"I'm in a perfectly good mood and I'm making a perfectly reasonable request."

"You're not in a good mood. You're hardly ever in a good mood. Whatever is the matter? Is it work?"

"No, it's not work. Nothing's the matter."

"Then why are you so grumpy these days?"

"I'm not grumpy. I'm just a bit tired and I want to get on with this review and I can't because you are making such a bloody noise banging away on the keyboard and crunching biscuits. Do you know that you type as if it were a matter of life and death." Stephen stood up, red in the face.

"Then I'll go away. You don't want me in the study. That's what you're really saying, isn't it?"

"My study." He was in a churlish mood.

"So where am I supposed to go?"

"You can stay in here but don't type as if your life depended on it. Slow down. Calm down."

"You're being ridiculous."

"You're being unreasonable."

"Why don't you just say: I don't want you in here."

"Okay. I don't want you in here. I can't concentrate without silence."

"I would like to be able to write."

"I'd like to be able to work," Stephen countered.

"Oh so you have work and I only…"

"Well?"

"That's obnoxious! That really is horrible. So the only thing we can classify as work is paid work? Not writing, not painting, not composing."

"Oh, don't be simplistic. You know perfectly well what I mean. For now I'm the bread winner and there are things I have to do."

"Why don't you get them done during the day?"

With this dumb question, Alice knew she had lost the

battle. Stephen did not tolerate sloppy logic. He twirled in his chair and stared hard at his wife.

"So you've forgotten, have you, that lecturers who want to do research have to make time outside office hours? You have forgotten about staff-student ratios? About a rising student intake? Have you forgotten how hard people worked in the Education Department to turn it into an elite..."

"Some people worked hard." Oh Alice Green! You fool! You idiot!

"Don't, for God's sake, start on that again."

"Sorry."

"Why must you always bring up the past?'

"Always is an exaggeration. And I said sorry. I mean it. I know how hard you work. You don't even have time to play your cello or cook like you used to."

"I cook when people come to dinner."

Alice sighed. "And I do the routine cooking."

"Point taken."

"Stephen, I said I'm sorry. What more do you want?"

"How about moving your desk?"

"Where to?"

"I wondered about the far corner of the hall?"

"Oh Stephen!" Alice dumped her hands in her lap and scowled at him. "Thanks for the delightful suggestion. I've always wanted a cramped dark space in the middle of a passage way. Perfect!"

"No-one walks through the hall in the evenings."

"That's hardly the point. It's still a hall. Don't I merit a room?"

Silence. Impasse. Neither budged. If the clock had had

hands, it would have ticked loudly but being digital, it remained silent.

"How about moving your desk into the nursery?' Stephen then said, slapping his hand to his forehead. "We don't need the single bed. No-one stays with us anyway. An eight year old doesn't seem to have the same attraction as a baby."

Anger had brought a solution where argument and reason had failed.

"Why didn't you think of that before?" Alice asked, still fuming.

"Why didn't you?"

"Because I don't worry about these things. I didn't know I irritated you so much. I didn't know I was so unwelcome."

"You're not unwelcome... just..."

"Noisy," she finished. Alice's attempt at a joke broke the tension and put an end to the mean-spirited point-scoring.

"Come on then," Stephen said, brightening. "There's no time like the present. We can have it sorted in half an hour."

Maybe he's missing the massive home improvement project, Alice thought, watching Stephen stride across the hall to collect his box of tools from the cupboard. In minutes he had dragged the mattress and bedding out of what had once been the nursery. While Alice folded the bedding and put it away, she saw a spark of enthusiasm as he folded up the wooden slats and knelt to unscrew the bed base. Bed parts were soon stacked neatly in the hall to be taken, later, to the council dump.

"Might as well get rid of this horrible bedside table too," Stephen said cheerfully as he dragged it to the front door. "There, Alice. A pristine room. A blank slate. Do with it what you will." He stood back to admire the emptiness.

"Thank you," Alice smiled.

"My pleasure."

And it clearly was.

AS THE WEEKS passed, the separation between husband and wife stretched well beyond the length of the landing.

IN A BID to establish her own territory, Alice bought a pair of translucent curtains from Ikea. Pink. Stephen said they were ghastly and whatever possessed her. She hung a purple trailing geranium from a hook in the ceiling, breaking the rule about exclusively white flowering plants. In Habitat, she bought some stacking boxes covered in shocking red velvet, and in a shop on the Royal Mile, a Renee Macintosh coffee mug which Stephen condemned as twee and touristy. An embroidered cushion appeared on her black office chair. Against the backdrop of the rest of the flat with its harmonious neutral blends with splashes of red and green, Alice's room was a clash of vivid colours and buzzed with vibrancy. Or tastelessness, depending on who was describing it. Even her pencils gave her pleasure – pink and covered with infant sparkle.

Stephen never went into Alice's study. And he asked her to knock before entering his because he might be mid-sentence. Alice agreed. Perfectly reasonable.

Instead of shrugging off Stephen's words about her writing being irrelevant, Alice took them to heart. Even while riding the first waves of euphoria at having a room of her own, her spirits sank.

ONE EVENING, SEATED on her spangle-encrusted cushion staring at her blank screen, she took her hands from the keyboard, put them in her lap, hung her head and burst into tears. You're self-deluded, Alice Green! You – a writer!? Your hope is founded in quicksand. What do you actually do? Plan the week's menus and go to Asda and hoover the floors and do the ironing and pick up Toby's shoes and dropped clothes while Stephen exercises his brilliant mind and earns a decent salary. "I look after Toby," she said out loud. "I have been a full time mother for eleven years."

Ah but eventually he will make his first bid for freedom and Alice will not cling and make a fuss, but will wave him off with a smile. There will be no emotional blackmail. If she feels maternal angst, she will hide it because it's her problem, not his.

Alice is not prone to weeping, but now she is crying uncontrollably and bitterly because she knows she does nothing productive or creative or of any significance.

She does her best to cry quietly because she does not want to disturb her husband. Fortunately, the old walls are sob-proof and the space between the two rooms absorb the few tearful noises that escape under the door.

Chapter 36

1998

What's Going On?

A FEW MONTHS later Alice chucked her retaliatory grenade at Stephen. Not that it caused much of an explosion.

Husband and wife were eating omelettes and tomato salad. Their default meal. Neither cooked much anymore. Stephen flicked through the Guardian. That's OK, Alice told herself. He had explained that he read the paper to loosen the springs of his taut mind after work, but as the silence between them became oppressive, and the back of the paper became hostile, tolerance flipped abruptly into tearful anger. And a sense of rejection. He held the paper like a barrier between them, to stop her communicating with him.

She picked up the bread knife and, with its serrated blade, sliced the newspaper down the middle, narrowly missing making a similar incision down her husband's face. The action was intensely satisfying.

"What's that about?" Stephen remained aloof and cool, refusing to react. He folded the two newspaper halves and placed them neatly on the table.

"You know perfectly well," Alice replied, blinking back tears. She would not cry.

"I'm not allowed to read the paper?"

"Not while we're having dinner together."

"I'm sorry. You should have said."

"I was hoping I didn't need to."

Silence. Stephen picked up his fork. Slowly chewed the last mouthful of omelette.

"I'm sorry. That was over-dramatic… only there's something I want to tell you."

"Okay. Well, tell me…"

His mild response extinguished her fury. How skilled he was at dousing her emotions when their relationship threatened to catch fire.

"I'm all ears."

"Stephen, I'm going back to work." She waited for the drum roll and a bright spotlight to beam down on her head.

"That's good."

Oh.

"Stephen? Did you hear what I said?"

"Yes. You're thinking of going back to work," he said, while his eyes darted sideways towards the folded paper.

"No."

"Then what did you say?"

"I said, I am going back to work."

"Oh, Alice," he sighed. "I'm not in the mood for linguistic conundrums."

"I'm not playing word games. That's your department. I'm saying it as simply as anyone can. I've been offered a job in Newington Library starting next Monday." Alice said very slowly, as though speaking to someone foreign or hard of hearing.

"I didn't even know you were applying for jobs."

Alice said nothing.

"What about Toby?"

"Toby's growing up. Haven't you noticed?"

"I don't want him to be a latch-key kid."

"He's nearly twelve. Besides it's a part-time post so I'll be back by three thirty when he shuts himself in his room."

"Well, if that's what you want... congratulations."

"Thank you," she said, biting back bitter disappointment. Why so tepid and begrudging?

"Why the stealth?"

Alice sighed loudly. "I've been restless for a long time, in case you hadn't noticed. I applied for a senior post advertised in *The Scotsman* and I got it. All very simple; no stealth or subterfuge to be seen." Alice put one word in front of another, like talking to a foreigner.

"Senior post? But you've been away from work for years..."

Well, thanks!

"And was by far still the most experienced and highly qualified candidate."

Stephen gave Alice a hard look, as if he had missed something in this story, before picking up one of the jagged newspaper pages again.

Alice stared long and hard at the paper shield and wondered, not for the first time, what had happened to the insecure, sensitive, endearing man who had hovered in the library alcove in a state of approach-withdrawal paralysis because he had fallen in love with her. When did this distracted, irritable person steal his place – this man with the short fuse and the warning sticker on his forehead. Alice walked on egg shells and kept her thoughts to herself.

It will be all right when I start work again, she reassured herself. I will not be fidgety and furious because my husband prefers the newspaper to my company because I, too, will have work in the evenings. She envisaged a set of scales; the old-fashioned sort with brass pans and little lead weights. Going back to work would even out the matrimonial inequality so that she and Stephen would swing, nicely counterbalanced, at each end.

Chapter 37

1999

I Will Survive

ALICE PUSHED OPEN the doors to Newington library because they didn't part automatically as they should have done. Then she spotted the discrete notice. *Due to high winds these doors are not set to automatic.* Inside, on the walls of the wind-blown lobby, were Sellotaped fliers: Help For Carers. Sing-along With Wendy. Do You Have Mobility Problems? Art For The Elderly. Alice remembered the burnished wood and the mezzanine...

Stop it right now, she said sternly. Comparisons are odious. And pointless.

Inside, she took stock of the dirt-resistant brown patterned carpet and the mobile book shelves which made the space claustrophobic and hard to negotiate. She had to stand on tiptoe and peer over the shelves to locate Biography or Travel or History. Alice noticed that all the books facing outwards had embossed titles or flowery covers or were by Ian Rankin, J.K. Rowling and Alexander McCall Smith – the famous home-grown literary trio who lived on what Edinburgh residents dubbed 'Writers' Block'. There was nothing on display by new and emergent writers, and literary fiction hid amongst thrillers and romance. There were two carousels for Mills & Boon, a stand for newspapers in a far corner next to a few plaid-covered seats, and the requisite sad little plants.

Alice's room was directly opposite the automatic doors, past the lobby and just before the tight corridor swept round into the library itself. How thoughtful of the architect, she muttered to herself. As a new boss wanting to set her own tone, she believed in open access for her staff, so each borrower carried in a blast of icy air that froze her legs and blew piles of papers off her desk. She wore woollen tights and thick jumpers, but the day finally came when her hands were too cold to strike the right keys on her computer and she kicked the door shut with a splutter of blue words, there to remain. Council run, and council funded, there would no money for improvements. The dirty striped wallpaper would stay, as would the bulky desk and brown office chair. She found a ladder and climbed up with a dust pan and brush to get the cobwebs out of the corners of the ceiling and rip down her predecessor's torn notices.

STEPHEN CAME ONCE, and once only; to visit his wife in her new domain, to offer advice on a topic that interested him. He loved decor. He hated public libraries.

"Enough to make you slit your wrists," he said sweetly as he stared around. He referred, she presumed, to the room rather than the practice of lending books. "How does the council manage to produce such ugliness? Outpatients, bus shelters, job centres, STD clinics, NHS dentists – all designed to send you running straight under the next bus."

"Could you say something positive?" she countered. "It's not that bad. You should see the Morningside branch, it's a dark rabbit warren. Now that place is depressing."

"I wouldn't want to work here."

"You don't have to, so thank you for the visit and the encouragement. Now bugger off back to your own magnificent office with the view," she smiled, relishing this glimpse of the old ironic, amusing Stephen.

"Tell you what...we'll come in the dead of night with a few gallons of ivory paint and redo the whole shebang. New Ikea glass desk, stylish phone instead of that filthy thing, some art prints and you'll feel cheerful instead of depressed."

"I'm not depressed."

"Oh. In that case you are quite exceptionally resilient. Or your sight is going."

Alice laughed.

"I'm not in the least depressed," she repeated. Was it a lie or a half-truth? "I like it here. Not everyone is as anal as you about colour schemes. In fact, I remember a few academics in Birmingham who were so totally oblivious of their surroundings that you could have put them in an air-raid shelter and they wouldn't have noticed."

"Well, at least let's go and buy you a decent angle-poise lamp because I bet that one has a forty watt bulb in it."

"I accept your kind offer."

"And I'll choose a couple of framed Rothko prints. How can you live with those Monet lily pads?"

"Done. Now go away and let me get on with my work."

"You are valiant," he said as he walked away. "Don't

know how you do it."

Alice smiled at his retreating back, savouring the small spark still between them. It just needed a long, strong puff of wind to blow it alight again. She'd have to pray for a gale before it went out. Maybe the library, even this ugly excuse for a library, took him back to memories of days long past, as it did Alice.

SHE WOULD NOT have admitted it, but her mood sank each morning when the doors swung open. Her kingdom was old fashioned, but that's what Edinburgh people seemed to want, so she made changes only gradually. Alice moved the mobile shelves to allow movement and ordered new stands for recently published books to be positioned near the entrance. She organised talks by local authors, but few people came. She made lists of books that would appeal to different groups of readers and placed them in bright folders with large-lettered labels. They languished, never consulted.

Barely a day passed without her missing the rarefied, golden atmosphere of the other library. She missed the smell of bees' wax, the acres of polished wood and the minstrels' gallery. She missed the atmosphere of silence and reflection, of belonging to a community who loved books and learning. She missed the eclectic mix of students and lecturers and professors and eccentrics.

Most of her clients here in south Edinburgh were either old age pensioners or mothers trailing small children. The adults wanted romance and crime and the latest book by Catherine Cookson. She wondered if she was running a library or a day centre for people who had nowhere else to go.

Here comes the old woman wearing a pleated plastic rain hood from half a century ago. Here is the strange, tousled-haired woman who comes in at least twice a week with nine or ten books in a Tesco carrier bag. Here's the sad-faced man who sits and reads the newspapers until closing time. And here's the dutiful daughter with the shaky, dithering mother complaining about the books she took out last week in a loud, hectoring voice. And after school, Alice welcomes the regular mums who haven't given up trying to interest their offspring in books while the noisy brats, who don't want books at all, twiddle with mobile phones and crawl under the tables and shoot one another with plastic guns.

YEARS PASS AND Alice makes no attempt to look for another job. Is it from inertia? Or a lack of confidence? Occasionally she opens the University Bulletin that Stephen brings home and checks for vacant posts but the moment passes, another day passes, and here she is in Newington Library, walking through the automatic doors, blown in with the gale, and settling herself in the hard brown chair for another day in her faded office.

Alice Green reassures herself that she is content, in an understated sort of way.

Chapter 38

2002

When You're Strange

"TOBY...."

She heard his key in the lock, then the thud thud of his Size 10 Doc Martens up the two flights of red-carpeted stairs. But Toby, now at the local secondary school, had long grown weary of his mother's infantile questions.

"How was school?"

"Good day?"

"Would you like a cup of tea?"

"Are you hungry?"

"Take your boots off please."

Aged nearly sixteen, he didn't need a warden, a carer or a spy, so he had perfected the strategy of doing a runner from the top landing into his room where he slammed the door to make his point. He had stuck notices all over it: a skull and crossbones, No Parents Allowed Beyond This Point, Zero Tolerance Of Intrusion. He would re-emerge in the kitchen, spot on time, as Alice was serving up spaghetti Bolognese or fish pie, his head moving in time to tunes relayed into headphones which also served as a barrier to conversation. He would grab his plate of food and vanish again into the bowels of his den. Alice collected the dirty plates when he was at school. For a while, she and Stephen had insisted that Toby eat with them each evening, without head phones, but his head-down chewing and passive resistance had ruined their own appetites and they'd given in. Alice had read enough books on adolescence to know to leave him alone and wait for the storm to pass. They lived in a state of siege, but between Toby and Alice something held. She would not lose him altogether.

STEPHEN'S FORTIETH BIRTHDAY tipped him into a wired search for another house, another project, which, Alice sensed, had been simmering for some time. He had successfully guided a lot of students through doctorates, written two well-reviewed books, and needed to throw the switch from burning brain cells to manic physical labour. Alice had given in, knowing his fretting would only escalate. By now, she recognised his mood cycles – the quiet, dampened times when he was withdrawn and preoccupied that morphed into fidgety, adrenalin-charged restlessness. When they had first lived together, the shifts from one state to another had been gradual and the difference not so marked, but now the troughs were deeper and the highs, perhaps in compensation, rose into jagged summits of mad energy.

STEPHEN STARTING NAGGING Alice about moving from their studenty Marchmont tenement as soon as the university promoted him to senior lecturer. Superficially, his arguments were about status and space and post codes but Alice knew that Stephen wanted another project. He had written a couple of books and felt like a breather. The tools of the DIY trade called him away from Aristotle.

They found their Victorian drawing room conversion in The Grange with comparative ease. No bigger in area than their tenement flat, it nevertheless had its own entrance, its own doorstep, red-carpeted stairs and a stained glass window over one of the two landings. A property developer had got there first but had retained the period features and dipped only into Magnolia paint. When she knew it was theirs, Alice breathed a sigh of relief because this time there would be no building site. Stephen was content to install new lighting, rip out the bath to create a monochrome and mirrored wet room, and buy a few expensive pieces of furniture for the formal drawing room.

For six months, Stephen plumbed and wired, busy and fulfilled. The drawing room conversion was already beautifully proportioned; after Stephen finished his cosmetic work, it was stunning.

After bumping into each other during the upheaval, they retreated back into three separate existences which barely impinged on each another. Toby chose one of the back rooms and turned it into a hell hole. Stephen vanished into the other – a replica of his previous study. Alice was the only one who roamed the flat, wandering from room to room. Toby at least was transparent. He couldn't hide overgrown adolescents who come to stay on a Friday night and cram into one room. You couldn't not hear the thump thump of their music, nor ignore the soundtracks of sickeningly violent videos. On Saturday nights, Alice put in yellow foam ear plugs and on Monday mornings she gathered up the rotting remains. She opened Toby's window to release the smell of beer and pot noodles and stale pizza and body odour. And something else.

As TOBY PUSHED and pushed at the boundaries, his parents leant harder against them to keep them in place. They insisted on a few clear-cut rules: they wanted to know where he was when he went out and told him when to be home, but their success rate was not encouragingly high. They talked and talked about him without a resolution because there wasn't one. They consulted friends with children of the same age who were similarly distraught, but none had answers. They talked to Toby's teachers who told them that he was very bright, very musical, and still just about working – which was one up on most of his mates. Alice and Stephen consulted books and newspapers articles and found conflicting advice.

Toby provided Alice and Stephen with an ongoing, if sometimes upsetting, mutual concern. They huddled in the same air-raid shelter while Toby fired adolescent bullets and lobbed hormonal hand grenades at them. They wore tin helmets in their own home. At night, they lay on their bed reading their books with a wall of sandbags stacked outside the door.

Yet in the end, it was probably Toby who drove Stephen back into his room. One day the talking simply ended. Stephen had had enough. Alice sensed the familiar spiralling down of his physical energy, as if draining away down an invisible plug hole. He slid back into the other place, where he shut himself away and shunned communication. The house project had lasted a year. Toby would continue for several more. Stephen battened the hatches.

ALICE KNEW NOT to interrupt because she would be given the cold shoulder treatment for days. Just once, she barged into his room late one night without knocking, upset because she'd just had worrying news about her elderly mother. Alice was the family telephonist because Stephen hated phones and Toby had his shiny new mobile. As Alice stepped into the room, she saw Stephen's computer, alive and animated. Three or four bright little windows flickered with multi-coloured images like adverts or jerky home movies. In one, for a split second, she thought she saw a naked woman, like those she'd seen framed in windows when she had walked through the red light district of Amsterdam. One thing was for sure – it wasn't the usual white background crisscrossed with lines of black writing. Alice noted how quickly Stephen clicked the icon which whooshed the windows down to the bottom of the screen as soon as he registered her presence in the doorway. Then he pretended to fiddle with some papers. Unconvincingly.

"Sorry to interrupt. What were you doing?"

"Oh nothing."

"Not writing?"

"Looking up something on the internet…"

Oh. The internet. The new playground for the techno-logically advanced. Information and entertainment at the click of a mouse. Stephen revelled in it. He lived in it.

Alice walked across the hall to her own study and quietly closed the door. Her GP had just told her that he considered her mother too fragile to live on her own; she needed a carer. With sadness, Alice acknowledged this inevitable step down the mortality ladder. She would deal with that later in her usual, competent way. Right now, it was Stephen she thought about as she sat alone for a very long time, the light off, the window lit by the yellow street lamp outside. She knew what she had seen, but when she tried to dismiss it, the reasons and excuses didn't stick. She placed the first piece of barbed wire around her heart.

There is something nasty in the woodshed.

And so began a heavy-hearted watchfulness. In the early hours, when she couldn't sleep, and there was still a flat empty space beside her, she would wander into the kitchen to make herself a drink and would see the lights from the screen sparking under Stephen's door. Flash. Flash. Flash. Blue. Green. Orange. Jumpy movie lights. His sessions on the computer now continued into the early hours. He woke red-eyed and desperate for a shot of heavy-duty caffeine. Alice felt her terra firma developing ruts the size of potholes which she knew, sooner or later, would fall down.

Mind the gap, she chanted.

Mind the bloody gap.

Chapter 39

2002

Papa Don't Preach

URBAN LEGEND HAS it that bad news comes in threes, like buses.

Bus No 1

"IT WAS ONLY a bit of hash, for fuck's sake, Mum."

The three of them were in the living room, used so rarely it had taken on the air of a waiting room in a private medical clinic. Toby sprawled in a chair, legs wide apart, head down. Stephen stood at the mantelpiece, fists clenched. Alice leant on the back of the sofa. Statues.

"Don't give me that crap, Toby! You're suspended from school and we've just spent an hour trying to persuade the Head to take you back. How do you think we felt? Or don't you care? I'm ashamed of you."

"Gently, Stephen," Alice warned.

"The hell with gently. My son is taking drugs and I have to sort the bugger out before he's expelled."

"Stephen…" Alice pleaded.

Anything salvageable in this situation would come from

diplomacy and calmness.

"Toby, just tell us the facts so we don't get any more nasty surprises," Alice said quietly.

"Fair enough. Me and Zac were smoking in the playground and some fuck-head of a teacher who'd forgotten to go home caught us. For Christ sake, it's not such a big deal. Everyone does a bit of dope on a Friday after school."

"For God's sake…"

"Stephen, shut up!" Alice interrupted. She rarely overruled him, especially in front of their son, but she knew confrontation would be futile. "Just shut up a minute."

"Wasn't it a bit stupid to smoke on school premises?" Alice asked, hoping that Toby would hear the morsel of sympathy she held out to him. Bad luck you were caught, she was trying to say. The experimenting with hash didn't worry her very much. From conferences she'd attended and from reports online she knew maybe a third of sixth formers were using drugs on a regular basis. Alice's generation did alcohol. This one did drugs.

"Whatever," Toby replied.

"If I catch you or hear about you taking drugs, here, there or any-bloody-where you can pack your bags and get out of this house. Do you understand? Drugs are illegal, bloody stupid and wrong."

Toby raised his head very slowly and gave his father a straight-in-the-eye look of utter contempt. "And porn isn't?"

Silence. Heat spread from Stephen's forehead to his face and down his neck. Like a menopausal flush.

"You're a hypocrite, right? I smoke a bit of hash, but you're the dirty old man in the raincoat. You disgust me."

"Don't you dare speak to me like that…"

"Whatever!" Toby snarled and stomped off, calling over his shoulder, "Mum, if you want to talk, you can come to my room later. But I'm not discussing ethics with that wanker."

"Stephen?" Alice's voice was deathly quiet, her face pale. Toby'd had the courage to confront his father while she had stuck her head in the sand. Up to her neck.

"No idea."

"So why did he say that?"

"My son is taking drugs and stoned out of his head half the time…"

"Oh for heaven's sake, don't exaggerate, and answer my question. I'm not that naïve, you know."

"Okay. He's talking rubbish. One way to crawl out of your own shit is to throw it at someone else."

"Look, he may be impossible, and he may be smoking dope, but he'll be all right. Most of his peers are doing drugs, some on the hard stuff."

"I've never heard such a load of liberal garbage. Soft drugs lead to hard drugs. Toby is a few bloody reefers away from heroin and cocaine. He's sixteen, about to go to university, and he's screwing up his life."

"You're entitled to your opinion. I disagree. And you're still wriggling on the hook, Stephen. I asked you a question. Why did Toby say what he did?"

"Revenge. Adolescent hatred. Forget it, Alice."

"I don't think I can." Alice looked hard at him. "Stephen, I know."

"Okay, later." And somehow the moment slipped away. "Right now we need to talk about our son. Make us some coffee and we'll work out how we can persuade Mr MacFarlane not to expel him."

Alice saw the quick sideways skid. The convenient change of topic. But the jack-in-the box had flown out, scary and grimacing, and could not be stuffed back inside. She left it lying on its side, floppy but menacing, while she ground the single estate Kenyan coffee beans and inhaled the aroma. This was her addiction. She sipped her first morning fix with a kind of ecstasy. Who was she to criticise others? But then again, didn't the three addictions come in some kind of order of seriousness?

Caffeine, porn, marijuana.

Beans, boobs, blow.

Percolated, perverted, pot.

Stop it! Shut up, Alice. Stop playing with words. Playing with fire. On cue, John Lennon joined in: *Whatever gets you through the night...*

Bus Number 2

A FEW DAYS later, Alice's mother died. Putting her worries about husband and son on the back burner, she packed her black suit and took the train to Essex to set in motion all the rituals and traditions that follow a death. She arranged the funeral, put a notice in the newspaper and phoned her mother's friends. Her father was too upset to move from his chair. She walked around him while he sat and stared out of the window, seeing nothing while tears rolled down his cheeks. He won't survive this, Alice thought, not after sixty years. Then reinforcements arrived.

Two aunts went through their sister's belongings and

took sad, bulging carrier bags to Oxfam. One of them took the broken old man home to put food in his mouth and to place a comforting arm across his hunched shoulders. Two weeks later, Alice was back in Edinburgh with a head full of worry about what to do with her elderly father. But, already dealing with the aftershock and fallout from both her son and her husband, he would just have to wait for the next space in the queue. *Till Number Five, please.*

Bus Number 3

THE THIRD BOMBSHELL went off at work. From newspapers and the grapevine, everyone knew that library funding was being slashed and stocks of books were not being replaced. Libraries were being closed or threatened with closure.

Up popped an email notifying Alice that Newington Library had been selected to become fully automated. She knew what that meant, of course. Instead of the curving wooden counter and the warm welcome her staff gave every borrower, especially the old and the lonely, there would be a couple of machines into which readers fed their books. And of course there would be staff redundancies. Already upset and out of kilter, Alice immediately picked up the phone. "Thank you so much for informing me about this in an email," she said icily when she'd finally managed to get through to a human being. "And am I to expect redundancies?"

"We'll be sending out letters to employees in the next few weeks. In the current economic climate, Mrs Green, this is one of the few ways we have of saving money."

"I repeat, which of my staff are you sacking?"

"Well, no-one will be sacked, of course. The reform and modernisation of the entire system means that some members of staff will be offered early retirement. Obviously we can't say any more until we have offered this package to the individuals concerned, but we are making every effort to select those who are approaching retirement age or who only work part-time."

"In other words, some of my best staff," Alice shouted. "Do I get any choice in this? A say?"

"I'm afraid not, Mrs Green. It's all being managed at a higher level involving the funding committee and the management…"

"Well, tell the powers that be that I thoroughly disapprove and am very reluctant to see any of my staff go."

"I will pass that message on, Mrs Green."

Automation, as Alice knew, was the first step towards making humans obsolete. Especially humans of a certain age. The unskilled would replace the wise and experienced because they were cheaper. Well, she would fight to the death for the rights of the older staff who served the community and provided a welcoming haven for people who wanted to escape the fairground noises and racetrack pace of the modern world.

Alice vowed to fight all plans – and she'd seen the suggestions – to turn her library into a social club, where choosing a book would be accompanied by muzac wheezing in the background. She would stand up against yoga classes and bingo invading one of the few remaining bastions of a gentle silence.

She prepared her case and presented it passionately at

every committee meeting, but the bright young things told her she needed to move with the times. 'Old-fashioned', they said behind her back. Damn right, thought Alice. Soon the books will be shunted into cupboards and we'll have Pilates classes and karaoke.

Three strikes and still not out, Alice went around chanting Henny Penny and Chicken Licken. The sky is falling. And still she ran along the line of spinning plates giving each one a twirl to keep them from tumbling.

Alice ran. And kept running.

Chapter 40

2006

Because I Got High

O N HER HALF day, Alice stopped working at twelve-thirty and left the library three minutes later after gathering her things and saying goodbye to whichever staff member stood between her and the doors. Heaving her bulging rucksack of emotional luggage on to her shoulders, she rehearsed her plan to go to Waterstone's to run her professional eye over the three-for-twos and to find a birthday present for a friend – a biography or a gardening book. It was a busman's holiday, not a candlelit dinner with her husband or a surprise weekend in Paris. How long since someone had given her a bunch of flowers? Alice Green's treat would be a cappuccino and a slice of carrot cake after staring at the shelves in a book shop. A bit sad, she thought. A bit sad.

On her way out of the library, she noticed how cold her hands were and pulled on her gloves, despite the mild weather. She felt trembly, as if she had drunk too many espressos. She was in fifth gear and hadn't got into the car yet. Not surprising, she reasoned. Husband. Son. Library. Careful, Alice, she warned herself. I don't think you're in very good shape. The trees shimmered and the familiar parking place looked vaguely out-of-focus. Inside the car, she breathed deeply and chose a CD of Einaudi to sooth her as she drove. She started the engine and inched carefully out on to the road, her foot pressing the pedal more gently than usual.

WHEN THE TRAFFIC light turned red at the top of the Mound, Alice was able, for a precious few moments, to look down on the monuments and art galleries side-lit by a low amber sun that rolled out of hurtling dark clouds. She recalled that moment, almost twenty years ago now, when she and Stephen had stopped at this very same spot and he had shown her the sandstone burnt golden by a similarly elusive sun. The traffic lights changed. Down the hill she glided, after placing the memory in a box and sealing it shut. With a sigh, she crossed Princes Street and found a parking space.

BECAUSE SHE WAS close to tears, and because the wind stung her face and she still had another two blocks to walk along George Street, and because she didn't want to look at books at all, she turned right into Castle Street – one of the many roads now spoiled by pizza parlours and shops selling tartan jumpers and golfing kick-knacks that led down towards Princes street. There, she plunged into the cavernous spaces of Marks and Spencer. Occasionally she came here to search for work clothes. Today she went in simply because it was there.

In Per Una, dozens of middle aged women just like her worked their way through swathes of calf-length gypsy skirts and spangle-encrusted tops and bold striped jumpers and cardigans with big buttons. Alice knew every garment fell just the right side of the Mutton-as-Lamb divide. Alice observed, distracted, as women clicked hangers along rails and perhaps, for a moment, dreamed of finding a fabulously cut dress, a subtle blue or dusty purple, made from fine fabric that hung in soft, flattering folds. Something which might make her beautiful again. Who are you kidding, Alice? Not here. Never in here.

In retrospect, Alice didn't know what happened next. Maybe the mood in the store – busy, hopeful, high – had sucked her in. This time she might find a dress or a top that would make her heart sing. She moved from rail to rail, rejecting the colour or the fabric or the garish trim. Half-heartedly, she hung a couple of garments over her arm to take to the changing rooms. And, having traipsed to the changing room and tried on her selected garments, she handed them to the assistant with a shake of her head and a "No, thanks".

She should have left the store then, but today her heart-ache translated itself into a longing for a garment that would – somehow – make her feel whole. She wandered towards stands of cocktail and party frocks, though Alice never went to either, but something caught her eye, a simple, cobweb-thin, grey silk top. She glanced at the tag – pricy for Per Una – and draped it over her arm. Then she found a plain white paneled skirt ruined by its 'free' garish gold belt. Alice headed for the changing rooms again.

The assistant must have headed off to replace an armful

of garments so Alice slipped into one of the cubicles and pulled the curtain tight across the opening. The skirt was a surprise; it fitted perfectly across Alice's hips and looked good without the belt. The grey cobweb top was 20% cashmere, 80% silk and so gossimer fine she could scrunch it up and hold it in the palm of her hand. It would look perfect with a sleeveless black T-shirt underneath and maybe a single strand of pearls. Alice got dressed again and lifted her hand to pull back the curtain.

Then stopped.

INTERVAL

"GOOD CHOICE. LOVE the top."

Alice jumped. "You! It's far too expensive. Anyway, where have you been? I've missed you."

"I know. I've been at your side, listening to you, and it's been pretty shocking. I've been shaking my head in disbelief and shedding a few tears. Sad, isn't it?" The younger Alice sat down on the bench and stared at her older self.

"I'd say my fifty or so years have been an ordinary sort of roller-coaster. Ups and downs."

"Are you saying that to reassure yourself?"

"Probably."

"You look wretched."

"I feel wretched. I'm at my lowest ebb. Utterly demoralised and worthless."

"You've said that before, you know, and you've found a way out. Something's turned up."

"I think I've had my nine lives."

"Four. If it's men we're counting. Relationships."

"So isn't there more to a life than a man?"

"Yes. But let's start there."

"OK. Four. I don't want any more. I'm alone now while

living with a man, so I might as well be properly alone and play loud music while I write and eat beans on toast in the middle of the night."

"Hurray! That's the spirit. Dump the bastard."

"I think we're coming to that."

"Good. Then you you'll be free."

"It feels like that'll never happen. I'm dragging around so much unhappiness."

"I wish I could help."

"It helps to have you here. It helps to remember that I was once your age and giddily in love with Cal."

"Having heard what happens with Cal, I'd like the narrative freeze-framed so I don't have to move on."

"Can't be done. As for me, I want to fast-forward to the time when I'm happily settled in a little flat all by myself, writing a bestseller, watering geraniums on the window sill and talking to the dog."

"It will happen."

They both smiled.

"Do you want that silk top?"

"Yes, but it's ninety-nine quid." Was this the cue? Or is Alice conjuring up a whopping lie?

"Stuff it in your bag. No-one's looking."

"Don't be ridiculous. You did that and got caught."

"That was a full-length leather coat with three assistants on to me. I was having a dumb day."

"Go away."

"No. You need me. I'm here to rescue you from disappearing. Remember when you used to waltz through these boring stores with a spring in your step and head for Biba."

"Biba is dead. Perhaps I am, too."

"No, you're not. You once had a sure eye for beautiful clothes. You were eye-catching and lovely. You wouldn't have been shopping in here."

"I'm fifty something now. We shop in here when we're fifty.'

"I know how old you are. But you're still lovely, you know, even when you aren't trying."

"You mean I look okay for my age?"

"I didn't say that. You are a very attractive woman but you're hiding in your uniform of beige slacks and clumpy shoes. When did you last buy a new lipstick?"

"Maybe I don't care about any of that. Maybe I'm content with my boring clothes and bare face."

"I don't believe you. You're wearing those things because you think no-one sees you. You think no-one finds you attractive."

"They don't."

"It's not true, but if you want to believe it, then buy something nice for yourself. What better reason? That top is a good start. Take it!"

"No! I'll have it but I'll pay for it."

"You'll feel more triumphant if you don't pay. It'll be a gift. A treat. Aren't you angry enough to pinch something? A small act of revenge?"

"On whom?"

"Everyone."

A pause.

"Yes, I am. Now go away before you tempt me with your clarity. You're incorrigible."

When the older Alice peered out of the curtains again, there was still no assistant in sight. No young Alice, either. She had vanished.

Chapter 41

2006

Just Do It

IT TOOK FIVE seconds to scrunch up the top and stuff it in her substantial shopper that already held an umbrella, a book, a notepad, tissues and her purse. Alice walked casually out of the changing room and handed back the skirt with a smile and a shake of her head. Rather than racing for the exit, because that, she knew from long, long ago, was guilty behaviour, she forced herself to linger amongst reds and navy and even fingered a few more garments. Raising her head as if to scan the garments but actually to sweep the store for security staff, she saw only engrossed shoppers. Women pushed past and around her. As far as she could tell, no-one followed her movements, so she worked her way along the rails towards the exit. If they had electronic machines that detected the colour of adrenalin coursing through people's veins, hers would have shown up bright, guilty red and electric orange.

No firm hand gripped her shoulder. No "Excuse me, Madam, but would you just step this way please." Her heart fluttered in little illicit leaps of joy. She bumped into several

pedestrians as she walked, lightheaded, back to her car. She
didn't notice the rain soaking her face or the wind howling in
her ears. Could she still be arrested? At what stage could she
be sure that she'd got away with it? Alice couldn't dredge up
the memory. She unlocked the car and scrambled in,
trapping part of her coat as she slammed the door. Beads of
sweat dotted her forehead. It took ages to extract her keys
from her bag and insert the right one into the car.

Quickly. Quickly.

Get the hell out of here.

Run, Alice, run!

SHE PARKED ALL askew in front of her flat, did one last check
in the mirror then grabbed her bag, scrambled out of the car,
opened the gate and headed up the path. Did she look guilty?
Slow down, Alice, for God's sake. Stop rushing as if there's
someone following you. Behave normally.

Alice hugged Hunter, burying her face in his shaggy fur.
Her dog loved her unconditionally; in return for simple
canine comforts, he rewarded her with adoring brown eyes,
body shakes of delight and a wagging tail. It was so easy to
please him. Alice dumped her bag at the back of the
wardrobe, changed into jeans and wellies, and the pair set off
up Blackford Hill for a long, tiring walk. She wanted to wear
herself out, never mind her beloved dog, and restore some
kind of order. She replayed the scene and felt no guilt, just a
small, spiteful triumph. A kind of two finger salute at life.
The adrenalin drained away as she made the descent and by
the time she arrived home, Alice was calm again.

With the nail scissors, she cut the tags from the silk

blouse and pushed them inside an empty dog food tin which she put in the kitchen bin. She felt a small stab of guilt because this tin would not be put out for recycling.

Chapter 42

2006

Can't Stop The Rain

A WEEK LATER, at work, Alice was drumming her fingers on her desk, and the voices that accompanied the heartbeat of her fingers were singing blues that were definitely not related to books or personnel. Usually so good at leaving her personal upset outside the revolving doors, today they had blown in with her and would not be quiet.

Stephen had not come home the previous evening. He had phoned to say he was assembling a fiendishly complex index for his new theoretical book and his publishers were hounding him to finish it in time for a big international conference. Since moving to Edinburgh, Stephen had started climbing and now he stood on the giddy top rungs of his academic ladder. Alice looked up at him from the bottom. Far from resentful, she was proud of him, but also aware that the gap which used to stretch across the landing of a tenement flat had opened up into a ravine which made her dizzy when she looked into it. He lived on a rarefied planet with star-studded colleagues while she, his faded and unfamous wife, handed out weepies and horror and violence memoir in the local, equally faded and unfamous library.

Why are you suddenly so upset about the difference in status? Alice asked herself as she tilted her chair back and stared at a strip of wallpaper making its descent from the ceiling. Be truthful. That's not what's upsetting you, is it? It's the emotional distance that's opened up between you. He's cold and indifferent. He doesn't notice your presence. He doesn't love you anymore. You are irrelevant in his life and surplus to requirements. What difference would it make to Stephen if you packed your bags and left? Exactly. You are no more than a convenience. Two new words rolled about among the verbal detritus. Separation.

Divorce.

Wait, leave that for now.

With a mighty shove, she edged Stephen out of her mind only to see that her son had moved in to fill the worry gap. Not now, Toby. Not now. I have enough to think about. Yet her maternal fingers itched to pick up the phone to find out if he was still alive. Six months after he'd left home, she still stared into his room and wished he would materialise once more with his raw music and edgy tactlessness and his raging, youthful anger at the world. She longed for the rare occasions when he would let slip his mask of rude indifference and lean down and hug her, telling her without words that she was still his mum. The thread that bound them was thin and stretched to breaking point, but it still connected them. With the phone somehow in her hand, her fingers punched in her son's number. You don't need this, she reasoned silently. Why torture yourself further? Toby has his own life now. Put the damn phone down. But she didn't obey herself.

The phone rang for a long time. Finally someone answered.

"Yeah."

One of Toby's flat mates. Ed or Phil. Their phone etiquette was identical. Was this a question or a greeting?

"Hello. It's Toby's mum." Alice glanced at her watch. 12.45 p.m. He should be up by now.

There was a pause as if this information was difficult to grasp.

"Is he there?" Alice asked.

"Toby!" yelled the voice.

Alice heard a shouted exchange up and down stairs.

"Yeah…" said Ed or Phil. "He's in the bath."

"Well, could you take the phone up to him?"

They wouldn't have anything as uncool as a fixed landline.

"Yeah… OK… hang on…"

Footsteps. Door opening. Sounds of water. Then clear as clear:

"Hey man!"

Laughter.

"Why the clothes on, man?"

"Hate launderettes. Who that?"

"Your Mum."

"Oh." More splashing water, which Alice interpreted as her son heaving himself to a sitting position in the bath, followed by retreating footsteps, then the deafening crash of the phone being dropped on the floor or banged against the bath, and finally, "Hey, Mum!"

"Hello, Toby. I just wanted to say hello because we

haven't heard for a few weeks. Are you OK?"

"Yeah, fine. Been busy, that's all."

"So, what have you been up to? Lots of extracurricular activities?" Maternal anxiety tripped her tongue into shaping ridiculous words.

"Gigs, Mum. They're called gigs. Save the long words for the library."

"Gigs," she repeated. "So...where have you been playing?"

"Wolverhampton last weekend."

"Did it go well?"

"Think so."

"Good."

Her next sentence tumbled out all by itself. It was none of her business. "Did your flat mate say you had your clothes on in the bath?"

"Yeah."

"Why?"

"Why not? Two birds."

"Oh, well, as long as you are all right, I'll let you get on with your bath and your, um...laundry."

"Whatever. Yeah. Okay."

The after image was of her tall, thin son wearing jeans ripped across the knees, probably leaking dark blue dye, a T-shirt with an angry slogan, and mismatching socks (a matter of principle) in the bath, with his dreads hanging over the end. Oh, heavens. Don't think about it, Alice. He has flown the nest and is no longer your responsibility. He will either sort himself out or not. She had never dared broach the subject for fear of making things worse. He will either get a degree or he'll become a rock musician. Or both. Or neither.

THROWING THE TAMEST of excuses about a meeting with the execs at a colleague who collided with her, Alice grabbed her bag and fled to her car. Her hands left sweaty marks on the steering wheel as she drove to almost the same parking space in George Street as the previous day.

She ducked into M&S via the Rose Street cafe entrance where a CCTV camera would have snapped the image of someone else. She was not Alice Green – worried librarian, unloved wife, anxious mother. She was Mrs Anybody. Mrs Nobody. Go for it, Alice, turn the tables on them and make the most of being anonymous.

THE ENTIRE PREMISES were baroquely complex with different levels and half-levels, escalators, mini-escalators, lifts and entrances. It was easy to mingle with the roving middle-aged shoppers. Having reached the ground floor in the lift, Alice wandered through shoes and tights, casual clothing and swim wear, then walked up a short flight of steps, down another flight, and took the escalator to the underwear department on the first floor. There was probably a simpler way of getting there, but never mind.

As she stepped off the moving stairs, a football pitch of pants and bras confronted her. It was worse than the Woolworth's pick-and-mix sweets counter. There were padded bras, push-up bras, platform bras, plunge-cleavage bras, diminishing, reinforcing and uplifting bras. Overwhelmed and very hot, Alice took off her heavy cardigan and hung it over her arm. Her first mistake. A deliberate one?

On the other side of this breast-bearing expanse were packs of plain cotton knickers and camis and strappy vests – the kind of garments Alice wore. She took a couple of the cotton tops and laid them over her cardigan. Some black pants with only one row of lace. A black cami. The assistants, preoccupied with women returning knickers that didn't cover their bottoms, did not see Alice discretely move her large cardigan so that it hid the smalls underneath. Then in an isolated corner, she deftly scrunched up her haul and slipped it into her roomy bag. Don't look down, keep staring at the racks. That's the trick. Don't draw attention to your hands.

Only someone who knew Alice Green really well would have noticed her slightly odd body language as she made crab-wise movements through the store. Alice rejoiced in the benefits of looking ordinary and in an anonymity which reduced the chances of being stopped and challenged. Sweating, she detoured through the jewellery stands. Around her, women held up shiny, tinkling necklaces and bangles. Alice paused and held up a necklace. Then a pair of earrings. She feigned interest. Then she retraced her complex trail and, breathing hard and almost painfully, she walked slowly out of the store into Rose Street.

A cami top, three pairs of high-leg pants and a pair of black lacy knickers for no reason whatsoever – all stuffed well down into the depths of her bag, still attached to their silly little plastic hangers. Alice's cheeks flushed pink with pride at her recklessness as her heartbeat slowed away from an imminent coronary. The muscle-clenching tension she had carried into the shop had been pricked as effectively as a needle going into the flesh of a balloon. Phuff!

WHEN SHE HAD upturned her bag on the bed at home, cut off all the tags and thrown them away with the plastic hangers, Alice totted up the total of her takings. Thirty-two pounds of underwear. Clever. Not exactly a gold bullion robbery, but not bad, not bad at all for someone who hadn't the slightest interest in the price or value of her thieving. The pants and bras she folded neatly among the old grey ones in the appropriate drawers, and that was that.

"Come on, Hunter. Walkies."

Dog and mistress set off up Blackford Hill at a very brisk pace.

Chapter 43

2007

Hit Me With Your Rhythm Stick

S TEPHEN WAS, AS usual, behind the closed door of his study when the phone rang. Alice went to pick up, but she heard Stephen talking. She heard shock in his voice and seconds of silence. Moments later, he burst out of his room, ashen.

"Frank's collapsed. Possibly a heart attack," he shouted to Alice before rushing out of the flat, one arm in a jacket sleeve, car keys in his hand. "One of the students looked in just now and found him lying on the floor. Don't know when I'll be back…"

"How awful!" Alice said to the cold blast of air that slapped her in the face.

ALICE SIGHED AS she crossed the hall, thinking of the stricken colleague, barely registering her husband's still-flickering computer screen. In his urgency, he'd forgotten to close his door. She retraced her steps, this time glancing in. Stopped at the door. Froze. Her heart hit her ribcage, missing a few beats here and there – like during the adrenalin rush of the slow-motion seconds before she stole something. It was the same thrill of doing something wicked and wrong. Wrong but necessary. What did he do in there? Computer games? Bullshit! Come on, Alice. Why carry on with the delusion? You know damn well what games your husband plays on his computer, and they have nothing to do with aliens or avatars. Stop playing the dumb innocent. Get in there and confront the truth – which you know already. Toby told you. Your instinct told you.

Alice harnessed her arguments against crossing the threshold. She had no right to invade her husband's privacy. If he had secrets, fair enough. Everyone had secrets – or thoughts and feelings they chose not to reveal to others. It's called survival. Alice knew who would suffer if she broke her self-imposed rule. At best, she would feel guilty. At worst, she would have to act on the information she discovered. The worms would writhe out of their can and crawl all over her skin. It wasn't worth the risk.

Don't! Alice told herself, half-turning away from the open door.

My marriage is a sham. What more harm can be done? She replied, turning back again.

A dizzying clutter of windows filled Stephen's screen. With a blush that spread from forehead to neck, she saw a male hand masturbating an erect penis, on and on and on. Was it really taking him that long or was it a tape loop? In another window, a woman squashed and squeezed her marshmallow breasts. Her face was coy but ordinary. Any woman.

ANOTHER WINDOW, NEAR the bottom, contained an online conversation of sorts – if jerky little phrases with tons of exclamation marks counted as dialogue.

Hope ur getting wet....

I'm as stiff as a concrete banana!!!! Are you sharing with me?

Wow look @ whoopee now. I can see ur pussy, whoo-pee!!!!!!

Alice-the-writer-and-librarian gave these amateurs two out of ten for their banal sound bites and predictable monikers: DaddysGirl, PerkyTits, Balls2, Sexdeviant, Mad4it.

But Alice-the-wife stood in front of the screen, too appalled to make literary judgements. She bit her lip as a new window popped up, revealing a Chinese woman who strutted to a chair and straddled it. A large carrot lay on the floor by her right foot. She undressed, later by layer, very slowly, until she was naked and her legs were splayed.

go go on, stick it in....

an orange dick lol!!!!!!

bet the check-out guy knew what you u were going gonna to do with that!!!!!!

that shud fill ur big pussy....

The woman tore open a pink condom and stretched it over the carrot. Licked the tip of the absurd vegetable. Inserted it into her mouth and pushed it in and out, in and out, sucking and sighing. She blew kisses at her camera. Then, with her eyes closed, she started to roll the carrot-dildo slowly, teasingly, naughtily over her breasts and stomach and groin until she was slipping its bright pink tip into her...

Alice fled.

Words chattered in a nasty tumble of painful dismay. Sad. Sleazy. Seedy. This isn't sex. This is mass masturbation. It's man-in-a-Mac territory, she said to herself, eyes wet and tears rolling down her cheeks. And with the words came the memory, as vivid and animated as the screens, of Toby staring hard at his father and challenging him to deny that he, too, was an addict. Toby had smoked hash. His father did porn. Why had Alice not taken it more seriously? When her son threw his verbal darts, she thought it was about saving face. Two males on high horses. Tit for tat. But Toby had been bang on target.

Stephen, do these images excite you? Why? Alice sat on the floor, leaned her head against the wall, and sobbed until there were no tears left. The thought of her husband watching anything tasteless seemed as improbable as him walking into the cheapest tat shop on Lothian Road and drooling over a painting of a kitten or a vase with rosebuds and a gold rim. Stephen didn't do garish or ugly or kitsch. He did exquisite and elegant. Quietly perfect. Of course she knew that some men masturbated to porn in magazines and adult videos, but she had dismissed these males as no-hopers – lonely, broken, sad, dysfunctional. They were uneducated, unattractive, inarticulate blokes with shaved heads and beer bellies and tattoos. They spoke in F words. They thought of women as meat. Their greatest pleasure was six or seven pints, a brawl and a quick, brutal fuck. They had the sensitivity of a cockroach.

Hang on, Alice. What's happened to your liberal sentiments?

Bugger my liberal sentiments. I've just thrown them out of the window. They can shatter on the pavement for all I care.

Those men aren't always to blame. Brutal backgrounds. They know no different.

I don't give a fuck about them. I'm talking about Stephen and Stephen knows beauty.

You think Stephen is different? Superior?

I did.

THE CONFRONTATION IN the early hours, when Alice initiated it – for even in extremis she was sensible enough to wait until Stephen had offloaded the news that his colleague, now safely in the Royal Infirmary, had had a mild heart attack – was short and bitter.

"Stephen, you left your computer on," she began while they nursed glasses of brandy. Both in shock. Stephen coloured. Looked at Alice.

"You had no business…"

"Don't interrupt. Don't give me your stock phrases. Don't accuse me of invading your privacy. Just shut up and listen to what I have to say." Stephen looked up from his glass. Alice's voice was measured and certain. "OK. Practicalities first. How long have you been looking at porn?"

"It's hardly…"

"Don't play with words. Don't twist meanings. I'm not interested. Answer me."

"Ages. What's the problem?"

Where was the man who loved the colour of mint and the taste of lime? The cellist who could run a bow across taut

293

strings with such fragile sensitivity that she'd cried? Who was this hard, harsh-voiced stranger?

"What's the problem!" Alice repeated, her voice glacial. "The problem is that porn is demeaning and insulting and damaging to women."

"Women take part."

"I know the ratios. I'm not interested in gender studies just now. Just tell me why, Stephen. What do you get out of it? Because for the life of me I don't understand your pleasure in watching this mind-numbing rubbish."

"You really want to know?"

"For God's sake, I wouldn't ask otherwise!"

"OK... it's an escape. It's a bit of harmless fun. I work damn hard and this is how I relax. It's a way of sharing sex anonymously with strangers. It doesn't hurt anyone or make them pregnant or give them STDs."

"It's group masturbation, isn't it?"

"Oh it's more than that. There are some beautiful people out there who aren't shy about showing their bodies, so why not look at them?"

"I didn't see any."

"You didn't look for long enough."

"For Christ's sake! It's a very poor substitute for making love."

"It's an addition."

"A subtraction."

"It hurts no-one."

"It's just hurt me."

Silence.

"You watch porn every single night, don't you, while I

cook and iron and hoover and tidy, and creep about because I think you're busy working. You'd rather watch women sticking carrots up their cunts than be in bed with me."

Silence. Alice clamped her hand over her mouth. Ugly words, Alice. Stephen shifted in his chair. Stared into space. Alice watched him, and found not a single, small sign that any of this touched him. Or moved him. Proverbial ducks and water.

"You have deceived me, continuously, for years. You've belittled and diminished me to the point where I feel I don't exist, certainly not inside this marriage. Can you understand that?"

"Alice, what I watch barely counts as porn. A bit of eroticism, that's all. Pretty faces. Pretty bodies. You are overreacting. It's a harmless, ordinary way to be…" Stephen's eyes became cold. He turned away from his wife's expectant face, studied his brandy as if it has just appeared in his hands. "Oh shit, Alice, I'm not going to justify myself to you about looking at young, beautiful bodies. Every bloody male does it. It's normal. The images are available. It's all over the internet. It's part of the way we live now. Grow up and stop hiding in the last century. In one of your domestic novels. Men watch porn. So do women. What's the big deal?"

If Stephen had shown some regret…

If he had reached out to her…

If he had acknowledged her hurt…

If he had apologised for the pain he had caused her…

If he had said, "Look, we have a problem. How can we work together to solve it?"

But Stephen rose, stormed off into his study and

slammed the door.

I don't get it. I don't even know whether I'm right to condemn it, Alice thought. How many kind, respectable, caring, upstanding husbands rummage in their trousers for an hour every night while staring at headless, open-legged women? And watching porn on a small screen is not a criminal offence. I bet policemen watch porn while their wives cook dinner.

Staring at images of naked women who look like inflated Barbie dolls is not a crime.

Shoplifting is.

Chapter 44
2007

Not Fade Away

O F COURSE THEY would separate. They had no future together.

Stephen and Alice rotated around each other like planets, each on its own destructive course, each feeding a habit both compulsive and insatiable. The playing field lay uneven, of course, for while no-one else would discover Stephen's nightly playtime, Alice walked a more and more precarious tightrope towards being caught.

DURING THOSE TIMELESS months, Alice felt emotionally anaesthetised. She went through the motions of running the library and managing the house, looking like she always did – quietly content and competent but without giving an atom of herself. Behind her perfunctory smile lay a wasteland of burnt out feelings. At the library counter, people continued to tell her their life stories, but now all she could offer was an absent nod of her head.

When the featureless landscape of her days became intolerable, she dashed for her car and drove into town. This was how she frightened the emotional numbness back to life, if only for a few hours. The alternative, she knew, was a break down and she might not be able to put herself back together. She was an old, fragile vase whose widening cracks daily challenged the glue which held it together. Then, the broken pieces of Alice would be taken to a psychiatric hospital. To hold back that inevitability, she drove up the Mound, knowing that soon her heart would start beating again and a river of adrenalin would warm her veins. But she also knew that the shelf life of this temporary resuscitation was nearing its end. Each time, it took more to shock her nervous system into even mild excitement. She needed bigger shots, larger doses, more dangerous hits.

In Laura Ashley, Alice peered around the curtain of the changing room and checked that the cubicle assistant was looking the other way. Without hurrying, she folded a pair of beige trousers and a shirt, laid them at the bottom of the carrier bag, and covered them with her cardigan. She didn't even bother to try things on anymore. She tugged back the curtain and walked out.

Jigsaw proved more of a challenge. An electronic tag weighed down every garment. The assistants were canny. The store had been created with wide, open aisles and minimalist racks. Foxed on several occasions, Alice had exited empty-handed. On she went, picking weird dark tunics and square dresses. In the changing room with the stable door, she quickly ran her hands over the silk top with the £105 price tag. Nothing. She stuffed it back in her bag. After a suitable time lag, Alice handed back the tunics, smiled her thanks and marched out.

In M&S, Alice helped herself to a nice black watch with a leather strap. On the lower shelves were art-nouveau glass jewellery boxes with little drawers. Thirty-five pounds. She could have treated herself but paying now seemed alien. Alice had never owned a jewellery box – she kept her earrings and her gold chain in cardboard boxes in her sock drawer – and she wanted it. The assistants on the check-out counter were busy serving customers. Shoppers milled around, but none too close. She fished out a big carrier bag (never go unprepared) and let it drift down to the floor. As she bent to retrieve it, she slid the jewellery box inside. It took less than five seconds.

If asked, Alice could not have said what items made their way inside her bags. The thrill was purely in the taking and in getting out without being caught. The surge of excitement mixed with terror kicked in when she walked past the unsmiling, uniformed guard whose muscled arms were crossed over his chest, and continued out, past the electronic machines (would they scream?), into the weak Edinburgh sunshine. Big breath out.

Back in her car, Alice leant her throbbing head against the headrest and waited for her heartbeat to quiet. She contorted out of her coat, dumped it in the back seat and stabbed at her wet brow with a wad of tissues from the box she kept in the glove compartment. The thrill of the chase had once kept her working the shops for hours. The aftershock of triumph used to last so much longer. Now, an expensive frock or a pot of outrageously priced face cream, adroitly removed from its packaging, no longer gave her the same buzz. Done that, she thought, too easy. The pretty silk top from Jigsaw would give her a shiver of pleasure, but satisfaction would be fleeting.

Maybe she should go bungee jumping on the Meadows instead. Or take up hang-gliding. Alice wasn't stupid. She knew exactly what she was doing. And why. On the back of her bedroom door hung garments she couldn't even be bothered to put away. Someone had removed her adrenalin drip and in its place a mind-numbing drug cursed through her veins. Nembutal or valium.

ALICE WAITED IN her study – her sanctuary – her hands in her lap, for her husband's return.

"Stephen, can we talk?" she said, getting up and moving to greet him as soon as he walked in the door. "Can we sit down and have a drink together? Like we used to." Her glance was straight, her intention firm.

He looked at her in surprise. Looked again, as if he hadn't seen her for a long time. She thought she saw a softening. It was her last chance, she reckoned, to mend the bridges of a marriage that was a pile of bricks worn away and fragmented by a fast-running tide of accusations and guilt and crime. She would wade into the water and pull from the river bed what was needed to lay the foundation all over again. Before everything was washed away.

"Sorry, Alice." Genuine regret coloured his voice. "I'm going to have a quick bite to eat and get back to a meeting. It's something I can't avoid. I'm sorry."

"I think it's more important that we talk. After the other night…"

Alice's fury had melted into one last and probably futile

wish to mend their marriage, or else to agree to part company in a kind and civilised way. To talk about compromise. To be open and honest.

"I agree, but I have to go back in. I'll try and come home early."

"But you never do." A fact, not a complaint.

"I'll come back as soon as I can."

"I'm so unhappy with all of this, Stephen."

"So am I." Said with humility. Honesty.

It was something.

She gathered those three short words to her and out of them made paving stones across the wreckage of their marriage. They were the first heart-felt sounds she had heard from him since Saturday's shock waves had sent them spinning into marital outer space.

THE CLOCK READ ten-thirty when Stephen quietly let himself into the flat. A timid smile played over his face, and his hands gripped a bottle of very good Pinot and a bunch of oversized sunflowers. Yellow for Alice.

From the top landing he could see into the lounge, and spotted pink socks belonging to the sleeping woman whose feet stuck over the end of the sofa. Stephen tiptoed into the room, bent over Alice and kissed her very softly on her forehead. While he had been gone, she had found a long pin and had reached up high to stick it with strength, with determination, and with vengeance, into the bitter, acid-filled balloon that floated above her head. Strange how easily it deflated. And with its collapse came her own. Suddenly aching with tiredness, she lay down on the sofa and blacked out into a deep, dreamless sleep.

"I came back as soon as I could," Stephen whispered. "We'll talk tomorrow, Alice. I've cleared the whole evening."

"Mmmm," said a barely conscious Alice.

But tomorrow was a day too late.

Act 5

Alice

Chapter 45

2007

Born To Run

TOMORROW IS TODAY.

Stephen tiptoed off to work, promising the still-sleeping Alice that he would come home early. That they would talk. Alice slept on. Her day did not connect with Stephen's early return from work. Four policemen parked their cars outside her house and interrupted any possible peace talks.

And now as Alice sits on the sticky plastic bench in the police station foyer, hallucinating with tiredness, the sixth act erupts in this nighttime play.

The doors are revolving and spitting out new actors. From the back of the stalls, Alice watches as one, then another, then another exit the real world and enter the spotlit stage of the police station. Three in uniform. One not. Three male. One female. Alice recognises the police woman despite the hat rammed down on her forehead and obscuring her eyes, but the police woman gives no indication of knowing Alice. She busies herself at the glass-screened counter. The man who is not in uniform stares straight ahead towards an invisible dot on an invisible horizon. If he sees Alice, he doesn't acknowledge the fact. On his face flash pain and disdain, fleeting emotions that come and go like storm-blown clouds across a round dull sun.

"A double whammy," says one of the uniforms, soto voce, to the guy on duty. "First one then the other. Who'd have believed it, eh?"

"What? In it together?" They look at Alice.

"Nah. Sheer coincidence. He'll wish he'd been selling stolen knickers on Ebay for her. That's nothing to what we got."

"What?"

"Smut. Porno."

"Ah. Does she know?"

Words said almost inaudibly. Almost.

"Doubt it."

Oh yes she does! Alice wants to call.

Oh no she doesn't!

Oh yes she does!

It's a pantomime! And I thought it was a tragedy.

At the desk, the uniforms begin the ritual that Alice herself so recently endured, this time with the man in civvies who remains silent. Alice watches and knows that by a trick of mind he has removed himself from this scene. He is in his late fifties with curly reddish hair turning grey. Black polo neck. Black jeans. A man who once effaced himself in library shelves but now has nowhere to hide.

A whole hive of buzzing insects have taken up residence in Alice's ears. The revolving door spins again and a young uniform staggers through carrying a computer; a shiny green machine trailing wires and plugs and connections. Floppy discs and CDs balance on top, all in transparent sleeves, all neatly labeled.

"Where's Hunter?" Alice asks as Stephen is led away.

"Mary'll walk him then put him back in the house."

"Stephen…"

He turns his head towards her. Tries to hold her gaze.

"I'm sorry," Alice says.

"I'm sorry too."

"Too late." Alice shakes her head slowly as an ocean of tears builds. Not now, she tells herself, trying to hold back the grief that rolls towards its breaking climax.

You can mourn later. Let him go.

And then Creases is back and sitting beside her. Does the man never go to bed? From the expression on his face, she senses she has been allocated to a new pigeon hole. The tags of criminal and thief have been replaced with victim.

"Look, Mrs Green, this may come as a bit of a shock, but when we were searching your husband's study to see if he was in this with you, maybe selling stuff you nicked, we found some incriminating material on his computer."

Alice says nothing. Creases looks at her to check she's heard. She has but gives him nothing.

"We've only looked at the chat rooms and websites in his recent history, but they've left a trail. Your husband refuses to give us his passwords but that's no problem. Just means he's in for a very long sit and he'll be done for non-cooperation as well… and if we find what we think we'll find… well…"

He breaks off and shakes his head. "You did better, cooperating with us," he says, on safer ground.

Oh, a marital competition? What is this nice, rather dim guy trying to tell her?

"It's OK. I know."

What he longs to ask her is printed across his eyes in capital letters, but he blinks and erases it.

"Don't most men... I mean it's so available. It's not illegal, is it?" Alice asks calmly, remembering Stephen's words.

"Depends what he's been looking at. Depends if it's just titillating stuff for, well, his own pleasure. There's porn and there's other stuff that's not nice, Mrs Green. Not nice at all." He waits. For shock? For tears? "Well, I'd better get back down. He'll be here all night. What will you do, Mrs Green?"

"I'll go home."

"Shall I call you a taxi?"

Why is everyone so keen to call her a taxi? They must be desperate to get her out of here.

"I'd rather walk. Thank you."

With a backward glance that speaks bafflement but also sympathy, he stands up and walks away, down the stairs where Stephen may be sitting in the very chair in which she herself sat earlier.

INTERVAL

"LET IT GO," someone says gently.

"I knew."

"You suspected… you certainly didn't know the worst of it."

"He's destroyed…"

"…himself. Just himself."

Alice gives her full attention to the girl in the red boots, who is leaning against the wall, watching her. Alice smiles. The girl smiles back. Stephen does not know this part of me, Alice thinks. The police do not know, and if they were to shine a bright light in my eyes and pull out my fingernails I would not bleed the facts. The girl in the red boots is less of a ghost now. She is sharpening into focus.

"Hi!" A cheerful greeting out of sync with the sympathy and concern on the young woman's face.

"You're back."

"Of course. I wouldn't leave you to go through this by yourself. And I've been at your side since just before Cal left. We're not separate people, you know."

"I suppose not."

"So here we are again. A long time ago, I spent a day in

the tardis-cell, sitting on the hard wooden plank. Very young. Petrified. I scraped by just the right side of a stint inside because I agreed to say I was a glamour model, not a student. Remember? Intelligent women don't steal. We're all Madonnas or whores, Alice." The young Alice looks relaxed. Almost amused.

"Of course, it doesn't matter in the grand scheme of things. Cause and effect, Alice. Stephen could give us a tutorial on that."

"Don't mention him, please."

"Whatever you've done, it's nothing compared to him. Pervert. Wanker."

"Someone else called him that a long time ago. Emma."

"I remember. She was right."

"You should have listened."

"Heads and hearts. We go where our emotions lead us."

"Well, at least it should make you feel better to know that you're an innocent by comparison."

"No. I'm not innocent. But I don't care what he's done or what happens to him."

"Good."

"All the same, I do wonder if I would have set out along this crazy road if I hadn't met any of them. Is it anything to do with the men who hurt me…who hurt us…and brought us down?"

"They played their parts, but it's not the whole story. Society, Alice. Once we have droopy boobs and wrinkles we have to shut ourselves indoors for fear of offending someone."

"True. So who's responsible?"

"We all are. Yes, women too. We're complicit in not putting up more of a fight. We watch the older men grab their trophy wives and feel failure instead of thanking our lucky stars that we've not been caught and shackled."

"We're abandoned though. We're alone."

"No. We're free."

"It's fine for you to talk. You had men falling at your feet…"

"That was then. What about the thirty-something-year-old woman who fell in love with a man not worth the paper she writes her stories on? Who did a detour from her own smooth path to follow his stony one? Under his rules, his reign, she started to unravel like an old jumper."

FOR A WHILE, Alice is lost in thought because in this conversation she recognises the truth.

"What shall we do now?"

"Take some time out. And then with our own nails we will tear at the chrysalis and crawl out healed and confident and beautiful."

"Beautiful? Does that matter? It's so long since I've bothered and… hang on aren't we going against everything we've just said? The pressure to stay young and trim and attractive?"

"Not if you do it for yourself. You haven't tried that for a very long time. Treat yourself. Find a good hairdresser, go to John Lewis and hope that they don't look at you suspiciously. Ask the personal shopper to find you some funky new clothes that make you feel comfortable and attractive."

"Am I reinventing myself then?"

"No, just finding the Alice who was always there but who's been rubbed out, year after year, by men and kids and a sick celeb society, and her own female vulnerability. She is being freed. She will be strong. Was always strong."

"So it's a sharp haircut and a purple hat and ankle boots, is it?"

"Not immediately. It'll take a bit of time to adjust, but you'll get there. Start with the sharp hair and some highlights to hide the grey."

"What's wrong with grey?"

"You'll look prettier with your blonde streaks back and you'll smile at your reflection in mirrors. When you're happy with how you look, it shows and people respond differently."

"I take your point."

"And join a gym or a choir or a drumming group. For heaven's sake, have a bit of fun."

"I like reading."

"You'll like drumming, too. Or dance again – zumba or salsa. Alice, there's so much still for you to discover."

"So this is a fresh start? There's still time."

"Absolutely."

"God, I'm a slow learner."

"But you got there in the end. Go and enjoy your life. Set yourself free."

"I've just been charged with shoplifting."

"But they won't put you in prison. A fine at worst. Anyone can see that you're a mad, middle-aged woman. It's what happens when we reach fifty."

"So how do you explain this... um... episode?"

"A digression. A somewhat eccentric cry for help. Forget

it."

"What if it happens again?"

"It won't. You won't. There's no need."

"And you?"

"No need for me either. I'll go on my way."

They exchanged one last look. Poignant but final.

"So this is the end?" Alice said, casting a lingering look at her younger self.

"No. The beginning."

Chapter 46

2007

I Can See Clearly Now

A LICE WAS ALONE again.

Just for good measure, she did a double rotation, because the St Leonard's police doors were the magical exit into her brave new world. Outside, in the crisp air, Alice looked up and saw the nail-paring of a new moon. That's good luck for the whole of the next month, she thought, treasuring one of her grandmother's many superstitions.

SHE TOOK HER return journey slowly and gently, relishing the crisp air and star-lit sky. She wandered through Marchmont and down the hill into Newington, glancing into the lit windows of the tenement flats and noting the colour of the ceilings and the arrangements of the furniture, the plants and the posters. How long since she had taken the slightest notice of how other people lived? My new flat will be a riot of colour, she decided. Clashing pinks and reds with not a shade of tasteful off-white in sight. A soggy cushion-filled sofa for reading and dreaming. Lamps that shed pools of warm light onto books instead of spots with a bloody dimmer switch. It will be as messy and cosy as I like. Alice watched the tiny moon playing hide and seek in and out of smoky wisps of cloud and laughed out loud. She too had been playing the hiding game, but without the fun.

I'll phone Toby, she decided. I have a hunch he'll pat me on the back and be proud. Hey, a mum with a criminal record. Cool! I'll tempt him out of his lair with a promise of a pizza or a curry, and several pints of beer. We'll celebrate. As Newington morphed into The Grange, Alice walked on, wondering, without the slightest quiver of anxiety, if her neighbours had given up their vigil behind the net curtains and gone to bed. I couldn't give a damn. I'll be gone soon. Out of their stuffy stuck-up territory. Perhaps Stockbridge would be fun. Or the old town where I can walk to the central library and galleries. Her heart gave only the smallest quickstep when she turned the corner into her own street. But there were no police cars. No officers opening their doors and walking their policeman walk towards her gate. Upstairs, her bedroom would hold no guilty secrets and Stephen's room would be bereft of computers – lime green or any other damn colour.

A BLACK NOSE was pressed against the glass panes of her front door next to dozens of wet smudges of worry. Left alone again, and at night, Hunter's whimpering had reached a desperate crescendo. The neighbours will report me to the RSPCA tomorrow for neglecting my dog and I'll tell them the police are the guilty ones. Alice flung her arms around Hunter's neck and smothered him in a long, loving greeting. A mutual snuffling.

"Good boy! You're a very good boy! I'm sorry you were

left alone."

Hunter nudged his head into Alice's hands wanting reassurance, wanting routine, wanting security. His trembling shuddered into breath-held sighs of relief as Alice's safe hands went around him and held him tight.

"Midnight walkies, Hunter?" she suggested, a lilt in her voice, lifting his lead from the peg.

Hunter put his head on one side. Then the other. Is she kidding?

"Then I'll pack up and we'll leave here. I promise the rented place will have a garden. We'll find somewhere wonderfully untidy and be very happy." And in answer to his raised-eyebrows question: "Yes, of course you're coming with me."

IF SOMEONE HAD been staring out of the window, they would have seen a middle-aged woman skipping through the darkness with a dog, bouncing with elation, at her side. The climb up Blackford Hill was steep but Alice breathed steadily and deeply in the knowledge that freedom like this was a gift that should never be taken for granted. At the summit she stared down at the sleeping houses and knew with an emotional sure-footedness that it was time to move on.

"Let's run, Hunter!" she cried. "For the sheer hell of it. We're not often up this late. Race you to the bottom!"

As if someone had fired a starting pistol, they were off, laughter punctuated by barks, along the narrow path between moon-touched brambles and purple heather painted black by the night. Hunter could do it blindfold, but Alice too knew every footstep and twist and stone and didn't stumble.

Praise for Lynn's Previous Works

The Red Beach Hut. Inspired Quill. 2017. Linen Press. 2018.

'From the first pages of this novel, Michell sets up an atmosphere of such convincing threat that the reader's expectations are on red alert.'

— Jenny Garrod. DURA. Dundee Univeriry Review of the Arts.

'Lynn Michell writes a beautifully innocent and endearing tale twisted by the tainted gaze of society's perverse darkness….She presents the reader with the delicate and fragile moments in which one reveals oneself to another and hopes that that this vulnerability will be met with compassion.'

— Isabelle Coy-Dibley for The Contemporary Small Press.

'A faded seaside town in Autumn is the perfect setting for this elegiac story of a vulnerable boy and the adult who befriends him…The sense of jeopardy is palpable. As the narrative flicks backwards and forwards, we're also reminded that in any part of Britain, ignorance and bigotry are never far away…I was left with the sensation of the fragility not just of seaside communities but of the knife-edge on which society is perched. A highly engaging and thought-provoking read.'

— Ali Bacon. *Between the Lines*

'The prose is achingly beautiful…I doubt there can be a better, more poetic or lyrical writer when it comes to sea and shore and to the timelessness of being out on the water in a boat…The boy Neville is exquisitely drawn, a wounded soul who counts stars and steps and grains of sand for security.'

— Avril Joy, Costa and People's Prize winning author

'A parable for our times…an intriguing book about secrets, assumptions, and consequences. I found it beautifully descriptive and the boy is beautifully realised.'

— Derek Thompson, Author of *Standpoint, Line of Sight, Cause & Effect, Shadow State.*

'A compelling book that examines bigotry, ignorance, redemption and friendship. Beautifully told too.'

— Heidi James, author of *Wounding.*

'Some of the best writing I've seen in a long time. The characterisation of Abbott and Neville is quite superb: the unease of the man and the perfectly credible affection he feels in response to the boy's humanity. The boy's moments of excitement, fear of happiness being snatched away and awareness of adult moods are all quite superbly drawn…Lynn Michell conjures up the somehow appealing desolation of a faded British seaside town. The opening paragraph is a tour de force. You want to jump right in.'

– Howard Sergeant, Writer and ghost writer.

'The innocence and trust of the relationship between Abbott and Neville is beautifully conceived.'

– Susie Nott-Bower. Author of T*he Making of Her*.

'The magnificent part of The Red Beach Hut … is its touching on the ugliness and beauty of human nature – to be alone, an outsider and still seek out human connection…'

– SipnSee

'Delicately beautiful and gorgeously descriptive.'

– SarahLouise writes

'The writing in *The Red Beach Hut* is enthralling.'

– The Bibliophile Chronicles

'A convincing and compelling read. Neville's thoughts and speech effortlessly reflect that of a young child. An incredibly consistent character.'

– Lauren Parsons, Legend Press

'Beautifully written. The small English seaside town comes to life in front of your very eyes, and pretends to fall asleep while it keeps one eye open, watching the goings-on.'

– Bookmarked

'A brave and brilliant decision to have a child as one of the central protaganists…Neville is so beautifully drawn.'

– Ninja Book Box

'A rain-streaked, deserted British beach becomes a place of pilgrimage, of mystical retreat; an old beach hut offers warm sanctuary, revelation, truthtelling, consolation and love. It is fable for our time: a cautionary tale, shot through with light and loveliness.'

– Kate: Amazon reader

'Quietly and without dogma explores the consequences of the widespread intolerance in our society towards anyone who isn't vanilla flavoured.'

– Amazon reader: Bookworm

'Beautifully constructed, the narrative flows.'

– Amazon reader: Dr. Heinrich Uhlig

'A compelling book that examines bigotry, ignorance, redemption and friendship. Beautifully told too.'

— Amazon reader: Nomenclature

Shooting Stars are the Flying Fish of the Night. Linen Press. 2013.

'In this book, I recognise many of the mistakes I myself have made. If you dream or plan to sail off into the blue, you will learn from this book. A great read for those who are going or want to go over the horizon!'

— Sir Chay Blyth

'*Shooting Stars are the Flying Fish of the Night* should be compulsory reading for anyone intending to make their first extended offshore trip under sail. It is an endearing human story of three members of a family; father, mother and son battling to survive both physically and emotionally. Few families put themselves through such a test and then have the courage to commit it all nakedly to paper.'

— Chris Hawes, Yacht Fractions

White Lies. Linen Press. 2010.
Runner-Up in the Robert Louis Stevenson Award

'A debut novel which possesses and is possessed by a rare authority of voice…It is the mother's voice that sings White Lies into unforgettability. Hers and Eve's. Their thoughts and writing ring like music.'

— Tom Adair, *The Scotsman*

'Hauntingly beautiful… with a bombshell of an ending.'

— Michele Hanson, *The Guardian*

'Moving, memorable and totally absorbing. Captures perfectly the trials of a middle-aged woman trying to care for and build a relationship with her distant father, now in his dotage, through the writing down of his memories.'

—Sophie Radice, *Guardian* & *Observer* columnist

'Credible and touching. Dramatic and tragic.'

— *The Torch*

'An anatomist of the human heart.'

— Wanda Whitely, HarperCollins

'A first class read. Transports the reader whilst exploring the reactions, feelings and fears of those who lived through the early stages of the Emergency.'

— Martyn Day, Lawyer for former Mau Mau insurgents against the British Government

'A wonderful evocation of Africa...Lynn Michell is an extremely accomplished writer. There are passages of extraordinary vividness and beauty and the characters spoke to me very convincingly. I love the sense, by the daughter, of unease at her father's painting of a golden era of colonialism, the spaces, the gaps that he is unwilling or unable to discuss.'

– Edwin Hawkes, Makepeace Towle

'A naturally gifted writer and not afraid of ambitious projects as this one is. It has great filmic potential.'

– Christopher Rush, author of *Will*

Readers' Reviews from Amazon

'This book is beautiful and well constructed. There are moments of playfulness and moments of love in the abandoned houses of Lake Navaisha. For the rest, the tenor is dramatic: beauty and war and human pain. This book that has shaken me.'

– Martignon

'Beautifully written and page-turning. The story is told in David's, Mary's and their daughter Eve's voices, and in places you get three versions of the same events. Everyone re-writing history, telling white lies, to suit themselves. I loved this book – picked it up two days ago and could not put it down.'

– A Reader

'The child Eve's vivid evocations of a life of great, if temporary freedom in her African garden and surrounding landscape are viscerally painted. I feel her younger sister Clara's hot skin under Eve's fingertips as they strip off their outer clothes and draw letters on each other's backs...Weeks after reading this book I am still thinking about the characters and their story.'

– Tracemyself

Shattered: Life With ME. HarperCollins. 2003.

'A timely and powerfully written book and Lynn Michell is uniquely qualified to write it.'

– Bernard MavLaverty, author of *Cal, Lamb, Grace Notes, The Anatomy School, Midwinter Break.*

'Inspiring stories, not simply of broken lives, but of survival and hope in the face of terrible adversity.'

– Dr Vance Spence, Chairman of MERGE

'Throughout this book, the reader is kept on a steady and reassuring journey of validation and support. The stories by other ME patients work to solidify Michell's broad but well-rounded overview of a life made more difficult by an invisible chronic illness. Identifying with the ME stories in this book reminds us that we are not alone in this fight.'

– CF Alliance Newsletter 2003

'Shattered is a powerfully written account of life with ME—an unpredictable and devastating illness. Definitely a 'There but for the grace of God go I' book, and one that should throw some much-needed light on this terrible condition.'

– *Tuam Herald*, June 2003

'I highly recommend it to all who suffer from ME/CFS…Shattered is a good eye-opener for carers, friends and relatives of sufferers who may not understand what it's really like to live with such a debilitating illness.'

– Sleepydust.net

Letters To My Semi-Detached Son: A Mother's Story. The Women's Press. 1993.

'A story of such painful intensity that tears poured down my face as I read it. No mother could fail to identify with her anguish and guilt, or her sense of failure.'

– Celia Dodd, *The Independent*

'A very modern situation that will send a sympathetic shiver down any parent's spine.'

– Hazel Leslie, *Mail on Sunday*

'A brutally honest account of how her own emotional needs and those of her little boy came into conflict. The sheer despair and desperate sense of guilt is something most mothers could identify with.'

– Jean Donald, *The Herald*

'Moving, tersely written and painful to read. The honesty is remarkable. I was left with some uneasy feelings, like I had read someone's diary, but then, perhaps, the controversial nature of this book is its strength.'

– Penelope Aspinall, *Event*

Growing Up in Smoke. Pluto Press. 1990.

'If you want your children to grow up healthy rather than kippered in tobacco soke, this is the book you need.'

– Claire Raynor

'Essential reading for evey adult who smokes.'

– Lynn Faulds Wood

Lightning Source UK Ltd.
Milton Keynes UK
UKHW020912300819
348617UK00002B/3/P